Snowmelt Wood

Book 1 of the Keepers

By Jo Erickson

ISBN 9798351600857

Library of Congress Control Number: 2018675309

Printed in the United States of America

Table of Contents

Chapter 1 - Accident

The car raced down the slippery snow-covered road past midnight, barely seen through the blinding snow that whipped around in the wind. It passed through a little town at full speed, not slowing the least bit. The few pedestrians out in the weather walking home from a late-night party stopped and stared as they tried to make out the speeding vehicle. It passed on into the night and disappeared, following the highway out the other side of the little town. The pedestrian group had begun walking once more against the wind and snow when a sudden roar and glare of headlights cut through the blizzard. They jumped back as one body when a large SUV materialized out of the snow speeding down the street, narrowly missing the huddled group on the sidewalk as it swerved on an icy patch in the road. The SUV recovered and disappeared after the car into the storm as the pedestrians hurried to their homes as fast as they could.

Inside the car, the view wasn't any better. Defrosters blew furiously at the windshield but only a small portion was frost-free, and all was black outside the headlights. Inside the headlights was a swirling maelstrom of snow which formed a blinding and disorienting tunnel. She gasped as her car slipped on an icy patch and began to swerve, then she straightened the car and continued, still mashing the gas pedal to the floor. "Oh, this is stupid! This is so stupid!" she muttered insanely to herself over and over. Suddenly a glare of headlights shone in her rear-view mirror, and she knew the SUV had caught up once more. She reached up and yanked at the mirror in frustration, ripping it loose from the windshield. "I don't want to see it!" she yelled stupidly to the car she drove, throwing the mirror down and grabbing the wheel again with both hands as the car swerved and spun crazily around, this time completely out of control. She saw headlights in front of her and heard a heavy crunch and screeching of metal; the impact flung the car end over end until it came to a stop upside-down in the ditch.

She breathed slowly, carefully, "Okay, the man hit me, but I don't feel hurt, and I can handle this. Just calm down." She listened to her heart thumping and closed her eyes for a few minutes, trying to calm herself before opening them once more to take stock of her situation. Everything was pitch dark - no, it wasn't. There was a red glow, what was it? Her confused mind tried to think as she hung upside-down, still belted into the driver's seat. She listened to the soft crackling and sniffed. "What do I smell? Is it smoke? Yes. Yes, I smell smoke, but it's not like a campfire or- oh no!" She scrabbled at her seatbelt ineffectually, "My car is on fire! That's what the red glow is! That's what the smoke smell is! Oh no!" She wondered just how far outside of that little town she was, and if the pedestrians would follow to see the crash. She started screaming "Help!" "Help!" and kept trying to unbuckle herself from the seat. It was stuck fast, and she couldn't grab hold of the buckle in her panic. She continued yelling "Help!" and suddenly the driver door was yanked open, and the man was there - the man from the SUV. The same man who had been chasing her all afternoon, trying to drive her off the road every chance he had. She didn't know why he was trying to kill her; she had first seen him as she left her workplace and headed to her car in the parking lot. She had requested an early day from her boss to enable her to drive the three hours from Kingston to the airport in Toronto; her youngest sister was getting married, and she had to catch a flight home to Kathmandu, Nepal for the wedding. The man had followed her as she left the building, tried to grab her. She fled to her car and the chase began.

"Help!" she cried to him, not caring at this point who was there to help her, "I can't get loose! Can you undo the buckle?" The man ignored her, pawing furiously around at her pockets, leaning under her as she hung in the seatbelt to open the glove box, snarling fiercely all the while "Where is it? Where?" She grew angry at him "Hey! Are you going to help me or not? Hey!" He ignored her and suddenly looked up startled, then backed quickly out of the car and ran. She heard sirens and saw reflected on the crumpled hood of her car flashing blue and red lights. Oh good, help! She began yelling again so they'd know she was stuck, and once more started fiddling with the seatbelt buckle, her fingers were clumsy with shock and she was unable to grasp the buckle.

She couldn't believe it. A policeman stood there on the road talking to the man; she could hear their voices as the conversation drifted across the snow toward her car. She heard the man tell the officer she was dead! She started yelling again at the top of her voice, "Hey! Hey! I'm here! I'm perfectly alive! Help me! Hey!" The officer walked over to the car, bent down, and looked straight at her, then nodded his head. She said, "Get me out, please!" in a panicked, trembling voice. He made no move to unfasten her seatbelt, but only walked back to the edge of the road, saying, "I hope the fire truck makes it here soon or this baby's gonna go." Her last thought before she passed out was that she was going to miss her flight.

She blinked and opened her eyes. She was lying in the ditch some distance away from the huddle of emergency vehicles. She could see the large SUV off to the side of the road, not a dent in it. She whispered, "Oh, wait; is there another car at the scene too?" She couldn't see through the swirling snow, everything seemed to be faded. "I must have lost consciousness," she whispered again, "but at least they got me out of the vehicle and moved me a safe distance away." She stood up and tried to brush the wet snow off as best she could with her bare hands, then started walking toward the activity; amazed that she wasn't hurting after the crash. She stopped several yards away as emergency workers pulled a body out of a burned-out car. She turned away suddenly, sick. "Ooh," she said softly to herself after recovering, "There must have been another car! I killed someone! Ooh!" She was promptly sick again. She was glad for the snow that blurred the scene and blocked out the details. It was a long time before she finally turned back around in control of herself once more. She started to walk over to the car and then she started to run, "Hey!" she shouted, "Wait for me! Hey!"

She stopped at a spot where blackened, trampled snow and withered grass was all around. No one was there, not even the car she had seen in the ditch. All were gone with taillights retreating into the distance back towards town, covered by snow in a heartbeat. They had forgotten her. She had been put so safely out of the way that they had forgotten her! She couldn't believe it. "Oh no!" she gasped, seeing a car after all, although not the one she wanted to see. It was the black SUV that had pushed her into the ditch, still parked at the side of the road, but where was the man who had driven it? She looked around and shivered, then walked over to peer timidly into the passenger window of the SUV. Nobody was inside, maybe she should get in and take this car back to town, to save herself the walk. She wondered if it would be considered stealing if she only drove it for the one or two miles to the town? She walked around to the driver's side and reached for the door handle, but somehow couldn't grasp it. "My fingers are just too numb with cold!" she muttered, teeth beginning to chatter with cold. She gave up after a few more tries and started walking back to town in the blinding snow, not wanting to encounter that man again.

"Hold there! You can't go that way, come back here!" She spun around looking for the source of the voice she had just heard yelling over the howling wind. There, back in the accident area stood a figure. She hesitated, wondering if it was the man who had chased her in the SUV, but realized that she was truly too cold to walk all the way back to the little town in this weather, and she would have to take her chances with the man and hope he would give her a lift to town. She sighed and trudged slowly through the blinding snow back to the accident site, then ducked behind the parked SUV, trying to see who the figure was. No one was there, not even in the SUV still parked at the side of the road. She shook her head in confusion, blinked. "Am I going mad, did I imagine a voice calling me?" she asked herself in growing consternation, not bothering to keep her voice down. "No," answered a voice from some distance away, "You are not going mad, and you will be safe now, I have banished the Daimon who killed you to a place far away. Come this way, out of the storm."

She spun around and saw the shape of a tall man standing just within the shelter of the trees at the edge of the road, surrounded by some golden sparkles, which she assumed was from her eyes adjusting to the darkness after all the emergency lights. She thought how foolish it was to follow a complete stranger at night on a deserted road in a snowstorm, and then she thought about turning and running for her life, but she knew that she would never be able to outrun him, and she was simply too cold to make it back to the town on her own, she was now shivering violently. She stumbled across the burned-out grass and then stepped forward at last into the woods and the shelter of the trees.

"Oh, the wind has stopped!" she exclaimed in surprise, feeling surprisingly warm all of a sudden, "The trees really do provide good shelter." She realized that she was no longer shivering and looked up at the tall man in front of her, he didn't seem threatening, but she couldn't see his face clearly in the dark night. She was relieved to see that he wasn't the man she feared, yet she still jumped in fear as she saw him replace a large sword into a sheath at his belt. He looked kindly at her a moment and then motioned her further into the woods without a word. She rubbed her eyes and looked around again. The golden sparkles were gone, but so was the road; she could see only an endless procession of trees in any direction she looked, there wasn't even any snow on the ground. "What did you say? Did you say a demon killed me? But I'm here and there was no demon, it was a man chasing me!" she said, confused, "There was someone else dead, though, I saw the body." She gulped, trying not to be sick again. He stopped walking and looked back to where she still stood, confused and scared, and he walked back to her and said gently, "I did not say demon, I said the man was a Daimon." He shrugged, "I know that doesn't explain much, because the words are pronounced the same way, but trust me on this. Come, we need to go so that I can get you to a place of safety." She peered back through the

woods, trying to find the edge of the tree line and
see the burned out grassy area again, then asked,
"Why do we want to go further from the road?
We'll get lost!" He looked sadly down at the petite
woman and shook his head gently. "You cannot go
back, that way is barred to you forevermore, as it is
to me. You are now a ghost and can no longer
walk the land of the living; I have closed the Gate
which opens on to the living world. You are now
standing in an entirely different wood than the one
you entered, and you must go forward; it is the
only way. Come, I will show you." He took her by
the arm, pulling her gently yet with a grip she
couldn't break, further into the woods and she
stumbled after him very frightened indeed.

They stopped at last on a high, rocky ridge beyond
the trees. She didn't know how far they had gone,
but morning was coming, and the sunrise glowed
below them in bright pinks and oranges as the sky
began to lighten. She stood quietly, wondering
what was next, but he stood there quietly also,
looking out over the land at the sunrise. She stole a
glance at him once or twice, a shadowy silhouette

in the pre-dawn darkness still on the ridge, then back to the sunrise as it grew slowly but steadily outward and upward. She gasped suddenly as the sky turned blue and the sun rose higher. The land below was green grass and bright flowers as far as she could see, bright and warm and welcoming in the blaze of morning sunlight. Countless buildings and farm fields dotted the countryside below, cows, goats and sheep grazed in pastures. It was a beautiful, warm summer scene. "Where have I got to, and in the middle of a Canadian snowstorm?!" she murmured softly to herself.

"Now do you see why you can't go back there anymore?" he asked her quietly. She turned from the scene and looked up at him, seeing him clearly for the first time in the morning light, then stepped back a pace in amazement. He was an extremely tall, strongly built man, dressed in soft, dark brown leather pants and boots with a matching leather vest pulled over a white cotton shirt, and he had a sword clasped at his side. His long, silky black hair was pulled back in a ponytail at the base of his neck, and he smiled kindly down at her, waiting for her answer. "What- uh, who are you?" she stammered. "I am one of the Keepers of the Gates, of course," he replied, "Does that help your understanding?" She shook her head, "No." She was very bewildered. He gave his head a slight shake and smiled again gently, "Oh, that's right, you've come through a Dragon Gate, I should have known better. Come," he said, taking her hand, "We must report to the Hall of Images. There everything will be made clear to you and your questions will be answered. It's not my place to tell you too much, for the masters of the towns prefer to do that task themselves." They turned from the ridge and followed a long, narrow staircase cut into the side of the cliff. She held tightly to his hand as she followed him, afraid of falling off the dangerous way.

Chapter 2 – A New Beginning

She gazed around in wonder as they walked across the valley floor; it was so beautiful here. Farm fields and barns were scattered about the landscape with a forested backdrop of trees in the far distance, and a small, burbling river swept alongside them as they walked. They were still holding hands. She had held tightly to his on the way down the stair out of fear but when they reached the valley floor, she didn't try to pull away even though he had loosened his grip. She stole small, timid glances at the tall, silent warrior from time to time as they walked through tall, grassy meadows and past farm fields toward the nearest cluster of buildings grouped around a splashing fountain. "What is this place called?" she asked as they walked, wanting to hear his voice again, "I don't recall seeing this town on the map?" He glanced quickly down at her as if surprised she had spoken, then forward again, nodding politely to people who were working in the fields they passed. "This world is called Arkady, and the town ahead of us is called Greenfield, but this place is not on any map which you would know, because you are no longer in the living world," he replied, still looking forward as he walked. "Do you have a name?" she asked. He stopped walking and turned, looking earnestly at her, "I do, but this is not the time for speech. You will understand in time, but I have a job to do, and I don't have much time now, I have many Gates that must be attended yet today. Come."

She sighed and gave up as they began walking once more. She studied the buildings they were now approaching; all were made of white marble and glistened brightly in the sunshine, there were eight larger buildings with golden symbols carved above the entrances and great pillars at the stepped entrances, and around forty smaller buildings which looked like personal dwellings. The larger buildings formed the central square around the fountain, and the smaller homes were distanced from this, branching off further from the town center along narrow lanes so that the homes enjoyed a more private setting. The pavement here was cobbled with white and pink stones, well-kept and grass-free between the cobbles.

At length they approached a long, low building in the center of the cluster, climbed the steps, and stopped just outside the entrance, their way was barred by the crossed halberds of two sentries. "Keeper! You have brought her?" one sentry inquired. "Yes, it is I, and this is she," the warrior responded. It struck her as a very ritualistic exchange. The weapons were uncrossed with a salute, and she was pushed gently forward by the man at her side. "Go now. Enter the Hall of Images and walk forward until you reach the center dais. I cannot come in with you, it is against Arkadian law for Keepers to enter any of the Halls." She hesitated, looking back fearfully at him. "Go forth!" he said again firmly, "I will be waiting for you when it is over." She turned hesitantly and walked timidly forward, clasping her hands together for comfort. She was shaking all over although there was nothing frightening about the surroundings, yet the words "when it is over" somehow filled her with fear. When what was over? What was this place full of warm summer sunshine, strangely made buildings and meticulously kept countryside? Had she fallen back into the past somehow and ended up in ancient Greece or some similar place? Who were these people dressed so peculiarly? What were they going to do to her?

All these questions tumbled around her brain as she walked slowly forward with faltering footsteps down the long, pillared hallway until she reached a circular center area. She stopped and looked carefully around before making her way to the center dais, then halted again before the dais, uncertain whether she should climb up or wait. She waited. No one was in the building, but she could hear a soft rustling and murmur as if people were nearby, moving quietly and whispering. The woman turned and looked back the way she had come and could just make out the warrior standing in the center of the doorway with the two sentries on either side. He motioned her further with one arm, so she turned and stepped up onto the dais at last, walking hesitantly out until she reached the exact center. People were suddenly around her on all sides dressed in white linen robes and seated on fancy, golden chairs like thrones. She gasped, but said nothing, hunching in upon herself slightly as she waited to see who, or what, these people were, and what would happen next.

"Greetings, She Who Has Newly Arrived," spoke a short man with white hair and beard, "I trust your journey here has not been too traumatic? Though it is true some of the journeys are. How was yours?" He looked kindly upon her as he stepped onto the dais, yet it was obvious to her that he expected an answer to his strange question. "I- I don't understand you," she whispered, unable to speak any louder. "Ahh!" a collective sigh arose from the group. She glanced around, still trembling, unsure what the group sigh could possibly mean. The man who had spoken to her came closer, "You do not know your own name, then?" he quizzed her, looking directly into her brown eyes, "No, you do not, I can see it in your eyes" he said, before she had time to answer. "You are one of those who have had a traumatic journey here. That is both good and bad." She shook her head, more puzzled than ever. "Sit," he commanded, pointing to a small stone bench with a purple cushion upon it which she was sure hadn't been there a moment before. She stumbled over to the bench and sat, clumsy with fright. The man spoke to her once more, "Do you know what has happened?" She nodded. "Well, then," he replied, "Tell me." She gulped and then said disjointedly, "There was a man chasing me, and I crashed my car, and another car was wrecked, and someone was dead, and they left me behind! I was walking for help and another man called to me from the woods and I went to him. And now I'm here." She gulped again.

The man shook his head slowly, "No, that is not what happened. You have started the story at the end, tell me from the beginning." She looked at him in surprise. As far as she was concerned, the car wreck is what led her to the strange circumstance she now found herself in, and it was the beginning. "What do you consider the beginning, sir?" she asked, feeling suddenly exhausted. He smiled, "That is better. Tell me your story from the time you were at work until the time you entered our world of Arkady." She did a double take, if he knew, why ask her? She stared at him, saying nothing. Who was this man? What was going on? He spoke again, sensing her unasked questions, "People often enter this world in confusion. You must tell me your story so that I know how much you are aware of and can help you to better understand your circumstances. Please begin." She sat up a little straighter and began.

"Well, um, at work today I worked only the morning shift, because my youngest sister is getting married, and the boss let me have the afternoon off to drive to the airport in Toronto and board a flight back home to Nepal. One of my coworkers gave me a gift for my sister. She wanted to do something nice for her because I've been a good friend of hers since I arrived in Canada. It's a locket that she found in an antique shop. It won't open, but it looks so nice. I put it around my neck to keep it safe, and I think my sister will like it." The man shifted and said, "May I see this locket?"

She pulled an ancient, heart-shaped golden locket with an engraved rose on the front out from under her shirt and held it forward. The man nodded solemnly and tried to pick it up from her hand, but he received a jolt of electric shock, and he drew back quickly, "Please continue with your story."

She exclaimed, "Oh!" and then said, "It must have been static, sorry! Uh, that's all, really. I left work at noon, and it was an ordinary workday except for the gift and getting off work early. When I walked out of the door at work, a man wearing a black and red hooded cloak was standing there and he tried to grab me, so I ran for my car and drove away as quickly as I could. But he followed in another car and tried many times to drive me off the road! It was snowing heavily, and the roads were very slippery. Finally, he succeeded, and I ended up in the ditch. I couldn't get loose from the seatbelt, and my car was on fire! I thought he came to help, but he didn't help! He searched my pockets and my car for something and was hissing as he searched. I've never heard anybody hiss before; it was weird. Then he left when the police and emergency workers showed up. But nobody would help me, and I lost consciousness. When I woke up, I found that somebody must have helped me because I was safely away. And there was a dead body. I think I kill," She couldn't say it. She stopped and gulped as a tear rolled down her face. She couldn't say it aloud. She killed someone. With her stupid reckless driving. She sat and waited, unable to speak further.

"I see you do not understand at all what has happened then," said the man, coming forward once more. "You are now in the land of Arkady, and it is a land the living cannot walk." She looked confused once more "Is this Heaven?" Laughter softly echoed all around her. "No, does it look like heaven to you?" She glanced back in the direction of the door and thought of the strange warrior once more; she blushed, turning away, and said quickly, "No! No!" The man said, "The body you saw was your own. You did not make it alive out of that wreck," he said calmly to her, "You are now in the realm of Arkady which lies between the worlds of living and dead, and you can no longer walk the paths of the living. You are a ghost, as are all who you see here. Those who are here have tasks, which must be accomplished before we are released to our final death. Do you understand now?"

She did not answer, but it did make a strange sort of sense to her once it was spoken. That explained why there was no snow, and strange dress customs. She looked down at herself, suddenly aware she must look stupid in jeans and sweater among all these people wearing linen outfits, only to find she was not dressed in jeans and sweater after all but in a light, flowing white gown belted at the waist with a braided leather belt, and sandals on her feet. How strange that she hadn't noticed before. She looked up quickly, eyes wide. "Yes," Silenus said, "your eyes are now opened to the reality before you. It has indeed been a troubled journey for you, and lucky for us that you still bear the locket upon your breast." She reached down and touched the locket as he spoke, wondering. "That locket is many living generations old and contains a seed which must be planted to ensure the safety of all things. The man who was chasing you is a Daimon from the evil world of Brimstone, and he was after the locket, indeed he has been following it for many generations and must not be allowed to get it, or it will be the death of us all."

She giggled suddenly. She couldn't help it. Before her was this stern and serious man speaking of dying when everyone was already dead here. She slithered off the bench in a fit of giggles, unable to stop. Soon she was joined by several others in the ring of thrones around her; they obviously had caught the joke and were just as humored by it. Finally, she got herself under control and, wiping the tears from her eyes, sat up on the dais and said, "I'm so sorry! I don't know what came over me!" The man smiled "That is alright, it was a poor choice of words, perhaps, yet as you can see death is not devoid of interest. This too will be wiped out if that man gets his clutches on the locket, and because he is a Daimon, he has the power to step between the worlds of living and dead and walk equally in all worlds, unlike ordinary ghosts, who cannot be seen or heard in the land of the living."

She sobered immediately, not liking that thought. "Here," she said, standing up and taking the locket off, "You take it!" She held it out, waiting. "No, I cannot. It belongs to the one it was given to. You are the one who must protect the locket and plant its seed." She pushed the locket into his hand, and he jumped as it shocked him again. "You see now?" said the man angrily, "The locket knows who should hold it. You must keep it safe." She stared at him for a moment, pulling her hand in at last and replacing the locket about her neck. "Oh, I'm sorry! Uh, what should I do?" she asked, no longer confused as to what happened, but very confused as to what they expected of her. The man said, "You will have to travel through the land to reach Snowmelt Wood in the south. There is a planting glade in the center of that forest and that is where the seed must be planted." She glanced around at the people looking at her, "Do not worry," he continued, "You will be given help for the journey. For now, you will remain in the town a few days and rest from your recent accident, while we decide the best approach to the area, as well as the best people to send with you."

The man walked back to the ring of thrones and then both he and the ring of people disappeared as the last words were spoken and she found herself alone once more upon the dais. Not even the stone bench was left. She stood there a moment in astonishment and then turned to face the long hallway she'd walked down. The warrior was gone! She spun around thinking she had simply turned to the wrong hallway but there were no other paths beyond the one she had come down which ended in the large circular area. She climbed down the steps hurriedly and almost ran down the hall in her sudden panic, feeling rather like a child who has lost her mother in a shopping mall. She reached the door after what felt an eternity (it seemed to her the hall had grown longer as she had gone down it, but she knew it was fear that made it seem so).

Just as she was about to step over the threshold, two long halberds were crossed smartly in front of her, barring the way. She stopped in surprise and looked at the sentries on either side, then looked ahead once more at the town square. There was the warrior standing by the fountain directly in front of her, and the older, bearded man who had spoken to her was facing him, speaking. She desperately wanted to hear what was being said and pressed her hands against the halberds blocking her exit. One of the sentries turned then and said, not unkindly, "Stay! Wait with patience one moment." She stopped trying to push through but kept her hands upon the halberd of the guard who had spoken, looking out and straining her ears to hear.

"And so, you see why this is so dangerous," spoke the older man pompously, "but from henceforth you must not come near the woman. Am I understood?" The warrior nodded and replied, "Yes, my liege, it is understood. I shall return to my duties." He turned immediately and strode away across the far side of the square as the older man turned back to the sentries and said, "You may release her now." The halberds were raised, and she stood numbly in the doorway, making no move to go further, looking after the warrior as he strode away into the distant fields at a rapid pace. "Come!" called the man to her, "You may come out now, for it is safe!" She still stood in the doorway not moving a muscle, not heeding the words spoken; her eyes remained on the warrior until he at last disappeared behind a grove of trees at the edge of one of the fields. She fell to her knees at that and cried "No! No! You can't send him away like that! No! I wanted to talk to him!" The two sentries looked down at her surprised, trading a swift glance with each other before turning to the older man who now came forward and stood in front of her. "Get up!" he said, harshly, "You do not know what you are saying! He is dangerous to you, as are all the Keepers of the Gates and you must not approach any of the Keepers from henceforth."

She ignored him, refusing to look up from where she knelt, and instead focused her eyes upon the marble step underneath. She felt dazed beyond any ability to respond; so much had happened in so short a space of time. The older man said sternly "You must not remain on the step of one of the Halls like this; I will send someone to show you to the quarters prepared. Mope there if you will!" He walked quickly away, and she snarled venomously "You rotten, rotten man!" She looked up in surprise, not quite believing she had said those words, and worried what the sentries would think. They both looked quickly away, trying to hide smiles. "You'll be alright," one of them said quietly, "They always come back." "Aye, that's right," the other one added, "Listen to Bert, he's been here longer than me, he knows. The Keepers, they always come back." She felt strangely strengthened by that and stood up, then walked down the steps and over to the fountain to look out once more upon the fields.

A young woman in her early twenties found her there half an hour later, staring down at her toes. "My name is Daisy Mae. Are you the newcomer with no name?" the girl inquired softly of her. The newcomer looked over at the young woman, startled, "No name? But everyone has a name! Why do they keep saying that to me? Where am I, really? What is this place? Some of what was said in there doesn't quite make sense to me." Daisy Mae brushed a stray lock of curly, dark brown hair out of her face, looked carefully about to see if anyone was near, then softly said "Come with me. I am to show you to your quarters, we can speak more freely there."

They walked away from the fountain, following a small lane to one side and eventually came out upon a meadow with little houses dotted about. The young girl walked up to a house off to one side of the path farthest from the town and close to some of the farm fields, then opened the door. "Here, this will be your place of residence for a few days at least. Come inside and I will show you around." They entered the house, and the young girl took another swift look around both in the house and outside the door, shutting the door swiftly and quietly as she did so. "Listen carefully!" Daisy Mae whispered, "I must speak quickly, for what you carry means there will be an almost constant watch on you!"

She glanced at the little window and back again, "All of us – all of us women that is – have been talking about what happened this day. Never has one of the Keepers of Gates brought someone here hand-in-hand as happened this day when you were brought! Keepers are not known for being overly friendly with strangers, although they are kind. The council members do not trust them and work hard to keep them at a distance from the towns whenever possible, but they are a nice people, whatever the council think. He must like you!" She stopped and put her hand over her mouth, trying not to giggle.

"We saw what old Snaggletooth did today, sending him away from you," she continued, "Oh! But do not call him Snaggletooth to his face! That is just what we women call him!" The young girl stopped, wondering if she had said too much and might get in trouble. "Who is he?" asked the newcomer, "Is he like the chief or something here?" The girl shook her head quickly, "No! Nothing of the kind, though he likes to pretend he is! His name is Silenus, but he insists on being called Chief Elder by the women, and by the men My Liege." But truly, he is only a steward, and not the most important of those because Greenfield is a small town!" Both women looked towards the door suddenly as they heard approaching footsteps crunching on the gravel walk.

Daisy Mae moved quickly to the bed and said loudly "And here is the bed of course, it has many pillows on it, but you can put them on the floor when you sleep, you do not need to use them all if you do not wish, they are only decoration!" She laughed and tossed a pillow to the newcomer, who caught it deftly, giggling. A short pillow fight ensued between them. The door opened and Silenus stood there, looking stern. The women stood still, pillows in hand, looking at him like children caught out in naughtiness. "Ah, good, you have made her forget. That is well." He turned and left once more, walking down the path but leaving the door open. They stared after him, still holding the pillows.

"So," the newcomer ventured after a long while, "can he just pop up and appear anywhere? I saw him disappear earlier, and in that hall an entire bunch of people appeared and then disappeared, along with a stone bench." Daisy Mae replaced the pillows on the bed and answered, "No he cannot, although he likes people to think he can. It is all tricks with mirrors and such and can only be done inside the Hall of Images, that is where he has his foolishness set up. He does not even have that many councilors, in truth, but the mirrors make them appear to be more than they really are. There are only five. They must have pushed the bench out when you weren't looking, and pulled it away again as well." The newcomer thought back to the chamber, "Yes! Now that you mention it, a lot of those people in the audience did seem remarkably similar! Only I was a bit caught up in the confusion of everything that was happening to me, and I didn't notice at the time, but it seemed like a great crowd!" The girl nodded, "We do not have to worry that he can suddenly pop up in the middle of a conversation in here, like he can in that Hall of Images, though if he wants to, he can be quite quiet and come quite near before we are aware. That's probably why he left the door open: he's keeping an eye on us from some hidden window, although I think he's far enough away not to hear us, even if he can see us through the open door. That's probably why he came here, to open it so that he could watch. But be on your guard not to speak carelessly!"

They walked outside together and stood at the entrance looking back down the path toward the town. "I must go now, or Snaggletooth will return again, he doesn't want anyone talking to you for very long, although I don't know why. I'm going to ask around and see what I can find out." said the young girl, "I will come again if I am allowed and tell you what I can!" she walked quickly away towards town and the newcomer turned and entered the house once more, thinking she had found a good friend. The newcomer looked around the house carefully. It was a small, one-room house with white marble walls and ceiling. A large, woven rug in bright reds and yellows covered the entire floor. Apart from the bed, there was an only a small table under the sole window which had upon it a bowl of assorted fruit, an unlit candle, a few matches, and a vase of flowers. There wasn't even a chair in the house or pictures on the walls. "What a bare little place!" she exclaimed.

She sat on the edge of the bed and wondered suddenly why there was food and a bed if she was supposed to be a ghost. Did dead people really need to eat, or to rest? This was all very strange, but Silenus did mention that death wasn't devoid of interest. She sat puzzling over it for quite some time. "What is my name?" She asked herself at last, looking up to stare out the little window, surprised she would forget her name. "How can I forget my own name? I know my name! Why, it's – uh, it's," She broke off, puzzled. She truly couldn't remember her name. She pulled the locket out from under her shirt and held it in her hand staring at it in confusion. "I was going to give this to someone, I know I was. Who?"

The living world was already beginning to fade from her mind and become dim. "Let me see, I work in an office on a computer." She glanced up at the window, then nodded, "No, I work on several computers. But what work to I actually perform? Hm, let me think. Oh yes! I'm with the technical team and I repair computers. That's right!" She frowned, looking down at the locket once more. "I don't remember what company I work for. Who was I going to give this to? Somebody important. I'm pretty sure I wasn't going to keep it." She was silent again, thinking, then began talking aloud to herself once more, "I was going to the airport. Yes, I was going to the airport and there was a car crash. Why was I driving to the airport?" She paused again, still frowning, then placed the locket back under her shirt and looked up, "My sister! That's it! I was going back home to Nepal for my sister's wedding!"

The newcomer stood up and went over to the open door, leaning on the frame as she looked out and sighing heavily, "She's going to be worried about me, oh dear! There must be a way for me to get word to her and let her know that I'm okay. I don't want to ruin her wedding." She thrust herself away from the doorframe with a burst of energy and walked quickly down the cobbled path until she was within a few yards of the town. Staring down the narrow lane between buildings, she concentrated, listening to the sounds of the day and the greetings people shouted to each other. No one was looking in her direction that she could tell, and she didn't really feel like talking just yet, even though she had questions. She sighed, then turned and stepped off the path, into the meadow, strolling slowly and looking at the flowers and butterflies all around, brushing her fingertips against the waist-high meadow grass. It was pleasant out here with a soft breeze playing through her long, dark brown hair and the sounds of nature all around. She began to relax a little as the quiet setting soothed her jangled nerves, and the sense of strange urgency began to leave her at last. The image of the handsome warrior who had led her to this place came to her mind, and she smiled, stopping to look around.

She saw a farmer in the distance, milking two cows outside a small stable, and began walking purposefully through the tall grass towards the stable. "Where are you going?" said a sharp voice close behind her. She jumped and spun around to see Silenus there. Drat the man! She hated him already. He must have been watching her from a window somewhere, just as Daisy Mae had said. She looked at him, saying nothing, and waited for him to continue. "Where are you going?" he demanded again. "I wanted to talk to the man with the cows over there," she pointed to the stable, "I like cows." She didn't really care two beans for cows one way or the other but felt at that very moment as if she needed to excuse her direction even though up to that point nothing had been said about her staying in one spot. He stared at her a moment longer, and then shifted his attention to scan the surroundings. Turning on his heels without a word, he walked quickly back to town, leaving her standing there with her arm still outstretched towards the stable. "How very odd," she said softly to herself, "how very odd indeed!" She changed her mind and let her arm drop, then strolled slowly back through the tall grass in the direction of her house, brushing her fingertips over the feathery tops of the tall grass as she walked.

Chapter 3 – The Farmer And The Women

The woman sat on a small bench at one side of her door and leaned against the house wall as she looked out across the meadow, replaying conversations in her mind. She remembered the words of Daisy Mae, "There will be an almost constant watch on you." It was best to remain in or near her little assigned place if she didn't want to attract too much unwanted attention. She wondered what Silenus had been looking around for when he accosted her in the meadow earlier today; it was almost as if Silenus himself were afraid of being watched by someone. Was he afraid one of the warriors would come after him if he went too far from the town? He certainly hadn't been very nice to the man who had brought her to the town, perhaps the warriors didn't like him, she knew Daisy Mae didn't. She snorted softly to herself, "I don't like him, either!" she whispered. What were the warriors called now, Keepings? No, Keepers? Yes, that was the word, Keepers. Keepers of Gates. She replayed the morning walk with the tall warrior in her mind and sighed softly.

She had once again begun to forget her past life as her memory of the living world began to tatter and fade like a dream, leaving only snippets of memories in her mind, but the sense of uncertain urgency had returned. Daisy Mae had appeared just before sunset with a supper tray and set it upon her table with a hurried whisper, "It's your locket! That's why Silenus is watching you so closely! He wants it, but he cannot touch it! Keep it hidden under your gown and don't let him or any of his councilors try to take it for any reason! I have to go now!" The newcomer had followed Daisy back out of the house and watched as her new friend hurried back down the path toward town, then she sat on the bench once more, wishing that Daisy Mae could have stayed to talk with her. The sun was beginning to set, and the sky was growing dark, yet still she leaned against the house wall, unwilling to go inside and be completely alone.

Town was quiet, no voices or footsteps were heard. People had gone home to their suppers and beds. Stars had begun to peep forth as the night grew darker and chilly, and the newcomer wondered if

Silenus might still be watching her from some dark window. She shivered, partly from cold, and partly with the thought of Silenus watching her. Finally, she sighed and went inside the house, shutting her door to escape the chilly night breeze. Overcome with exhaustion at last, she ignored the supper tray on her table and sank down on the bed, where she slowly slumped down and fell asleep, not waking again until late the following morning.

When she awoke, she sat up and rubbed her eyes blearily, blinking the sleep out of them and glancing around. "Where am I?" She asked herself, confused and momentarily forgetful of all that had passed the previous day. She stood and slowly walked the two steps over to the small table. As awareness returned to her, she noticed that the supper tray had been taken away and the bowl of fruit had been changed out with fresh fruits, and a small plate had been placed next to it with two blueberry muffins on it. "How nice!" she exclaimed, "But, I'm just too worried to be hungry. I wish I knew why I was worried, though." She glanced around the bare room once more until her gaze settled on the small window. She could see the farmer in the distance as he released two cows out into a field to graze. "Arkady," she said softly. She glanced through the open door of the house and tried to remember if she had shut it the previous night. She sighed, walked out of the door, and sat down on the small bench again. "I've forgotten the name of the town! I'm sure Daisy Mae mentioned it. I'm pretty sure that I've never been a forgetful sort of person before now." she sighed to herself, resting her chin in her hands.

The day passed slowly for the small woman, she spent her time sitting outside her door and thinking, trying to remember her past and her name, but most of her memories were now too fragmented to recall. At midday, the young woman Daisy Mae came walking merrily down the path towards the newcomer's house, carrying a tray. "Hello!" she greeted the newcomer cheerfully, "Are you feeling better today? You were sleeping soundly when I brought breakfast. I've brought you some lunch! It's just a turkey sandwich and some fresh vegetables, but you're probably

hungry!" The newcomer stood and smiled, glad to
see a friendly face, "Thank you! It's Daisy Mae,
correct?" Daisy Mae nodded and entered the house
to place the lunch tray on the table. "That's right!"
she said as the newcomer followed her in. "Why,
you haven't eaten anything! Don't you like
muffins or fruit? You didn't eat anything
yesterday, either!" The newcomer replied, "I'm
sorry, I appreciate the care you've shown me, but
I'm just not ready to eat yet. I'm still feeling pretty
nervous and confused." Daisy Mae nodded and
said, "I can't stay long, Snaggletooth is on the
prowl today, but I'll try and bring something
different for your supper. You need to eat, even if
you are worried! I'll leave the blueberry muffins
here for you as well." She left shortly afterwards,
and the newcomer followed her out of the house
and watched her walk down the cobbled path and
turn into the town square, disappearing in the mass
of people who were moving swiftly about on
errands of their own.

"Alone again!" the newcomer sighed, entering her
house once more and walking over to the table.

She looked at the tray and returned to the bench outside of her house without touching it, sitting down once more in the warm sunshine to watch the activity in the town square. That evening, supper had been brought to her by Daisy Mae, who once more did not stay to talk, or even speak a word. The young woman tilted her head to the brush at one side of the path as she entered the house with the tray, and the newcomer glanced over to see a hint of white behind the brush – Silenus! Daisy Mae left quickly, after changing out the food trays, and the newcomer remained outside the house, her supper untouched, as she kept her eyes on the brush. She was rewarded with a glimpse of Silenus moving quickly towards the town, hunched over as if trying not to be seen until he at last entered a house just beside the town square. Now she knew from which house windows he was watching!

Late that evening, the newcomer stood once again within her doorway, leaning on the frame, and staring at the silent town. She had walked down the narrow lane and into the town square after people had returned to homes and closed their doors for the night, but she didn't remain there long because the deserted square made her feel nervous and she wondered if Silenus might come out from a doorway at any moment. She returned to her little house after quickly glancing about the town but didn't go inside. The stars were now shining brightly down on her from a dark sky as she stood quietly within the open doorway. A red fox trotted out of the brush nearby and stopped in front of her house, looking keenly at her. She returned the gaze, fascinated that it would come so close.

The fox sat on its haunches and faced her, and she knelt slowly down, coaxing softly, "Here little guy, come here, I won't hurt you!" It stood and walked up to her just as if it had been a tame dog; she reached out and stroked it gently. "Hey, what is that around your neck, little guy?" she felt something under the fur and scratched him behind the ears, working her way back down his neck to where she had felt it. The fox yipped softly, and she thought she heard words, "Take the string off."

Working her fingers through the thick fur, she caught the string between her fingers and pulled lightly. The fox jumped back, and the string snapped. She watched as the little fox trotted back the way it had come, then glanced down to see the string between her fingers, and a scrunched-up piece of paper tied into it.

She peered nervously around, then took the paper and carefully pulled it loose from the string. Smoothing the note on her knee, she read the words in the bright moonlight, "I am watching, do not be afraid. Do not trust the old goat in town but show him respect. Burn the note tonight. We will meet early tomorrow morning and I will talk with you." She glanced towards the bushes behind the house and saw a tall, dark figure striding away across the field on the other side of them, with a fox at his heels. Her heart leapt within her chest. It was him! She knew it; he was not lost to her! She stood up and looked down the path to make sure no one was about, then went inside and shut the door, walking swiftly over to the little table with the supper tray and bowl of fruit upon it. She read the note one more time, wanting to keep it, but knew better. Finally with reluctance she held it over the candle on the table which Daisy Mae had lit when she dropped off the supper tray, and watched the hungry flames lick at it until it was gone. She looked at the supper tray on the table; suddenly hungry now that she knew he was out there close by. "But do dead people eat?" she asked herself again, then shrugged and grabbed a piece of cold, fried chicken as her belly rumbled.

She woke early on the following morning and sat up in bed, then ran her fingers through her long, dark brown hair to try and untangle it. "I really need a comb, and a bath!" she murmured softly as she deftly wove her tangled hair into a loose, messy braid to neaten the mass of tangles as best she could. She sighed, "I need something to tie this, or it'll fall out again!" She got out of bed still holding the end of the braid with one hand and glanced around the small house, but there was nothing she could use. "I suppose I could use the locket chain, but somehow I think I'd better keep that hidden." She walked to the door and threw it open. Birds were singing and the sun had just begun to peep over the horizon, tinting the sky pink. She looked around thinking how beautiful it was here, suddenly remembering the first sunrise standing on the ridge with the strange warrior.

She wondered when he would come today to talk to her. She walked quickly to the edge of the path and pulled up several long strands of green meadow grass with one hand, then carefully tucked the end of her braid under the front of her shift collar so that she could twist the grass strands together. Her nimble fingers made short work of the task and soon her braid was secured, and she let it drop down her back, messy, but out of her face.

Almost as soon as she had finished, she noticed a tall, tanned, figure with short brown hair, short-sleeved, light blue cotton shirt and brown leather pants striding across the meadow towards her house: it was the farmer she had tried to approach yesterday. She stepped out into the meadow a short way, waved, and waited for him. "Greetings!" he said to her upon arriving, "I see you are up and about early, that is good! Silenus and his bunch of friends tend to sleep in so we should be able to have a good talk before they are up. I was hoping you would be awake. You did burn the note, didn't you?"

"How do you know about the note?" she asked, looking up into his blue eyes with surprise, "I mean, good morning! I didn't mean to be rude." He laughed and said "It is I who gave you the note last night, through my friend the fox. I see you enjoyed his company, you are good with animals, he told me that you understood him. That is good to know. I will be able to get messages to you at need that way." Her eyes opened wide, "So, it was you I saw last night walking away with the fox?" He nodded, "Yes, who else would it be with a wild animal?" She was confused. So, it wasn't her warrior friend after all that she had seen last night. What a strange turn of events. "Well, aren't you a farmer? I saw you milking cows the other day. I didn't know farmers had much to do with wild animals. I thought perhaps you were, uh," she broke off, not wanting to sound rude by letting him know she wished he were someone else. The farmer smiled and said "I know who you look for each day, you will meet him again, do not fear. However, it is not wise just yet for you to encounter any of the Keepers; you must know more about your situation here first and then we can decide how best to approach the problem at hand."

She nodded and then said abruptly, "Last night, the fox yipped and told me to take the string off. At least, it seemed like the fox telling me that, but it couldn't have been, could it? Was that your voice I heard?" He grinned and replied, "No, it was not my voice! You did hear the fox. I said you were good with animals. Some of us in this world are gifted with understanding animal speech, and you are one of them, as I am. This world brings out many, varied talents in people that the living world doesn't have. You'll enjoy it once you're settled in properly and back on your feet." He motioned to her house, "Come, let us sit on the bench outside

your house and talk; I have much to tell you."
They walked the short distance to her house and
sat down next to each other. "To answer your
earlier question," he continued, "I am not exactly a
farmer. Here there are no farmers, although many
occupations do tend to overlap the old familiar
ones of the living world. I am known as a Tender
of Beasts. I, and others like me have a special
knack with animals both tame and wild, being able
to understand their speech, as you discovered last
night with the fox. So, we tend to them as needed,
feeding the farm animals, milking them, that sort
of thing. In regards to the wild animals, it is mostly
a matter of mending their hurts when they get
injured. Some of the wild animals are used as
messengers, such as the foxes and owls. Then there
are those folk who work in fields and gardens who
are known as Sowers of Soil, and of course there
are Shepherds who tend sheep and goats. Oh, the
list goes on, and I do not have time to tell you all
now since I wish to focus on the things you need to
know, but those are the three occupations which
you might consider a farmer."

She nodded, waiting for him to continue. "It is rumored that you are one who does not remember her name, is this true?" he asked her curiously. "I wasn't sure why Silenus kept calling me that when I arrived," she answered, "but I've tried recalling my name ever since, and I just can't do it!" She was dismayed about it once more; it seemed such a stupid thing. He nodded and answered, "It happens sometimes that a person will die before their time has been set. In those cases, the person who has died cannot remember their name. Most of the people cannot even remember any of the details of their past life, or very few details, and what little they do remember tends to fade away as the days go by. You were not supposed to die the other day, and I believe I know the answer although I am not entirely certain of it."

She waited as he continued, "You see, the man who killed you is an evil one both in the living world and in the world of Arkady. He is a type of ghost known as a Daimon. The Daimons are people who have entered one of the ghost worlds as a living person and been killed by a ghost, and they are much stronger than ordinary ghosts such as you and I. He knew that he should not approach you, because those in the living world who are touched by one of the ghosts in harmful manner will die. It was not your time. It is a good thing the Gate was closed in time, or he would have followed you here and perhaps acquired the treasure you bear, or taken you to Brimstone where you would have been made a slave to the evil Master." Her ears perked up at the mention of a gate, "The warrior said something about gates too, but I don't remember seeing one!" she said, "Where was it? Can I get back home through it? I really need to talk to my sister and let her know I'm okay."

The man sighed sadly and looked around carefully to ensure privacy, "Listen, I wish to tell you much, but the sun is already rising higher, and I must be gone before there is any chance of us being seen together: Silenus does not trust me because he knows I speak regularly with the Keepers, and he is afraid of the Keepers. Firstly, I'm sorry, but you cannot contact your sister in the living world from here. Even if I could open a Gate as the Keepers do and place you right beside her in the living world, you would still not be able to talk to her because you're a ghost, and we ghosts are invisible to the living world, sight, and sound. I'm very sorry." He placed a strong hand on her shoulder and squeezed it reassuringly, "It will be alright." She shook her head in denial, "No! I saw the man who you said was a ghost. Why couldn't my sister see me?" The Tender of Beasts said gently, "That man is a stronger ghost, a Daimon, and those type of ghosts can walk both worlds and interact with them. You are an ordinary ghost, as are most of us here, and you cannot interact with the living world." She brushed a tear from her eye, nodded, and collected herself once more as the Tender of Beasts continued, "Now, listen carefully and let me speak quickly. You will have to interpret my words later after I have gone, and if you are confused, I will try to answer them the next time we meet." He leaned closer to her so that he could speak softly.

"When we talk about Gates here, or the Keepers of Gates, what we mean is that split-second opening between worlds which occurs when someone crosses between life and death. When someone dies in their proper time, the Keepers are ready for them and open the Gate for them to come through, and then escort them to the town they will belong to in this world. There are specific areas in Arkady where people come in, and the Keepers wait there for them. If you look out there, you will see two tall pillars of red stone," Here Harold pointed to a pair of gigantic, red stone columns in the far distance and she followed his pointing finger with her eyes, "That is one of the regular Gates. The Keepers built them long ago, and they wait near these places each day to help people through, then take them to the towns." She nodded again, still peering at the pillars to see if she could spy a Keeper standing guard. "But when someone dies who was not supposed to die at that time, as it was in your situation, the Keepers are not aware of the death ahead of time and do not open a Gate. It is evil which has made an opening and pushed the person through, or tried to. The Keepers must find that opening, and then try to save the person if they can."

He paused and looked at her to make sure she understood, and when she nodded, he continued, "The Keeper who came to help you did not arrive in time to save you and so he did the next best thing by guiding you to safety in this town." She shook her head, "But, what would have happened if he hadn't? That man was already gone when the Keeper arrived." Harold said, "No, the man was still there, but the Keeper chased him away, and banished him back to his own evil world, which is called Brimstone. If the Keeper had not done that, then you would have been kidnapped by the man and taken to Brimstone, where you would have been treated badly and made a slave to the evil Master there." She shuddered in revulsion as Harold continued speaking, "After the Keeper banished the man who killed you, he went searching for you, because you had been flung from your body. That is probably why you didn't see the fight, you were unconscious, or too far away. I do not have time now to explain all to you without Silenus waking and catching us, but you do need to understand at least a little of what has happened to you." He paused and looked carefully at her to make sure she was following his speech.

"There are special Keepers who are known as Keepers of the Dragon Gates. At least, that is what we call them here in Arkady, but I do not know what they call themselves, none of us do, they are a bit of a mystery to us since they don't live here but only enter Arkady to work and then return to their own world, and Silenus doesn't allow them to talk with us Arkadians more than necessary. We Arkadians don't actually know much about the Keepers Rites or their way of life, but we have our own tales about them. But, back to the matter at hand, the man you met is one of those type of Gate Keepers who constantly move around Arkady looking for forced entry, and work to ensure the Dragon Gates wrongfully opened are closed again. Sometimes they can arrive in time enough to send someone back through to the living world before their bodies have entirely given up, so that a person may be 'brought back to life' or 'saved from death' as they say in the living world. But most often they are not able to reach the Dragon

Gate in time. Then it is their job to close the Gate, first defeating, or at least forcing the evil back to Brimstone; after which they escort the person to the nearest town for care. That is what happened in your case." Her eyes were wide listening to this strange information, it flew in the face of everything she had ever known or believed.

"I believe that you were told that you had a traumatic journey here. Let me tell you this: you did have one, for the fight at that opening between worlds was for your life, between the Keeper who brought you here and the evil one who killed you. The force of the battle flung you from your body and away from the area where you died. That is why you found yourself alone like that, and it should not have happened, but it was a fierce battle from the account I have heard. That is why you were disoriented, and everything is so strange to you. Most people who come here are aware that they have died, and they make the transition fine, but you did not have an easy journey, and so things are confusing for you. When the transition happens so fast like that, a person has no real closure, and cannot grasp that they've died or moved into another world, another life. This is why you are so confused right now.

Things will become clearer in time, but we need to make sure that Silenus doesn't catch you talking too much to me or some of the others who are known to be in regular contact with the Keepers. He is very distrustful of them, and of all who talk with them daily, such as me, so I'm afraid you'll be learning information in small bits and pieces, but I will do what I can, as will others you meet in the days ahead. The women of the town are trustworthy. You can also trust Bert the sentry; he's the older, slightly heavyset man with grey hair who stands at the Hall of Images."

The man looked up as a blue jay flew low and perched on his shoulder for a moment, then flew off. "I must leave soon, or we will be caught, Silenus is awake. Let me tell you one last thing and I hope I have not confused you too badly. Do not trust Silenus, he will tell you some truth, but only that truth which he thinks will gain your cooperation. Try not to question him about certain things, for instance it would not do for you to talk about the Keepers. Ask him innocent things to put him off guard if you run across him, nothing too deep. Talk about the Hall symbols, or ask about the work that is done here, things like that. Avoid the locket subject if you can although he may wish to speak on it, but especially do not let him or any of the town elders touch it and keep it hidden under your clothing at all times.

He has only been assigned to this town recently and things have changed for the worse since he has arrived, I suspect he may be one of the servants of the evil Master of Brimstone, working undercover. You do not know about that yet because there's been no time, but you will soon. Just trust me as best you can and I will talk to you again this evening after the sun has set if all remains quiet, then I will explain things more fully. Try and talk to the women in the town today, they will help you to understand, and they will ease your loneliness as well. Silenus should ease his watch over you a little if he sees you happily engaged with the women."

He stood up and strode quickly away and she stood to watch him leave before turning and going into the house for a piece of fruit. She ate the apple slowly, replaying the conversation and trying to place everything in her memory. Finally, she stepped outside again and looked around, but there was nothing to do here. Now that she had some answers and was beginning to understand this new life, she didn't want to be alone. She started walking, taking the path towards the little town. She wanted to think, and she always thought best while walking; she also liked the man's idea of meeting with the women of the town to ease her loneliness.

"What do you think you're doing here?" The query came from behind her. It was the voice of Silenus. She didn't even jump this time but turned from where she had been gazing at the fountain in the middle of the town square and looked straight at him, sighing audibly with exasperation. "I didn't realize that being dead meant I had to sit in one spot and do nothing forever." She said in a short, curt statement, looking him straight in the eye and crossing her arms over her chest. He seemed taken aback, "Oh, well it does not mean you must sit still and do nothing. Why would you think that?" She sighed deeply again and answered, "Twice now you have questioned my presence in certain places: the other day in the field when I wanted to see the cows, and today here in town when I wished to find people for companionship. Am I not allowed to walk freely now that I am dead, or talk to people? And another thing, why does Daisy Mae keep bringing food to my house? Do dead people really need to eat? And sleep? I'm very confused. I've been watching the town square trying to figure things out, but why do some people seem to have jobs and others wander around and relax? Do dead people have jobs like living people? What am I supposed to do now that I'm dead? Should I work, too? I'm so confused and lonely, and I don't know anything about what I'm supposed to do. I don't even know the name of this town. Daisy Mae told me the first day, but I forgot. For that matter, I still can't remember my own name! How can I get by without a name?" She fired the questions off one after the other at Silenus, setting him back on his heels in surprise.

The older man stood staring sternly at the small, fierce woman in silence after she had finished and then smiled nicely as he had at their first meeting, "Of course you may walk freely about! I only thought you might get lost in the field yesterday and today I was simply surprised to see you up and in town so early because many people who aren't working sleep in. Besides, as you said just now, you haven't even learned the name of the town, which is Greenfield, so if you wandered too far, how would you find your way back home?" She returned the smile, not trusting him and yet wanting information. He continued, "You will eventually be assigned work, but I wanted you to rest after your hard journey. Now that you're rested, I think the best thing for you to do this day is to visit with the women about town, I know all women love to talk and they will be able to answer all your questions! That will also give you good company and a chance to make some friends so that you won't be lonely, and they can help you to choose a new name to be known by. I have meetings this day so I cannot take time to answer your questions right now. I was just on my way to the first meeting. Why don't you visit the women?"

She nodded and replied eagerly, "I'd like that! Do you think I could visit with Daisy Mae? Perhaps she could introduce me to the other women since we two have already met?" Silenus nodded quite agreeably and answered, "Yes, that is an excellent idea! You will find Daisy Mae in the Hall of Crafts this morning, along with most of the women." He turned to go, and she stopped him with a last question, "Please, which Hall is Crafts? They all look the same to me." He pointed across the square towards one edge of town and directed her gaze to the top of the building, "Do you see the engraved sewing needle and thread above the door of that one? That is the Crafts symbol. Each Hall has an engraved, golden symbol above the door which specifies what the Hall is used for. The women can explain all the symbols to you." She smiled her most charming smile and replied, "Thank you very much!" then turned and walked in the direction indicated.

Silenus smiled to himself as he walked towards the Hall of Images and said softly "Ah, perhaps this is going to work out fine after all! I had thought yesterday that she was being difficult and wondered what trouble she was plotting as she sat by her door, but now I see she is simply curious and still confused. She should be easily manipulated after all. My Master will be most pleased with me when I turn her over to him tomorrow!" He nodded several times to himself, walked past the two saluting sentries standing guard and entered the Hall of Images. The sentries traded a doubtful glance at each other after Silenus had passed them and then resumed watch duties. One of them gave a quick, upward nod of his head to a passing boy and the boy ran over to him. The sentry leaned down, whispered something in the boy's ear, and then stood still, once more on guard, as the boy ran off as if on fire towards a distant barn.

The newcomer stopped outside the Hall of Crafts and peered in a window before entering. A pleasant, happy chatter of women's voices could be heard drifting out through the open front doors upon the morning air. "Well!" she thought to herself as she walked up the steps and stood in the doorway, "The Tender of Beasts had a good idea to throw innocent questions at Silenus! That should keep Silenus off my back for at least a little while!" She smiled and entered the building. There were dozens of women working around the large, open room at various crafts and chores, and Daisy Mae looked up from her knitting in time to see the newcomer walk in. Daisy Mae ran to meet her, dropping the knitting project unceremoniously on a table. "She is here! The newcomer is here!" and, grabbing the newcomer by the hand, almost dragged her into the circle of women who were now abandoning their work to come over and talk. Daisy Mae spun quickly in circles as she pointed to the other women one by one and named them,

"This is Caroline! This is Maggie! This is Betty and next to her is Georgia! This is Mary over here and this is Jenna, and this is Jill!" The newcomer smiled and said hello to each of the other women as they were introduced, but she knew that she'd never remember a single name because of how fast Daisy Mae was introducing them. "This is Denise, and this is Freya!" Daisy Mae continued naming the women, and the newcomer kept smiling and saying hello, but her ears had long ago tuned out the young woman's voice as she felt herself becoming overwhelmed.

Finally, the introductions were finished, and the newcomer was shown around the big, open room, taking in the various needlework, clothing, and knitting projects lying on tables where they were dropped when she came in. There were weaving looms at one side with half-finished tapestries and rugs, and a large kitchen with a delicious smell of baking breads wafting over the room was situated at the back of the Hall. The women talked quietly and cheerfully, loudly telling her small bits and pieces about life in the town and the assorted work that people did, but mostly giving her whispered advice about staying as far away as possible from Silenus and his band of town leaders.

The voice of Silenus drifted in through a window and the women hushed, looking tensely towards the front door. "Quickly! Quickly!" whispered the woman named Caroline, "There are things we need to tell you before old Snaggletooth comes along to take you away or hear what we have to say!" The women bustled back to the kitchen in a straggling group, some of them chattering and laughing loudly about the Hall symbols to provide a cover in case Silenus entered the building. Daisy Mae hurried in last, speaking softly, "He was speaking to one of the sentries, who he now has posted outside our door, and he has gone by after looking in the window, he's walking back to the Hall of Images now, I think he's satisfied!" Caroline asked, "Who did he post here? Was it Bert?" Daisy Mae shook her head, "No, it was Jack. Bert is still standing at the Hall of Images entrance." Caroline looked swiftly at the newcomer and said quietly, "You won't be able to go out the front door. Bert would have let you past, but none of the other sentries will!" The women grouped together whispering urgently to the newcomer. "You will have to leave today!" "That's right, he may lock you up soon!" "I'm surprised he hasn't already put her under lock and key, the way he's been watching her so closely!" "You must be brave!" Suddenly, Denise pushed a cloth covered bundle into the newcomer's hands with a hurried, "Here, you'll need this for your journey. You'll find some bread and cheese in there and – something else. We can't say more about the other item here. Don't ask questions, there's no time, just keep it safe! We have to get you out of this town before Silenus decides to lock you up, and he will!"

The newcomer clasped the bundle tightly to her chest and tried to take in all the hurried, frantic, whispered advice and information. Everything was very jumbled and confusing because the women around her kept taking turns to speak loudly for the benefit of the sentry posted outside, and the whispered advice was difficult to hear. She began to feel panic rising within her. "But why would he lock me up?" she whispered. Daisy Mae answered, "Because of that locket which you bear; he wants it desperately! It's dangerous in the wrong hands and he mustn't get it, he is evil. We heard Harold tell one of the sentries yesterday afternoon that he was planning to lock you away soon because he's afraid you'll run away once you have a better understanding of our world." Freya said, "The Keepers will help." "That's right," Maggie said in a hushed whisper, "Harold's animals will guide you to the Keepers, but you must go soon!" The newcomer was dazed, "Who's Harold?" she asked.. Caroline said, "Never mind that now, we have to get you out of here quickly so that you can get to safety!"

"Hurry!" hissed Jill, who stood at the edge of the kitchen looking towards the front door. She turned and grabbed the newcomer by her wrist, ushering her to a small, open window at the back of the building, "You can't go out the front door now without being seen and reported. Climb out the back window and run; they won't expect that! Avoid the roads and pathways. Go across the crop fields and into the woods as quickly as you can, and don't let anyone see you! We'll keep up your cover here and pretend you're still with us as long as we can to give you time to reach the Keepers."

Daisy Mae rushed up and hugged the newcomer quickly, "That's right! Don't stop running, whatever you do, just run! We'll meet again." Caroline hurried over and whispered, "Run in the direction this window is facing, get to the woods, and don't let anyone see you!" The newcomer tried to protest but was pushed against the window frame with another frantic "Hurry!" The newcomer climbed awkwardly out, clutching the bundle, and Caroline leaned out and pointed toward the distant line of forest, "That's your goal!" She whispered, "Stay out of sight, and keep going straight across the fields until you reach the trees, then get under cover and one of Harold's animals will guide you. Hurry!" The newcomer looked briefly to left and right to make sure nobody was watching before running to the edge of the town and out into the tall grass toward the nearest farm field, crouching low as she ran to allow the meadow grass to cover her from view as much as possible. The feeling of swelling panic threatened to overcome her but she pushed on, keeping low and moving as fast as she could through the tall grass in the direction that Caroline had pointed out to her.

Chapter 4 – Run For Freedom

The newcomer lay very still trying to calm her ragged breathing. She had made a long, hard run as fast as she could away from the town and across the meadow and four exceedingly long crop fields, standing up and running as fast as she could whenever she thought no one was looking, and then crouching low to run awkwardly if she heard voices or saw someone in the fields. She was now lying quietly in the dirt of a bean field, trying to catch her breath, and hoping that Silenus or his men hadn't heard her running footsteps. Her breath burned in her throat, and she had a terrible stitch in her side, which she was trying to ease by rubbing with one hand. The women in the Craft Hall had told her to run across the crop fields and into the woods, but the newcomer hadn't realized what a long way off the forest was!

At last, she raised herself carefully up off her stomach and onto her elbows, listening for any sounds of pursuit and peering cautiously about the field of thickly growing green beans. All she could hear were a few beetles flitting lazily among the leaves of the bean plants, some crickets in the distance, and the ominous sound of rolling thunder signaling a coming storm; the field workers had all gone home when the thunder had begun to rumble. The air was muggy and humid, the sky was growing darker by the minute, and it wasn't even midday. She winced involuntarily as a stroke of lightning crossed the sky. "This is a bad time to be on the run!" she whispered to herself, still looking out past the large green leaves, "A bean field won't be much shelter in the pouring rain, and it certainly isn't going to hide me from a search for long! I have to get under the trees, quickly!"

As she continued looking out over the thickly growing green leaves of the bean plants at the land surrounding her, she realized why the forest was so far away: It wasn't the wood on the cliff that she had walked through with the Keeper when she entered this world. This was a different forest, the much larger one she had seen in the distance beyond the town and fields as they had walked together. She turned to look at the forest she was making for, it was much closer now, this was her last field, and then there was a short stretch of meadow between bean field and wood that she needed to cross.

She knew she needed to get into the shelter of the woods fast, both to shelter from the storm and to hide from the pursuit she was sure wouldn't be far behind, but she was afraid to stand up and run again in case anyone was out looking for her; the more time passed, the more chance someone would discover her disappearance. Instead, she pulled her shift up past her knees and belted it in place, then grabbed the cloth bundle lying in the dirt beside her before turning around to face the forest. She began crawling steadily along one of the rows in the field as fast as she could manage, switching her burden from one arm to the other as she crawled to rest her arms as much as possible. At last, she reached the edge of the field and sat up carefully, scanning the tall grass at the edges for any sign of a guard or watchman on this end. Not a soul in sight, not even a farmer. She stood up into a crouch and brushed some of the dirt off her knees with one hand as she stumbled out of the field and into the meadow grass before the forest, keeping herself low. A fifteen-minute steady, crouching jog, brought her to the edge of the forest. Stopping before the edge of the trees and still hunched down, she looked in but could see nothing; she hugged the cloth bundle to herself tightly, hoping the bread wasn't squished after holding the bundle so tightly.

She hesitated now that she was here; the forest looked ominously dark and quite scary. A shout echoed in the distance, and she instinctively flattened herself into the grass before slowly raising her head to gaze back apprehensively towards the now-distant town and scan the horizon. She saw no movement in the fields, but the sentry that had been stationed at the Craft Hall was now striding across the town square. Had she been found missing already, or was he simply answering a call? Without wasting to find out, she stood up and stepped hastily into the forest, plunging relentlessly into the darkness, swallowing her fear.

An owl hooted and swooped silently down to perch on a low branch in front of her. She jumped, startled, and then put her hand to her chest, feeling her thumping heart. The thunder was closer now and she could hear the wind rocking the trees high above, the tree branches clicking against each other far out of sight. The storm wasn't far off and still she had found no shelter deep within the woods beyond the general closeness of the trees. Light pattering footsteps along branches, chirps, and croaks of various night animals, all sounded louder than they really were to her straining ears. She was jumpy, expecting one of Snaggletooth's men to grab her at any moment. She hoped the weather would hold the search off until morning and give her a better head start. The owl hooted again and flew a few feet away, perching on another tree branch not too far ahead. She thought she heard the word "follow" but wasn't certain. She could barely make out the large eyes in the darkness. It was acting strangely interested in her.

The newcomer thought suddenly of the farmer with his fox and wondered if the owl had been sent to guide her; the women in the town did say someone was going to send animals to help. Going with her gut instinct, she walked carefully towards the owl, just as she reached the owl it spread its large wings and flew silently ahead of her, landing again and looking back with its large glowing eyes. She followed silently but quickly, keeping her eyes fixed on the bird lest she lose her way in the dark, now certain the bird had been sent as a guide. As she walked after the owl and tried to keep her sandals free from the tangling undergrowth, she wondered if the farmer had sent it and if she was going to meet up with him soon. The owl led her on until it reached a small clearing about ten feet in diameter. She stepped out into the center of the clearing after the owl and then watched carefully for the eyes to appear again, but they didn't reappear.

A sudden crack of thunder sounded, and she looked up in time to see a bolt of lightning branch out across angry looking clouds. Pouring sheets of rain came down, drenching her to the skin in moments. She ran across the clearing and into the trees at the other side for shelter, clutching the small cloth bundle under her arm tightly. She screamed and skidded to a halt as another flash of lightning stroked across the sky and a long, metallic broadsword shone in reflection directly ahead of her. She turned to run back towards the clearing, but she was grabbed from behind and held tightly with a hand clamped firmly over her mouth. "Quiet!" a voice hissed in her ear, "You will be found, for they are in the forest this day!" She stopped squirming and stood still, frightened and trembling, clutching the cloth bundle so tightly that she knew the bread would certainly be squished this time.

"That is better, do not fear." whispered the voice reassuringly, "Come, we will go to a place I know where they cannot follow." A sudden gleam of electric blue shone to the side, and she shifted her eyes to see the sword once more, but it was not reflecting the lightning this time, it was glowing with its own power. She stood mesmerized,

momentarily forgetting her fear, and watched as
the electrical blue light spread out and up the arm
holding the sword, then she felt a tingle and shifted
her eyes down to her feet to see that she was
engulfed in the blue light and glowing. Suddenly,
the glowing stopped, and she heard the soft hiss of
a sword being replaced in its sheath as a few
random blue sparkles floated gently down about
her.

Quiet. The storm was gone, the dark forest was
gone; she stood dripping wet in a large dry cave.
The cave was furnished with wood and stone
furniture, fur rugs were scattered about the floor,
books, cards, dice, and dominoes were strewn
carelessly upon small tables here and there, and
tapestries hung on the walls between oil lamps
spaced at regular intervals. A large wood stove
crackled merrily in one corner, giving off abundant
warmth. The hand was removed from her mouth,
and she was allowed to stand free. She gazed about
the room taking in the homemade furniture and the
grey cave walls; she looked left and right, seeing a
few narrow hallways to the right and a door to the

left. It struck her as a cozy place, yet also as a sort of prison, since she could see no exit from it. She looked down at her bundle and said, somewhat sadly, "I, I think I squished my bread and cheese." There was a merry laugh behind her, and a familiar voice said, "That's alright, we have plenty of food here, you won't starve!" She turned around and looked up to see who had brought her to this place. She stood face to face with him – with him! "Oh!" she gasped, dropping the cloth bundle, and flinging herself onto the warrior she remembered, wrapping her arms around him, "At last!" Overcome with the exertions of the day and the emotions of the moment, she collapsed into unconsciousness.

He caught her and carried her over to a bed in one of the sleeping rooms down a narrow hallway, placing her on it and covering her with a blanket of furs. "I shouldn't put you to bed in wet clothes," he whispered, "I guess I have no choice, though; you're exhausted." He grabbed a second fur blanket from a nearby bed and put it over the top of her, then, walking back out, he bent and picked up the cloth bundle from the kitchen floor, unwrapping it and laughing softly. He set the flattened bread and small block of cheese on the counter, and then glanced curiously at the object that was left in the cloth. It was a fist-sized, elongated clear crystal, multi-faceted with strange runes glowing deep under the surface. He placed the crystal in his pocket and strode over to a desk in another room in the cave, across from the sleeping rooms. Taking a small scrap of parchment, he scribbled a quick note upon it in a neat, flowing script, then he strode down the long, wide hall to the bathing room, where he took a towel down from a shelf. He walked quietly back to the sleeping room where she slept and placed the towel upon the table at the end of the room, near her bed, then set the note on top of the towel. He watched her sleeping for a moment, a smile playing upon his lips, then he bent down and reached for her long braid, which was lying outside the cover. He tried to untie the knot of grass she had wound about it, but it was now a thoroughly sodden mass of knots, so he drew a small knife from his belt and carefully cut the grass loose, pulling it away from her hair. He kissed her softly on the forehead as she slept and then straightened and left the room, shutting the door softly behind himself so that only a small sliver of light entered the room.

Chapter 5 – In The Care Of Keepers

Silenus paced the small dais in the Hall of Images angrily, glaring at the young woman standing there. Daisy Mae cringed as Silenus began to yell at her once more, "Where has she gone to? Where did you women hide her? She was last seen entering the Hall of Crafts yesterday where only women go. What have you women done with her?" His shouting echoed through the empty Hall of Images, pounded in her ears; Daisy Mae shrugged slightly and shook her head a tiny bit, "I do not know, Chief Elder," she answered respectfully, repeating what she had already said to him, "She came in to visit with silly questions about food and sleep and jobs, and then we ate the midday meal with her After the meal, she said that she was going to see if you were done with your meetings as she wished to speak with you once more, and she left. None of us went with her, because we needed to get back to our work, but we told her that you would be found in the Hall of Images, and Denise showed her which Hall that was. When I brought her supper tray, she was picking flowers in the field next to her house, and called thank you, then she walked towards the house with a handful of flowers as I went back to town."

Silenus stopped pacing and frowned, thinking. He had walked by the Craft Hall the day before and heard all the women in there talking and he had even peered through the window two different times to see the newcomer there, yet nobody in town had seen that girl go anywhere else. When he had gone to her house early this morning, no one was there, yet the supper tray that he watched Daisy Mae bring to the house last night was empty and the bed rumpled, so the newcomer must have been in the house last night and eaten supper and slept. There was also a handful of freshly picked flowers in a cup of water, so that part of Daisy Mae's story also checked out. Silenus had quizzed all the women this following day one by one, but all had said the same to him about the newcomer's visit to the Craft Hall as this young one. It must be true if they all held the exact same story, yet he couldn't help thinking they were holding some piece of information back from him that would lead him to the newcomer. "I should have locked her away the day she first came here!" Silenus growled angrily, "The Master will not be pleased."

A messenger entered the Hall at that moment and bowed low before the dais, holding out a golden platter with a scroll upon it. Silenus frowned even more as he stepped down from the dais. He walked over to the messenger, took the scroll, and unrolled it. "Hmm," he murmured after a moment's reading, and then looked at Daisy Mae. "Your presence is requested at the dairy barn outside town, there is butter to churn. You are dismissed, go to the dairy barn and report to your duties." The girl sighed with relief and stepped off the dais, walking past the messenger. "Wait!" Silenus shouted, looking up once more from the scroll, "On your way stop at the house of Caroline and take her with you; she is needed for some mending of curtains. Take my messenger and he will get you past the sentry." Daisy Mae nodded and continued out the door, followed by the messenger. She was relieved to be away from the old goat at last but confused at needing the messenger to get by a sentry. She looked for the sentries as she exited the building, but they were not there. They were instead stationed in front of each of the private houses, along with many others who she had never seen before. "How odd!" she thought, glancing at the tall messenger by her side before she hurried to Caroline's house as fast as she dared.

The newcomer awoke feeling refreshed and safe at last. Opening her eyes, she looked around but saw nothing. She was upon a bed with furs over her, in a dark room. Sitting up, she pushed the furs back and swung her feet to the ground, then stood and peered carefully around in the dark. She shook her head, it was useless; this room was almost pitch dark. She put her hands out and felt carefully around, knowing there must be a door to the other, larger room she remembered. Shuffling her feet carefully so as not to trip, she felt her way slowly along to the foot of the bed and beyond it, encountering another bed. She stopped as a thought occurred to her, "Maybe he's sleeping in one of the other beds?" She stood still a moment, listening carefully for any sounds of breathing, not wanting to wake someone. Finally, hearing nothing, she turned carefully again and saw a sliver of light from the partially closed door and made her way to it with shuffling footsteps. The wooden door was closed partially upon the room, leaving a small glimmer of light to shine through from the other side, as the Keeper had left it. She pulled it gently open and stepped through to the other room. Nobody was in sight.

She glanced back at the room she had just left and looked it over thoroughly with the aid of the light streaming in from the open door. Several beds lined two sides of the room, and at the further end of the room nearest to the bed she had slept in was a table containing baskets and a towel. No one was there. She walked over to the bed she had slept in and folded the fur blankets, placing them neatly upon the end of the bed, then looked over at the table. Seeing the note on top of the folded towel, she picked it up, walking slowly back to the lighted chamber as she read it. "If you feel the need of a bath when you wake up, you'll find a bathing room down at the end of the wide hallway. There are cups of soap flakes near the pools, and I've brought a towel for you to use. There will be plenty of time for you to clean up before people return for the evening because everyone is out working, so you don't need to feel rushed. I cut the grass out of your hair; it was knotted badly. Also, I found a small crystal with your bread and cheese; it shouldn't be left lying about so I've put it in my pocket to keep safe. I'll return it to you later!"

She walked down the narrow hall and looked again at the large room she had been brought to earlier, still in the same state she had seen it in upon arrival. Books, dice, dominoes, and games of chess and checkers were strewn about, fur rugs were on the floor, chairs and tables arranged about the room in small and large groups and a few oil lamps spaced about the walls which gave off a smoky, yet bright light. A large wood stove stood in one corner. It was an incredibly large cave that would comfortably accommodate a hundred people. She gazed silently at it for several minutes, taking it all in and wondering how many people lived here.

There was a doorway across from the hall she had left, and she peeked inside the room. The back wall of the room held strange wooden cubbyhole shelves which were filled with rolled scrolls of paper, a line of desks were arranged underneath of it. All of the desks contained ink bottles, scattered pens and pencils, and stacks of blank papers, along with curious stacks of rounded, square stones. An abacus stood proudly at the center of each desk, and the woman stared curiously at one for a moment, trying to remember the last time she'd ever seen one of those. She turned to look around the room again, shaking her head with amusement, "They must not have computers or calculators here!" she whispered to herself. There was a large map on another wall, and shelves with stacks of parchments, ink bottles and cups of pencils underneath of them. Along the opposite wall from the map were more desks.

She walked back out into the large room to look around again. The wall nearest the kitchen stove had rock shelves carved out of it, filled with all sorts of clay jars and dishes, metal pots, and pans, and both metal and wooden utensils. Joints of meat hung from the ceiling near the stove, and baskets full of fruits and vegetables, breads, cheese, and eggs lined the walls. A long counter separated that area from the rest of the cave, and upon one end of the counter were her squashed bread loaf and block of cheese. She giggled softly and then looked past the kitchen to see an extremely long table which graced one end of the cave, lined with wooden chairs. She walked down the narrow hallways to peer into the other bedrooms, which looked much the same as the one she had been in, except a few were smaller, with only a single, large bed, table, and chair.

At last, she walked to the end of the wide hall leading off the open area and discovered a door that opened into a large chamber with rock shelves carved along the walls and steamy pools all over the floor, with water falling down into one end of each pool from the ceiling of the chamber. Towels were stacked up neatly on the shelves, as well as near each pool, buckets of soap flakes stood in one corner, with small cups stacked in a nearby cubby, and more cups containing soap flakes were arranged neatly around each pool. She stared for several minutes at the bathing area before remembering his note. "Oh, how lovely!" she breathed, rushing to the sleeping room again to get the towel from the table. She glanced quickly around the large cave once more, peering into the other sleeping rooms, to make sure no one else was present, then she hurried back to the bathing room and quickly undressed and stepped down the stairs into one of the warm pools of water. "Oh, yes!" she breathed, reaching up to untangle her braid with her fingers before ducking under the steaming water.

The newcomer finished her bath and then reached for the shift she had been wearing, pulling it into the water to clean the mud off as best she could by using a second cup of soap flakes and scrubbing it against the smooth rock wall of the pool. She rinsed it under the waterfall and then wrung the garment out in her hands before climbing the steps at the side of the bath and grabbed her towel, drying off quickly before trying to rub the shift dry. As she rubbed the shift with her towel, she looked around the room and spied a long, low stone trough at one end of the room, with curling wisps of steam rising up from floor vents behind it. "That will work much better!" she said, wrapping the towel about herself and hurrying quickly across the room to drape the shift over one of the long poles that were situated directly over the steam vents behind the trough.

She left the shift hanging there and walked back across the room, peering out into the wide hallway as she passed the door to make certain that nobody had returned to the cave. She swished her sandals quickly in the bathing pool to remove loose mud and dirt and then picked up the belt and swished it through the water as well, before using it to fasten the towel securely about herself. Walking quickly back to the steam vents, she carefully positioned her sandals over one of the vents to dry. Now, with her hands free, she began to work her fingers through her long hair to loosen it and allow it to dry faster. "This is silly! The steam will dry it even quicker." she murmured, leaning forward and holding her head over the steam vents as she worked, allowing the warmer air to dry her hair. Her hair and clothing were dry in a surprisingly short amount of time, and once fully attired and clean, she felt much better.

Not knowing what to do with her towel, she left it hanging neatly over one of the steam vents before leaving the bathing room. "I wonder if there are any brushes in that bedroom?" she said, wandering back down the wide hall and into one of the narrow hallways where the sleeping rooms were, "I know there were baskets on the table, but I didn't look closely at them." She entered her room again and looked around once more. She saw several brushes and combs lying in the baskets upon the table and moved thankfully over to pick up a comb to thoroughly untangle her hair before then using a brush on her hair, hoping nobody would mind if she used the items. "Hm, there's nothing here I can use to tie my hair back," she thought, looking in the baskets as she worked the tools through her hair, "I'll just have to let it hang loose for now, but at least it's clean!"

Once finished, she carefully cleaned the loose hairs from the brush and comb and replaced the tools in the basket, then picked up his note and read it again. She folded the note and tucked it under her braided belt, then walked out into the large common room to look around again. She was amazed that anyone could turn a cave into such a grand living area. But where was he? Was he truly a friend to her, or was he a "bad guy" after all? As far as she could tell, this could be a prison, she saw no exits whatsoever. She was stuck. She shook her head decisively, "No," she whispered to herself, "I think he's good! This place feels right. I just feel so alone and lonely all of a sudden! I suppose it's because I feel so much better now that I'm clean, and I feel safe, too, so the little things are what bother me now." She walked over to the wood stove in the corner of the common area and opened the door, then dropped the bunch of hair she'd cleaned from the brush and comb into the fire, not knowing how else to dispose of it. She shut the door of the stove again, then choose a chair with pillows in it near the stove, feeling chilled, and sat down, aware almost for the first time that she was lonely, depressed, hungry, and most importantly, still confused. "What is my name? Why is it that I remember I can fix computers, but I can't remember my name?" She whispered to herself yet again, the uncertain urgency returning to her now that she was comfortable and safe.

"What is it, Harold?" asked Daisy Mae upon entering the dairy barn with Caroline, "It is not often that you request me for churning butter. But I thank you for getting me away from that awful questioning session!" The Tender of Beasts smiled warmly at the women as they wrung out the rain from their hair and clothes and he shut the door, "Yes, I knew what was happening and sent the messenger to free you from questioning and to free Caroline from the house-arrest." He handed them two towels to dry off and Caroline looked surprised as she took hers, "House arrest!" she exclaimed. "Yes," returned Harold, "all of the women are now under house arrest by the old goat's orders, did you not notice the sentry at each door?" Daisy Mae nodded, "The messenger who accompanied me from the Hall of Images to Caroline's house had to tell the sentry it was alright for me to take Caroline along!" Harold nodded as he continued speaking, "Silenus is terribly angry, and very evil. I wish I had caught on to him earlier, when he was first sent to us, much sadness and trouble might have been averted."

The two women were stunned. They traded quick glances with each other as they dried off and then looked back to Harold. He nodded, "Yes it was the newcomer's disappearance that has led to this, but it was a good thing you told her to run, all the same. He was going to turn her over to the Master of Brimstone this evening when all was quiet. If you hadn't told her to run the other day, I would have risked coming to you to get her to safety." The women looked really shocked this time "You know we told her to run?" Caroline asked, "Do you know also about that which we gave to her?" Harold nodded again, "Oh yes, I do. Yesterday morning, Bert overheard Silenus talking to himself after sending the girl to you and immediately called over a boy to send to me with the message, and I sent two of my wild birds into town to listen, one to the Hall of Crafts, and one to the Hall of Images. Silenus came twice to peer in your Hall windows, though I do not think he heard anything that will aid him; only the birds could have heard your whispers from so far away as the front window. I know much and I say again, you have done well to send her off, and better yet in giving her the artifact before it came to the awareness of one who should not know of its existence. But come, this is no time for talking. I must send you off also, because the newcomer will need someone to be with her, and she will feel better having people she knows there with her. Will you go now where I send you?" Daisy Mae started to laugh softly, "I will go, I did not truly wish to sit at a boring old butter churn anyway!" Caroline smiled and nodded, "Of course we will go, Harold!"

"Good!" Harold replied, motioning them to the rear of the dairy barn, "Come with me, I have a secret exit here that Silenus does not know about, and it will keep you safe from the storm and the search and get you deep within the woods quite quickly." The women hung their towels over a stall partition and Harold turned to lead them to another stall at the end of the barn. Pushing the red and white cow out of the way and kicking some straw aside, he leaned down and opened a trap door in the floor. "Quickly now, climb down the ladder and follow the tunnel to the end. One of the owls will be waiting at the exit of the tunnel, she will guide you the remainder of the way, it is not far, and you'll be under the tree cover once you come out, so you won't get any wetter. Do not be frightened!"

The women climbed down the ladder and Harold lit a small torch and handed it down to Caroline, who reached up and took it. "Extinguish your torch before you climb up so that the light doesn't give you away! You can leave it lying in the tunnel once you put it out. There are council guards all over the forest this evening, be silent and speak no words once you open the trap door and be certain to close it again and kick some leaves over it to disguise it!" Daisy Mae looked suddenly frightened, "What if we are caught, Harold? What then?" "Hush!" replied Caroline, "We will not be caught, there will be Keepers nearby." She looked up and said, "Do I guess correctly, Harold?" He nodded and answered as he closed the trap door gently, "Yes, Keepers are on the lookout this night and know you are coming. The owl will guide you to them! Go quickly and quietly!" The door shut, leaving them in fluttering torchlight. They stood silent a moment and listened as the latch was secured above, and straw was scuffed over the trap door once more, then they turned and walked quickly down the earthen tunnel, anxious to get their journey over with.

The newcomer lifted her head from her chest, she had been dozing curled up in the chair, and stood up quickly, glancing toward the empty space between the kitchen counter and the scattered chairs as she saw a soft blue glow in the center of the room which began to grow in size as she stood waiting and watching. The blue glow spread out and began to sparkle a little as human shapes appeared within. The glowing ceased and she gaped, open mouthed, as a dozen tall warriors and two women appeared before her eyes. Swords were sheathed in leather scabbards, and the women ran forward to greet her, chattering at once. "Oh, it is good to see you again!" "We had thought you might get lost in the forest once the storm moved in!" "The council guards are searching everywhere for you!" "Have you kept it safe?" "Did Harold send an owl to guide you?" "Do you still have your locket?" "Was your journey long?" "They say the storm has been brought by the evil Master of Brimstone and it will never end!" "The women are all under house arrest by Snaggletooth's orders!" "Many of the men in town have disappeared, we do not know where!"

The newcomer stood silent and stunned as the words poured out of Daisy Mae and Caroline in rapid succession. She looked over at the warriors who were now moving about the room quite at home, making tea and sandwiches, laughing, adding wood to both of the stoves; she looked back to the two women in front of her. They stopped, seeing her bewilderment. "Didn't you know that you would be brought here once a Keeper found you? We did mention it, but there were so many of us talking at once that it probably got lost in the mix." Caroline asked, concerned. The newcomer shook her head mutely, staring at the older, plump Polynesian woman with an empty gaze; this was simply too confusing and muddled. So much had happened in so short a time span.

"Well, sit down and I'll explain things better," Caroline said, "we were in rather a hurry yesterday and there was no time to tell you everything, especially once Snaggletooth started prowling around!" The newcomer sat down and finally found her voice, "Yesterday?" It was Daisy Mae who answered this time, "Yes, and it is already evening of the following day in Arkady." Caroline glanced around, taking in the cave with a swift turn of her head, "Yes, I suppose it is easy to lose track of time when you have no windows. Also, this place is right out of the world so there isn't truly any time here," Caroline hesitated before continuing with a shrug, "at least that is what I have heard tell of it." She noticed the continued confusion on the newcomer's face and added, "This is the Keeper's world! It is a separate world from Arkady, where we were, but we don't know where it is or how to get here, only the Keepers know that. You're safe now! Silenus can't get to you here."

One of the Keepers walked over to the small group of women just then and set a tray down on the table next to them, and then pulled the table forward so that it stood between their chairs. "Eat and drink, it is not supper, but this will tide you over until it is time for the evening meal." He said kindly, smiling at the three women and then turning to address the newcomer, "You have many questions, no doubt. We have heard from Harold about all that has happened since you arrived in Arkady. You three women shall rest and visit while we tidy up around here and prepare supper.

The rest of the men will arrive soon and then we will begin."

He walked away again, and her eyes followed him, then she scanned the other men, looking for the warrior she knew, but he wasn't there. She looked back at the other two women who were now busy with the tea tray, "Who," she asked at last, deciding upon her first question "is Harold?" Caroline handed her a teacup and replied, "Why, Harold is one of the Tender of Beasts in Greenfield town of course. You have met him already; he talked with you the other morning in front of your house. Harold is the one who sent us to you this day. Would you like some sugar or cream?" The newcomer nodded, reaching for the sugar tongs, and adding a couple lumps to her cup, stirring the tea with a spoon, and placing the spoon upon the tray. Caroline motioned the newcomer to help herself with food from the tray and then leaned back in her chair to enjoy her tea.

The newcomer leaned back in her chair, tired and yet glad to have company, and sipped the tea. It tasted good, and she realized for the first time since coming here how hungry she was. She leaned forward again and reached out to the tray to choose one of the small sandwiches, then relaxed back into the chair with a sigh. The other two women watched her as they all enjoyed tea, waiting for her to speak. At last Daisy Mae could take the silence no more and spoke up, "Well, don't you have questions for us? You had so many in the Hall when we had no time to answer them because of the danger. Why don't you ask now?"

The newcomer looked up and sighed, "I don't know, I just don't know. I had so many questions, and I know that some of them seem so important and pressing to me. But now that I find myself here, a lot of my questions have disappeared, they don't seem to matter anymore. I can't even remember everything that I wanted to ask, to tell you the truth. I've been forgetting more and more of my past life.." she broke off, shaking her head in frustration, then looked up again, "This may seem stupid, but am I really, truly dead? This all seems so real. I'm not transparent like a ghost should be, neither is anyone else here, and I'm hungry, and tired, yet I've always heard that ghosts don't need material things; and except for the strange surroundings it's just like life always has been from what I can see." She hesitated, "Well, not exactly, I guess, since I have this feeling on me of being very forgetful, like there's something extremely important I need to remember and can't. It makes me feel incredibly nervous and jumpy because I know I've never been forgetful before. Is this some sort of elaborate trick?"

Caroline set her empty teacup down and looked the newcomer in the eye, "Listen, you are dead. There is no denying that because the living cannot come here to these worlds. And yes, ghosts do eat and drink, sleep, and tire: The same things the living people do, the ghosts do." Daisy Mae giggled suddenly and cut in, "Not all things, Caroline! Ghosts don't use the toilet!" Caroline smiled at the young woman and amended her previous statement, "Almost all of the things that the living do, the ghosts do. Daisy is right, we do not need toilets here because our bodies work differently now, and the food we eat is expended entirely in energy. Ghosts also don't age in this world. We remain the age we were when we first entered Arkady. We are all ghosts here, and we are just as real as the living." Seeing her still doubtful, Caroline reached out and took the newcomer's hands, "Let's see if I can explain it another way and perhaps it will make more sense to you: There are different levels of reality. Think of it as a mirror reflection. Who moves first - you or the reflection?" The newcomer said, "I do, of course! The reflection just follows my movements." Caroline answered, "Right! But now, you are the reflection - is the other side still real? Or are you, the reflection, real? Did you say we are not transparent here like ghosts appear in the living world? No, we aren't, because this is your new reality: Looking at the living world now, you would see it as transparent, less 'real' than the life you now have, and you wouldn't be able to interact with anything there. No one living would be able to see or hear you, although you could see and hear them. You wouldn't be able to touch anything there in the living world, either. Just as a dream is real when you're in it, and yet less real when you wake, that is how it is here. A new reality." She let go of the newcomer's hands and watched, waiting to see if she had gotten through.

The newcomer sat still, thinking, nodding her head slowly. "Okay," she answered, "that makes a sort of sense, especially when you put it in terms of a dream." The newcomer hesitated and after a few moments said softly, "I guess that's why I can't remember things now. Just like a dream fades, so my past life is fading, and only little bits are left to me, coming, and going." Her eyes widened and she said softly, "That also explains why I couldn't get myself out of the car! I kept trying and trying to loosen my seatbelt but just couldn't grab hold of it!" She pulled on her lip, then said, "I couldn't grab the door handle of that SUV either." She looked up at Caroline and asked, "But what is happening in this world? Is it always so terrifying when someone new comes? People die every day in the living world, so they must be coming into Arkady all the time, yet I don't see any other major fusses happening, or other new people brought in like I was. Do people always get spied on, and have to run and hide like I did?"

Daisy Mae answered the question, "You've been spied on because of that locket, remember? I told you that earlier. Snaggletooth wants it for himself. People come all the time to Arkady but the town and fields you have seen are only one small area of this world, and people are brought into all different places all the time. Arkady is several times the size of the living world! They say there are even lands across the Great Sea, although none of us know anything about those lands." The newcomer's eyes widened as she took this information in, then her glance wavered and she looked over to the center of the room as the blue glow started again, signaling new arrivals. The other two women also turned and watched.

Four Keepers and Bert the sentry arrived. The newcomer remembered the sentry; he was the older, grey-haired sentry who had spoken kindly to her that first day outside the Hall of Images as he held his halberd across the door. The other men seemed surprised to see Bert and one came forward to question him curiously, "What brings you here?" Bert twisted the halberd in his hands nervously and looked around, "Harold sent me with a message for all the Keepers. He says that the forest is burning, even as the rain pours down. Silenus has finally gone mad and means to have the newcomer at any cost, even if it means burning all the land to remove hiding places! His men have started fires in more places than Harold and his team can combat, and they are not ordinary fires because they burn through the rain. The old goat has also started capturing all the people his guards can get their hands on, meaning to use them as bargaining power or turn them over to Brimstone as slaves." The Keepers exchanged concerned murmurs among themselves at this news, then another spoke to Bert, "Has Silenus discovered you, or does he still believe you to be loyal to the ruling council?"

Bert shook his head quickly, "No, I have not yet been discovered, but I will be when I don't return to him. Please do not send me back there! Let me remain here and help in whatever way I may! Silenus sent me in a cart on an errand to Thornapple Center to gather chains, whips, and other terrible things, but I turned aside once Greenfield was out of sight and hid the cart and horse in a barn, then ran the back way across the fields to find Harold. He sent me through his tunnel to find a Keeper and that's how you guys found me. He means to turn the Hall of Crafts into a makeshift prison to keep people in! The women of Greenfield have already been dragged from their houses and placed within the prison, and a few of the men also. A few women have managed to escape, and the rest of the men have taken refuge in the tunnel of Harold's, where they may plan how best to save the captives." The three women gasped in unison and stood up.

Daisy Mae rushed over to the new arrivals and grabbed tightly to Bert, "We must do something, Bert! We cannot sit here and let them be tortured!

We must go back!" Bert shook his head and two of the Keepers pulled her away, guiding her gently back towards the other two women. "That is not the way to fight this one, Daisy." Bert replied as she reluctantly allowed herself to be led back to the other women, "This one is crafty and evil. Harold says he works directly for the evil Master in Brimstone. We must be wary. Besides, I didn't return, so he has nothing to torture people with yet." One of the Keepers questioned the sentry again, "Has word been spread to the other Keepers of this news, Bert?" One of the four Keepers who had arrived with Bert nodded and replied, "Yes, we four came here with Bert, and we sent Baldy to report to the other eastern Keeps. All Keepers should be returning shortly to their home Keeps and we can begin planning how best to deal with this new threat. Gatemaster Summersong said he would call a meeting of the eastern Keeps here after supper tonight. Summersong said that it's only one town, so we don't need to call in all the Keeps for an isolated problem."

The Keepers nodded and continued going about their business in the cave once more. One of them said kindly to the sentry, "You may remain here for the time being, Bert, and enjoy supper with us and stay the night. Our Gatemaster may have other orders once everything is decided, though. Until then you are free to remain. Perhaps comfort the women while we finish supper preparations here and wait for the return of the company." Bert nodded and moved to sit with the women, and Caroline poured him a cup of tea.

It was only a short hour later before all the company of Keepers had gathered once more in the cave. The newcomer felt a strange thrill run through her when she saw again the man she liked so much. He motioned the women and Bert to come sit at the long supper table with the Keepers, and then reached into his pocket and showed the crystal to the newcomer, saying quietly to her, "This is what you had in that cloth bundle with the bread and cheese, but until you have clothes with pockets, I will hold it safely for you. That shift isn't good for much, especially for keeping warm, we'll find you some new clothes very soon." He returned the crystal to his pocket and then withdrew a long, yellow ribbon from another pocket and handed it to her, "Here," he said, "I picked a ribbon up for your hair when I was in Lindentree Town today after my last Gate call. It'll work much better than grass!" She laughed and thanked him, and he motioned her to sit down once she'd pulled her hair back into a loose ponytail and tied it out of her face with the ribbon.

When all were seated, he addressed the company loudly, "There is a great danger upon our lands this day, and we will be in harder battle than ever before from this point forward. Much work must be done, much planning also, but it does not do to plan and work when men are tired and hungry. Therefore, let us partake of this meal in peace and leave all talk of our problems until afterward when we are ready to deal with things properly. As you know, time does not pass as quickly here as in Arkady; we may relax yet a short while." He sat and they all began the meal.

At first the newcomer sat silently, toying with her food and not truly eating. She felt guilty for causing all of the problems that now beset this beautiful world. Bert, sensing what was bothering her, leaned towards her, and said quietly in her ear, "It is not your fault that these things have happened. If the locket had not been given to you then it would have landed in another's hands. This is not the first time that news of this locket has caused uproar in our world. The enemy has been searching for it for many years. You did well to keep it away from the old goat! Do not fear, we will get through this and come out right, you will see!" He spoke with a great deal more bravado than he felt, but she fell for it and cheered up enough to begin eating.

The food was simple, but delicious, roast beef, mashed potatoes and gravy and several kinds of vegetables and fruits, along with fresh bread and butter. There was much talk around the table; stories were being traded of Gates, Rides, Riders, and rescues. She listened hungrily to the talk, wanting to know more about the place she found herself, longing to understand this new way of life. As she listened, she imagined the warriors riding on large draft horses, galloping across fields, and jumping fences, swimming rivers, and chasing bandits, like a cross between a medieval knight and an old west cowboy. She wondered idly about the strange names and terms that were being bantered about the table, trying to associate each person with their proper name and then realized with surprise that she didn't yet know the name of the Gatemaster. She was just about to ask, when he stood and said, "Okay everyone, let's clear up and get ready for the meeting tonight. We're going to have to clear the entire cave to make as much room as possible so that we can fit everyone in here tonight for the meeting!"

Chairs were scraped back, and people began standing up. The newcomer stood with them, reaching for the nearest basket of bread to carry it over to the kitchen counter. "You don't have to help with the cleanup, my lady, you are our guest!" The man said with a smile, smoothly taking the basket from her hands and placing it upon the counter behind him. "That's alright," she answered, smiling back, "I'd like to help, it makes me feel useful. By the way, what's your name? You wouldn't tell me when we first met, and I got a little lost with all the strange new terms and names that were being thrown about the table tonight." He grinned and answered, "My name is Summersong, and I'm the Gatemaster of this Keep. I'll let you, Caroline and Daisy Mae help clean the table off since you three ladies look like you want something to do," he glanced over at the other two women who were bustling about gathering dishes and silverware from the table, "and I'll ask Bert to help us move the furniture." He walked swiftly away, patting Bert's shoulder to get his attention, and motioning him to follow.

Chapter 6 – Meeting Of Keepers

Supper had been cleared, dishes had been cleaned and put away, and all the furniture in the cave pushed back against the walls, then rugs, pillows, and blankets had been laid on the floor for people to sit on. A few Keepers sat on the chairs pushed against the walls, but over three hundred more Keepers sat cross-legged on the floor in a great semicircle several rows deep, filling the large cave. Harold the Tender of Beasts from Arkady was there, as were Caroline, Daisy Mae, and Bert. The four Gatemasters of each company of Keepers were standing up at the front of the audience, taking turns speaking so that all the information each had gathered from various towns in Arkady would be shared and they might better plan their attack against the evil storm now raging in Arkady.

Through listening to the conversation, the newcomer had figured out that the Keeps were arranged according to the towns in Arkady, with each one in charge of a different section of that world. There were also many more Keeps that weren't in attendance, and those Keeps covered even more towns and cities. It seemed a vast expanse of territory to her, and she wondered briefly how they had all managed to gather so quickly in one place, then almost laughed out loud as she remembered those glowing weapons which they used to transport themselves from place to place like magic.

The newcomer sat quietly in the front row of the circle along with the other few Arkadians, listening avidly to all that was said, trying desperately to understand the situation. She had at first been surprised to see women among the Keepers in the crowd, but then felt a strange thrill of excitement race through her, a longing she had never known before to be a part of this group of Keepers. Next to her, Daisy Mae tittered and giggled, feeling that she was having quite an adventure to find herself among so many strong and brave warriors. The newcomer held a hand over the ear nearest to Daisy Mae, finding the girlish antics quite distracting. Caroline and Bert sat on the other side of Daisy Mae, whispering quietly to each other, they were old friends. Harold the Tender of Beasts sat beyond them, paying quiet attention to the speakers. The newcomer was pleased to see the Tender of Beasts again, and had greeted him warmly when he arrived with one of the other Keepers.

The talk seemed to be wrapping up at long last. "So, we come to it, three of the Dragon Gate pillars have been broken beyond immediate repair and evil can come and go at will between the worlds of living and dead through these breaches. This does not bode well for any of the worlds, especially for that of the living, for they know nothing about the other worlds and are ill prepared to deal with such things. Men have been sent to the Deep Mines in the northern reaches of the Great Barrier Mountains to gather the supplies of diamonds and red slate needed to repair the pillars. It is a work of many days to mine and gather enough material and will take almost as many to rebuild the pillars. The Smiths are at work cleaning out the placer holes and reweaving the magic in them while they await supplies to begin the build.

In the meantime, Keepers are currently posted in pairs at each of the three broken pillars, with relief contingents in waiting at the Keeps nearest to each to trade off with them as rest periods are needed, and more men are posted in pairs down in Arkady to patrol for breakthroughs."

The listening Keepers nodded approval as the speaker, a tall, muscular, and blue-eyed man named Silverwing who was the Gatemaster of Grimhold Keep, tossed his head to flip a lock of his shoulder-length, wavy brown hair out of his eyes, "Moreover," he continued, "we know that the locket this woman carries is sought after by the enemy. It does indeed carry a seed within it as she has reported that Silenus told her. But the seed is not one that will save the land in the way Silenus led the woman to believe. We think that it does indeed need to be planted in Snowmelt Wood, but if it is planted under the influence of evil, then evil will reign."

The newcomer looked straight ahead at the speaker, not liking this news, yet determined to learn as much as she could, and not moving a muscle. A woman Keeper sitting behind the newcomer raised her voice, "How then must this seed be planted, and by whom?" Silverwing answered the question quickly, "The seed if planted in Snowmelt Wood in Arkady will grow towards evil and if planted in the location of Snowmelt Wood in the living world will grow towards good, that much we know from our Loremasters. At least, that is what our Loremasters think, they are not entirely certain and are still searching through their scrolls and tomes for answers. We do not yet know who must plant the seed or how it must be done, since none of us can touch anything in the living world."

A tense silence filled the cave as everyone looked around, realizing the dangers ahead of them. The newcomer continued looking straight ahead at Gatemaster Silverwing, waiting for more, and was surprised to hear a whisper in her ear. "What Silver really means is that you will have to plant the seed, since you are the only one who can touch the locket." The newcomer turned to face Lady Evenflower, a tall, tanned woman with twinkling green eyes and a long white braid who sat next to her, and Lady Evenflower continued with a smile, "My mate doesn't want to scare you because you're new to this world, but I think you can handle the news." She winked, and the newcomer smiled at her, turning to face the center once again.

Silverwing spoke again, "The Keepers of course know their duties. However, we need further help if we are to accomplish our task so that we can concentrate fully upon the Gates and the matter with Silenus. People from Arkady that could help us with our daily chores such as baking breads, gathering fruits, repairing torn clothing and even farming would be very welcome. That would leave us free to concentrate on the battles and Gates with more of our people, thus ending this situation and getting Arkady back to normal as quickly as possible. I would ask those of you folk from Arkady here tonight to think about who you know that might be willing to join us in this effort and let us know who we could contact in the coming days." He paused and looked towards Caroline, Bert, Harold, and Daisy Mae.

"Also," Silverwing continued, "I suggest that it would be good to have one leader over all the Keeps to unite and direct us in the days ahead. Doing so would ensure that we have our resources deployed in the most efficient way possible. We can bring it before all the leaders for confirmation later, but tonight, let us elect a leader to begin this work." He turned to Summersong and spoke, "Gatemaster Summersong of Kingscannon Keep, since you have brought this newcomer and her locket to our world, will you lead us from here?" Summersong stepped forward from the other Gatemasters and answered evenly, gazing around the circle as he did so, "I will lead if all agree, but if there is one dissenting voice then you must choose again, and of course the matter will need to be voted on again with all Keep leaders present to confirm it, as Silver has said." Quiet murmurs of assent, quick nods of heads moved around the room in a circular wave as all the Keepers one by one agreed to accept Summersong as leader of all Keeps in the coming days.

Summersong raised his hands over his head in the Keeper signal for silence and said "Thank you for your trust. First off, as Silverwing mentioned, we shall need help from many directions. Harold here," he said, nodding in Harold's direction, "has already agreed to connect with the other beast handlers in Arkady known to be friendly to our cause. They will together call as many animals into service as can withstand the evil storm. Those animals will aid us as Messengers between here and Arkady, and as guides for the innocent folk in towns that we need to move to safety. Harold assures us that we shall at the least have the foxes, who can lead people, and the owls to carry messages, for they are not afraid of the storm. That will be a great help."

He looked around the circle slowly, then pointed to the sentry, "You, Bert, are familiar with the ways of guards and councils, having been a sentry for so long. You will be a help to us in providing information, as well as in contacting other sentries without attracting too much attention. Can you tell us who is loyal to our side and who to Brimstone, both among the sentries and among the councils and ordinary folk? You must know many people through your work." Bert looked uncertain, "Well, yes sir, for the central and eastern towns I can. But some of the farther cities, I don't know well enough to say, since I've never traveled so far." Summersong nodded, "That will do. I will ask you to stay with the company of Grimhold Keep, for they are the information center of our world and will be working in close contact with Harold and the other Tenders of Beasts to get everyone gathered in." Bert nodded and went to stand by Silverwing, who motioned him over. Harold stood and followed Bert.

Summersong looked next at Daisy Mae, "You, young lady, what are you good at doing? Have you any special talents? I do not want one as young as you to be returned to any location in Arkady while it is in such a dangerous state because you are known to be a friend of the newcomer, so you will remain with us for your own safety, at least for the time being, and longer if you so choose." He had spoken kindly but Daisy Mae began shaking uncontrollably, frightened out of her wits as she realized that she was going to be separated from all those she had known. Caroline patted her on the shoulder gently and answered, "Sir, young Daisy here is extremely good at both drawing maps and interpreting them, she has been tutored under Maximilian, our chief cartographer. She knows the lay of the land for many miles around Greenfield, having been taken out around the land by Maximilian and tutored extensively, and she is good at plotting and measurements."

Summersong nodded approvingly, "So, you are a young mapmaker, are you? In that case you should also travel to Grimhold Keep and help them with the task of marking maps with information as we find it; we need skilled Cartographers. Are you willing to do that? Your friend Bert will be there, as will others in time, and Harold will be coming and going so you'll see him as well." Daisy Mae brightened at once and said, "Oh yes, I could do that!" She was guided over, still somewhat shaky, to stand with Bert, who put a protective hand on her shoulder. Turning to Caroline, Summersong asked, "And you? What is your specialty, my lady?" The short, somewhat plump woman stood and smoothed her dress nervously, then patted her short brown curls, "Well sir, I had no real specialty in Arkady, but I've got a special knack for tending the sick and wounded and can pull small amounts of magic from the Crystal Time Stream as your Healers do. No doubt you'll be needing that before long?" Summersong nodded approvingly, "Yes indeed, we certainly will! You shall abide in Windspeak Keep, for that is to be where the Healers will be stationed as time comes, since it's in a central location to all of our Keeps, and we've made the decision to turn it into our Healers center. Gatemaster Stormchaser is in charge of that Keep, and he also a Healer who cares deeply for the sick and wounded." He pointed to a tall, muscular man with crinkly blue eyes and a black mullet, who motioned Caroline over with a smile.

Summersong turned at last to the newcomer. She looked steadily back at him, thinking that she should be nervous after all the confusion of the past several days, yet not feeling it in the least, having finally found herself among friends and reconciled with what had happened to her. "Come forward, lady." He said to her, and the small Nepalese woman rose gracefully and walked forward to stand before him. "You are different," he said, "You are not like most others who have only been here a short while. There is a certain something about you that sets you apart and I cannot place it. Tell me, how much do you understand tonight of what is happening? I need to make up my mind what part you shall play in all this, but I do not wish to put you in danger. Are you afraid at all? You do not look it."

She shrugged her shoulders, not certain what he wanted, "We are on the eve of war, of course, I've figured that much out," she stated quietly, "there is a great battle ahead to clear the path to Snowmelt Wood so that we can plant the seed that I carry in this locket. This enemy from Brimstone will try to stop us, and we will have to fight both in this world and at these Gates, possibly in the world of the living. Harold has told me a little, but I still don't fully understand what a Gate is, and I don't know much about this enemy, but no, I'm not afraid, for once. I don't know why, but I'm not. I guess I've just finally accepted that I can't go home again." She waited quietly to see if that was the answer he wanted.

Summersong looked at her for a few moments, studying her and thinking over her words. "You are stronger than you look, and you are not afraid to take risks, that we have seen already. It also seems to me that you have already grasped a rough layout of the land through our talk this evening and will be able to find your way around quicker than most people who are new to this world. You are good with people, making friends fast and able to play a hand at need. You have fooled Silenus into thinking that you are a pawn, but you have chosen position as a knight on the board. Harold here told us you have a knack for communicating with animals. Can you control a horse?" The question surprised her, but she answered quickly, "Yes I've been riding almost before I could walk." Her mind went briefly to a forgotten scene from her childhood in Nepal, riding a horse as she and her sisters helped their father to round up their herd of horses. He nodded slowly and then said, "Can you manage a horse out of control?" She shrugged, "I have many times before, yes. I like a little spirit in my ride." She added without thinking.

Quiet laughter was heard around the circle and Summersong looked over at Gatemaster Firestorm of Jumpriver Keep to ask, "How many available Rides have you in your stable at this point in time?" Firestorm looked up at the ceiling, tallying the number of Rides in his head, before finally turning back to Summersong and answering "Jumpriver Keep has fifteen Rides ready to hand, none tested. Any of the fifteen are available this night to one who can tame the Ride." An expectant hush fell over the crowded cave, and the newcomer cocked her head curiously at the man who had spoken.

Gatemaster Summersong turned to the newcomer to find her waiting curiously for an answer, "Well, what shall it be, lady?" he asked her in a voice loud enough to be heard throughout the crowd, "Will you travel this night to Jumpriver Keep stable and there try your hand at pairing with a Keeper's Ride? If you succeed then you will earn your place and position as a Keeper in this world, and you shall belong to Kingscannon Keep, for we are low in numbers and one of the few with no women among us." Everyone waited with eager looks on their faces, eyes sparkling; it had been over a year since a new Keeper was added to their ranks. She stood frozen a moment, excited, not believing her luck: To be a Keeper herself! To work with this man who she so desperately wanted to be with! She spoke and was amazed to hear no quiver in her voice "Yes, I will travel. I will pair with a Keeper's Ride!" The crowd burst into noisy cheers and shouting, and she grinned from ear to ear, turning to wink at Lady Evenflower.

Chapter 7 – Of Rides And Riders

A short half hour later, the newcomer found herself in a small bedroom in Jumpriver Keep, changing into clothes provided by the Lady of this Keep, Lady Songbird. The two women were almost the same size, and the clothes fit the newcomer well. Finally dressed in closefitting and soft leather pants and boots in a light brown color, with a short-sleeved, white cotton blouse, she looked over to the shift lying on the bed and reached over to take the folded note, unfolding it and reading it once again with a smile, then folding it and placing it in a pocket of her new leather pants. She quickly untied the yellow ribbon from her ponytail and then deftly braided the hair into her preferred style before retying the ribbon once more, then she stepped out of the bedroom and walked over to Lady Songbird, a slightly taller woman than herself with long brown hair and green eyes, who was standing in the entrance to the narrow sleeping room hallway. "Thank you for the clothes, it's nice to wear pants again!" she said, approaching. Lady Songbird turned and smiled,

"Oh don't mention it! We always give the first set of clothes to a new Keeper from another, established Keeper. It's tradition!" Lady Songbird laughed suddenly, "We have a lot of traditions here, as you'll soon find out!"

The newcomer said quickly, "I don't remember too much about the living world anymore, but I do know somehow that all the names here are very different from what I'm used to back in the living world. I love your name! Did someone give it to you when you came here, or have you always had it?" Songbird smiled, "You will find out soon enough. Are you ready for the test? You'll find it isn't difficult if you really do have Keeper's blood in you, and I'm sure you have." The newcomer nodded, "What do they mean by 'pair with a ride,' don't the horses need to be tamed? Firestorm said tame, but Summersong said pair. Are the horses really that wild here? They must be fast and strong to carry the warriors."

Songbird smiled gently, "Oh yes! A Keeper's Ride is always wild and can never be tamed, they are also magical, each with its own special power! Only the Keepers can pair with them, and each is loyal only to its own Keeper, that is what pairing means: You'll share a magical bond with your Ride that no one else can. Bear in mind that you must make friends with your Ride, not try to break, or tame it, so make sure to talk to them when you're in the stable; they understand human speech. Also, do not worry about the words that my mate Firestorm will speak before the stable, they sound intimidating but are only tradition." Both women giggled a bit and then Songbird said, "Come, it is time." Lady Songbird took the newcomer's hand and stood next to her, unsheathing a small knife. It glowed blue and then spread out to engulf both women until they disappeared from the Keep, reappearing moments later before the cavernous entrance to a rock stable where the entire crowd had gathered.

The newcomer glanced around at the strange setting, an impossibly large, grey rock pillar which stretched up high into the sky, with a cave entrance at the bottom. The pillar was in the center of a flowery, grassy meadow clearing surrounded by green woodland. A soft, cool night breeze was rustling the leaves of the deciduous trees around the clearing and made the newcomer shiver momentarily. Lady Songbird led the newcomer over to Gatemaster Firestorm, who stood in front of the cave entrance rubbing his buzzcut, flame-red hair, and left her there with him, walking back quickly to join the audience sitting further back in the grass.

The newcomer looked up at the starry night sky and then back to the tall pillar of grey slate rock before her, with the cave entrance at the bottom. An excited babble of voices filled the air as people discussed the upcoming test. Daisy Mae stood at the front of the crowd and shifted nervously from one foot to the other, afraid for her new friend. "Do not worry, Daisy! Sit down with us and relax!" exclaimed Bert, "The Keepers know what they're doing; besides this is a landmark achievement tonight! Never has one of the folks from Arkady witnessed a Keeper's Rite and look how many of us are here this night! It will be fine!" Caroline nodded and pulled the younger woman down to sit on the grass beside them, adding to Daisy Mae and Bert in a conspiratorial whisper, "I'm excited! I don't think anyone from Arkady has ever seen a Keeper's Ride before, especially up close like this! Just think of all the rumors and stories that fly around the towns about the Keepers Rides, and we're going to find out the truth tonight!"

"Are you ready?" Firestorm asked her quietly, after allowing her a few moments to look around. She turned her attention from the pillar of rock and glanced at the cave entrance once more, noting the steam billowing out and strange multicolored lights dancing within, and thought that any kind of horse that would bear the steam and flashing lights so readily must be rather fierce. For the first time since accepting the challenge, she felt slightly nervous. She looked up into Firestorm's deeply tanned face and took comfort in the kindness radiating from his piercing blue eyes.

She smiled as he twitched his neatly trimmed mustache and grinned at her mischievously. "Yes" she answered, suppressing a giggle, and trying to look brave as she smiled back at him. "Very well then" he replied, raising his voice, and turning to the crowd, "It shall begin! Lady, within this stable cave await fifteen Keepers Rides, untested and untamed. Enter within and choose your Ride while we witness. We are prepared to watch and to wait. You do not have to choose quickly but choose wisely, for the Rides are unforgiving of mistakes. When you have made your choice, mount your Ride, and come forth to prove to us that you are worthy to join the Keepers!" The newcomer turned and investigated the crowd, scanning the faces for Summersong's. He sat in easy posture at the very front center of the crowd next to Harold, leaning back on his hands, and nodded reassuringly to her. Harold gave her a thumbs up and grinned delightedly. She turned, walking across the short grass to enter the cave.

An enormous roaring and thudding noise split the air and shook the ground as she disappeared among the steam billows. The multicolored lights flashed and danced within the steam, brighter than ever, streaming out of the stable entrance. Daisy Mae screamed in fright and Lady Songbird turned to comfort her, "Do not be afraid! The Rides always do that with an untested person, to see how firm they stand, it is only noise used to evaluate courage! They are not dumb beasts, but understand much, and know well how to test for a Keeper's heart." Daisy Mae glanced at Songbird and nodded but scooted back into the crowd just a bit further.

The audience went quiet as a frustrated voice was heard from within the cave, over the noise. "Oh, do be quiet! Good heavens, it's not like I can't hear you. You are such silly critters! Just because I like a little spirit in my ride doesn't mean you have to be so noisy with feet and mouths!" The roaring and stomping stopped and the Keepers in the crowd gasped: rarely had anyone quieted the Rides so immediately, if at all. Everyone strained their ears to listen, but they could hear only loud snorts and snuffling, and the shifting and rustling of the beasts within. They waited expectantly as the steam continued to billow forth and the lights flashed brightly.

Within the middle of the stable beyond view of the audience the newcomer stood, hands on hips, glaring around at the large beasts as they arched their great necks and bent towards her, stunned at having been told to be silent by such a small, yet ferocious woman. The newcomer realized as she stood there in the center of the ring of beasts that the steam wasn't coming from them, it was simply warmer stable air rolling out into the cold night air. Inside where she stood was perfectly clear, with dancing, colored lights radiating from the beasts. She held her arms out and let them sniff her thoroughly, warm blasts of breath snorting from their noses as the fifteen great beasts snuffled her up and down and nudged her roughly to see if she would run away. She could feel the soft, fine fur as they brushed against her bare arms, and she longed to bury her hands in the thick, feathery manes that ruffed out around their faces. Finally, all stood silent before her and watched with their great eyes as she gazed back at them.

"Well?" she asked them quietly, "Which one of you shall it be? You're all so beautiful that I don't know which to choose! I've been told that each of you has their own magical ability. Tell me what you can each do so that I can choose which talent fits my need best!" The beasts snorted and pranced in place, preening delightedly, swishing their tails as they fluffed out their feathery manes, uttering small chirps and squeaks, purrs and whistles, yips, and barks. She walked slowly around to each one, gently stroking the long noses, gazing upon the upswept and curling horns at the top of each head, running her hands gently down the warm, furred flanks and feathery wings, amazed at the size of these beasts. They were dragons, without a doubt, yet unlike any dragon she had never seen or imagined. "The faces are like horses, with the long nose," she thought, "But the bodies and paws are more, well, like cats, long and lithe and the manes are definitely like lion manes all around their heads, except that they're made of feathers. The wings are like those of a great bird, but the twisting horns remind me of eland antelopes."

She kept walking slowly among the huge beasts, reveling in the feel of the soft fur and smooth, glossy feathers, admiring the twisting horns which blended smoothly into the manes, each dragon's horns were colored the same as their fur. She was awed to think that beasts who stood about fifteen feet high – half again the height of a large elephant - would be so gentle. She noted how some of the dragon ears sticking out of the manes were rounded, or pointed or ears that flapped over, some of them had tails that were fringed, or were bushy with feathers all over and some had furry tails that had only a tuft of feathers at the very end, reminding her of a lion's tail, some of the dragons had manes which flowed down their chests, some had shorter ruffs, and all of them sported furry, bearded chins, the beard fur sticking out well below the jawline. The fur of each dragon was also slightly different between them, all were very soft, but some of the dragons sported longer fur, some shorter fur. The dragons were very alike and yet subtly different, and each was a different color from the others, giving off a softly glowing light the color of their fur and feathers. She felt as if she were walking inside a living, warm rainbow as she listened to the happy dragon sounds and the many purrs that were rumbling deep inside of the beasts, marveling in her ability to understand what they were saying. "Heaven," she chuckled softly to herself, breathing deeply of the earthy dragon scent, and remembering the question Silenus had asked her at that first meeting, "Yes, I think this is a very good heaven!"

A loud cacophony of sounds rolled out from within the cave and the crowd waited expectantly. Daisy Mae said in whispered horror "Oh! What if the beasts are eating her alive?" Harold laughed and answered her, "Do you fear so much at the sounds of delight? Those are happy beasts in there, they are telling her all about themselves. Do not worry, she has made friends already with them and needs now only to choose with which one she will pair." Summersong glanced over at Harold and raised his eyebrows questioningly. Harold nodded back,

"Yes, she understands their speech as I do. She will make a fine Keeper!" Summersong turned to focus his attention on the cave once more, glad to know that she would pair, even before he saw her choice. "I wish I could understand dragon speech!" He whispered to Harold. Suddenly, the multicolored lights streaming out of the cave dimmed and went out and all sounds within were hushed. The cave was black save for the curling steam that still issued forth from the entrance: She had made her choice and the beasts were showing respect to the one chosen by dimming their lights. The crowd quieted, waiting to see which color would shine forth brightly and signal the newcomer's choice.

A great heavy padding gallop was heard, and the cave entrance lit up in brilliant purple light as a dazzling amethyst dragon shot out of the entrance at full speed. The dragon whirled and bucked and twisted in wildly convoluted circles when it reached the meadow, but the rider held her seat. At last, the dragon unleashed its feathered wings and took flight up into the air, lighting the sky with an aurora of dancing shades of purples, lilacs, lavenders, and deepest violets. The dragon whirled twice above the crowd, somersaulted in mid-air, and then landed softly in the space between cave and audience in front of Firestorm, sitting up on its haunches and holding forepaws to chest like a large puppy as it breathed hard from exertions.

"Are you quite through now?" she asked it good-humoredly. The dragon roared loudly and then purred like a gigantic cat, setting her forepaws on the ground at last and standing calm while her Rider dropped to the ground and walked forward. She ruffled the large, feathered mane around the dragon's head that looked so reminiscent of a lion's mane, and it chuckled softly, lowering its head for more. A great cheering and clapping erupted from the crowd as they welcomed their newest Keeper to the ranks.

Gatemaster Firestorm stepped forward to face her. She stood by the side of the dragon's head and waited, unsure what was expected of her at this moment. Firestorm said, "You have made an unusual choice this day. The purple dragons are generally considered untamable and do not accept Riders willingly, they are only kept for breeding because of their exceptional ability to produce multicolored broods, but we have never been able to handle any of them before. Yet this one has accepted you and allowed herself to be paired." The newcomer stood silently, unable to move since the dragon had by this time placed a large forepaw on each side of her and was resting its enormous, bearded chin upon her head. She reached up her hand and pulled the long, furry beard to one side of her face so that she could see Firestorm. The Gatemaster continued, "The dragon colors each have their own magical abilities, unique to that color." She replied, "Yes, I know." He looked at the dragon, so quiet after the initial wild display, then back to her, "Due to the fact that none before having ever tamed a purple dragon, we do not know what magical abilities this color holds, and it may be that the purple dragons do not have any abilities beyond siring the more desirable colors, indeed, they are one of the rarer colors. If you would like to choose again, in order to gain a Ride which will better help in the coming battle, you may do so."

The dragon reared up and roared mightily, splaying her claws, and beating her wings. The stars went out and the sky flashed as lightning branched across the breadth of it in all directions, thunder crackled in the night air. "Enough!" she shouted to the dragon over the noise, "I will not choose another! Be calm!" The dragon quieted, coming to rest on four paws once more, but pacing back and forth while growling dangerously low in her throat and showing her large fangs to the Gatemaster. The great long tail with the tuft of feathers at the end swung violently back and forth, and she glared at the Gatemaster. The newcomer turned to Firestorm once she was certain the dragon was under control, and said, "The purple ones control the weather; do we not have a storm to deal with?" The crowd gasped in amazement, control the weather! The very thing they needed!

Gatemaster Firestorm spoke loudly so that he could be heard over the continuing growls of the dragon, "How did you discover this talent? None have done so before, yet you who are new to our world and did not know what you were going in there to face have made the discovery?" He looked at her, eyebrows raised in question. She shrugged and replied, "Well I asked the dragons what they could do, of course, and they told me. I couldn't choose by beauty because they're all gorgeous, instead I asked them what they could each do so that I knew which would suit me best." Firestorm looked askance at her, replying with hesitation in his voice, "You – asked them." She nodded, uncomprehending. "How did you ask them?"

She gave an exasperated sigh and looked up at the dragon, "Tell me again what you can do, sweetheart." The dragon stopped pacing and chirped, squeaked, barked, ruffed, and made all sorts of animated happy noises as she threw her paws and tail out in all directions to gesture. The newcomer turned back to Firestorm, "Like that. How else is there to do it?"

Firestorm stood there, perplexed at this weird display. Finally, the silence was broken by a few people laughing and a voice from the crowd, "I don't see the problem here?" It was Harold, the Tender of Beasts, "I heard quite plainly what the dragons said to her in the cave and what this one has answered her just now. It is just as she reported to you. The purple dragons control the weather by both making and breaking it. Didn't you just witness the thunder and lightning overhead when you made this one angry? Didn't you notice the aurora lights in the sky when she flew into the air? Why are you so surprised? I said earlier that this woman has a knack with beasts. She understands their talk perfectly, the same as all the Tenders of Beasts do. Need I remind you that she is not the only Keeper that has this ability?"

"Harold is right!" said Lady Songbird, "Do you forget that I myself can understand dragon speech, dear?" Firestorm muttered, "I forgot," and looked embarrassed for a moment, rubbing a hand over his buzzcut. There was an excited babble among the crowd after this, everyone talking at once of the advantage they now might hold in being able to control the weather and fight the evil, magical storm that was sweeping Arkady. Finally, the crowd quieted and the Gatemasters in the crowd smiled and nodded agreement, "Of course," Silverwing said, "it's just that you're so new to our world, we didn't expect you to be one who could understand dragons!" Gradually, the crowd quieted and became silent.

Gatemaster Firestorm recovered his dignity and turned to her once more. "This time I speak the words of tradition: It is time for you to name your dragon here in front of us so that all may witness." She turned and stroked her dragon's nose, thinking quietly. The dragon thrummed a low answer and waited, gazing back at her. At last, she turned and said, "I shall name her Thunderstroke, since she will fight the storms in this world." The Gatemaster turned to the dragon, "Do you accept this name, dragon?" The dragon pranced in place, squealing with delight, arching her neck, mane fluffed out to the fullest and swishing her tail happily. "Then let it be so!" said the Gatemaster, turning to the audience, "This day the Ride has found a Rider and the amethyst dragon shall be known as Thunderstroke!" He turned towards the newcomer again, "Lady, you will take your ride back to Kingscannon Keep, where she shall make her new home along with you – who shall now be known as Lady Thunderstroke of Kingscannon Keep." The newcomer started, surprised, and then looked quickly over to Lady Songbird to find her smiling widely. So that is how the names were done here: the Keepers named their Rides and themselves were named after their Rides. Tradition. She grinned back at Lady Songbird.

Chapter 8 – Learning Curve

Lady Thunderstroke put the last of the grooming
tools away in the tack room, replacing the basket
that had held them back in the stack of baskets in
one corner, then she lifted the stepladder up on to
one of the large wall hooks inside the room and
stretched, reaching her arms over her head. She
was stiff and tired; it had been an exceedingly long
night with all that had happened, then coming back
home – home! She was thrust into more action,
settling her new dragon in the stable, being taught
how to groom and feed her, being shown around
the stables to learn where everything was and
finally to be introduced to the dragons in residence
there and introducing her dragon to the others. The
stable was not a stable with stalls, but an
enormously large and irregular open cavern with a
packed dirt floor. It was very bright and beautiful
with all the dragon lights intermingling and
brightening the space in multicolored rainbows,
and all the dragons gathered in groups or pairs or
singly as they wished. A few separate rooms with
doorways spaced along the sides of the stable held

food for the dragons (they ate magical fruits and berries which the Keepers gathered from the land), cleaning & grooming supplies and basic medical supplies.

At last, all was done, and she could rest. She had enjoyed an exciting and fulfilling day, but she was so exhausted that she just wanted to sleep. Her new name filled her with a feeling of belonging to this world, of satisfaction. That nagging feeling of doubt and urgency now felt like a distant and fading nightmare, and she no longer tried to remember her past life. She sighed with contentment, fastened the equipment room door, and walked over to have a last look at her dragon before retiring, but where had she gone? There was no sign of the amethyst dragon where she had been left. She glanced frantically around and there, over in the far corner, she found Thunderstroke curled tightly together with the large tawny golden dragon Summersong. They were twined about each other like furry pretzels; purple and gold intermingling and inseparable.

"Does it surprise you to see them such fast friends?" His voice from behind made her jump in surprise and she turned to face Gatemaster Summersong, who was sitting on a flat rock opposite the dragons, "No, well, yes to see them such close friends like that so quickly, yes it does rather surprise me!" He smiled, answering "They are not dumb beasts; they know that you and I are for each other, and the Rides will choose like their Riders." He stood and took her hand, drawing his knife, "Come! It is time for rest. Tomorrow there is much to do, including teaching you how to transport, which means getting you some weapons." They disappeared from the stable in a blue glow as the dragons snored on.

The next morning found Summersong and Thunderstroke walking hand in hand in a meadow by the edge of a small lake as their dragons frolicked like large ungainly puppies in the tall grass behind them, chasing each other and scattering flower petals and grass seeds everywhere as they played. "I don't fully understand this yet," she said to him, picking up an earlier conversation, "this world is multilevel, with distinct areas that don't overlap, and yet they do overlap." She looked at him, wanting an explanation. He motioned her to a small bench at the edge of the lake and they sat. "I should probably be explaining this in the map room, and I will later, but for now let me try to explain it this way," he answered, "The Keeper's world and the world of Arkady are completely separate worlds, and yet they also form part of the same world because they belong to each other. That is why the Keeper's world has no name, it belongs to Arkady and is, in essence, a reflection of Arkady. There are many other worlds besides these, for example Brimstone and the living world, but for now let's concentrate on the two you need most to know about and will be dealing with on a daily basis.

These two worlds are separate as the living world is separate from Arkady, and yet they are connected to each other, which the living world is not. The living world is separate from all other worlds, and when we walk in that world, we are ghosts and cannot be seen by the living, nor interact with anything in it. In all of these other worlds, we are real, alive, and can interact with everything and be seen by all." He glanced down at the short, slender woman by his side to see if she was following. "Yes, that part I understand now, but you said that the locations are the same between Arkady and this Keeper's world. How can they be if the worlds are separate? I'm very confused." He nodded, "Well, think of a map on a desk, I'll show you later today. Let's say I put a map of Arkady on the desk. For the sake of the explanation, we'll work with the little town of Greenfield where you first arrived." She nodded as he went on, "Now over that map I lay another map, that of the Keeper's world. Pretend the map overlay is transparent, so that you can see through to the map below of Arkady." He looked at her. "Yes," she answered, waiting for more explanation. "Do you know what location on the Keeper's world map would be directly over Greenfield in Arkady?" He asked her.

She closed her eyes a moment, trying to think it through, but finally shook her head with a small sigh, "No I'm afraid I don't." His eyebrows went up in surprise, "Are you sure that you don't know? Think about what was said last night during the meeting about Keep locations and which Keep was closest to each town. Remember that it was I who brought you to Greenfield, and not one of the other Gatemasters." He waited again as she looked over at the two dragons now flattening great swaths of meadow grass by rolling in it. "Would it be, uh, Kingscannon Keep?" He nodded, "Now you're getting it. The two worlds are separate, but the maps for them are identical, except the names are different of course. Each Keep corresponds to a set of towns and fields, such as Kingscannon Keep does to Greenfield town and its surrounding countryside, or to a city area, such as Windspeak Keep does to the largest city of Arkady which is called Thornapple Center."

She nodded, understanding at last, "So, if I learn one map, I've learned two?" "Well, not quite," he answered, "For the roads and pathways are different, since we don't have roads here like they do in Arkady, and the layout of the land is different as well. Also, there are some smaller hamlets and villages in Arkady that don't correspond with anything here and aren't actually listed on the maps, but the major town centers and Keep locations are identical. When we're in the Keep of Kingscannon, we're directly on top of the town of Greenfield in Arkady." Lady Thunderstroke looked puzzled, "Are we up above Arkady, like beyond the clouds?" "No," Summersong answered patiently, "We're in the same place as Arkady, we're just in another dimension of time-space. That's why the time passes differently and varies between all of the worlds. You were only here for a single afternoon when I brought you, but in Arkady, two days had passed. Time varies between the worlds, but that is another lesson."

She puzzled over things a little more and then asked "But Summer, why do the Keeps and the Keep stables need to be arrived at by transporting? Yet every other part of this world can be walked to or flown over just like in Arkady? If I stand in front of the stable, I can see the land about it, and I can see the tall pillar of rock. I know the Keep is up above the stable, but I can't walk down to the stable or up to the Keep. Also, I can't walk out into the land that I see surrounding the pillar, there's some sort of invisible shield which prevents me from going far, and I can only access the packed dirt area in front of the Kingscannon stable and the small grassy area that circles around our Keep. I can't get to the trees surrounding our Keep. When I'm outside of the immediate Keep area and I look around the land, I can't see the stable or the Keep at all, nor are there any windows in a Keep to look out of. Are the Keeps and the stables each in their own world as well, in a separate time-space dimension?"

He shook his head, "No, they are part of this world but are protected by a barrier of the same type that holds the Dragon Gates in place. If the barrier was broken somehow, then you would see them standing on the plains like gigantic pillars of rock, just like you see them when you're inside the protective shield of the Keep, with each Keep being positioned on top of each stable. It's a safety feature designed to protect us in case of attack." She looked at him questioningly. He went on, "There have been many attempts at breaking into this world by the Nevilem, who are the evil men from the world of Brimstone. They have their own world but are not satisfied with it and are constantly prowling Arkady trying to control the people and the land there and have made repeated attempts over the years to break into this world. Once they did break in, long ago. After that attack was repelled, we redesigned the Dragon Gate pillars to not only power the Dragon Gates in Arkady, but also to protect this world and hide our Keeps. You haven't seen those pillars yet because we have them scattered in the wild places about our land. You will learn more in time, I promise. For now, understand that our job is not only to keep the Gates, but to keep Arkady as well. We are the protection of Arkady, that is our job and that is why we are called Keepers."

Just then the two dragons came over, flower petals and grass seeds firmly embedded within their fur from noses to tails, chirping expectantly.

Thunderstroke laughed and said, "Well, the morning grooming session didn't last very long, did it?" The two dragons purred, nuzzling in to the two sitting humans and knocking them off the bench to the ground. Summersong laughingly said, "Okay! Okay! We'll go now!" They got up and the dragons crouched down so their Riders could mount, then Summersong looked over to Thunderstroke, saying, "Now, how well do you remember what I've taught you? Remember, on the dragon, they do the transport, not you, but you give the direction. A dragon cannot transport without a Rider touching them or giving them the order to transport." She nodded nervously, "I think I remember."

"Summer," he said, looking down at his dragon, "We'll go ahead to Kingscannon Keep stable alone. Don't help Thunderstroke, she needs to know how to do this on her own." The golden dragon chirped in reply and licked his amethyst mate, then tossed his head up as his twisting golden horns glowed blue. He and his Rider shimmered out of existence as the glow faded, leaving amethyst Thunderstroke arching her neck backwards and staring at her rider upside down, waiting for the command. "Uh, yeah! How do we do this again, Thunder?" The purple dragon twisted her head almost completely around in place like an owl and chirped, "You just tell me where to go. I will do the transport." Lady Thunderstroke nodded and answered, "Yes, I know, but when I must do it without you, how do I do it? Summersong said to think of where I want to go and then think of the power of my dragon, but how? Do I imagine lightning bolts, or thunder? Or should I just imagine you?"

The amethyst dragon gazed thoughtfully at her Rider for a minute before chirping again, "I have never done this before, so I do not know, I only know that I can do it now that I have a Rider. Once we have transported, ask me again, and maybe I'll have a better answer." Lady Thunderstroke sighed and shook her head, looking over at the lake once more and trying extremely hard to concentrate as she watched a soft breeze ripple the water. "Okay, let's go home to Kingscannon Keep stable, beautiful girl!" she announced to her dragon. The dragon untwisted her neck and looked forward as her Rider watched the dragon's purple horns begin to glow blue.

A moment later, they appeared in the dirt area in front of the stable and amethyst Thunderstroke galloped over to golden Summersong squealing with delight as Lady Thunderstroke tumbled off. "Well," she asked her Ride quietly, "How?" The dragon answered in a conspiratorial, soft series of barks and chirps, "All I did was think that I wished to come here, and I came! So, I think that you will have to do the same, and maybe also think of me transporting you." Lady Thunderstroke whispered her thanks, rubbed the soft nose of the dragon, and headed towards the stable, where Gatemaster Summersong was standing in the shade of the entrance talking with a younger man from the company and holding a sheet of parchment.

The two men turned as she walked up to them, "Lady" the younger man bowed to her, and she stepped back a pace, embarrassed. "That's alright, Baldy, you don't have to do that with this one. She isn't like some of those Jeweldance Keep women; she's just one of the guys, right Thunder?" She smiled gratefully and nodded, holding her hand out to the young man, and staring at his mop of tousled blonde hair as she asked, "I know I haven't got all the names memorized yet but, uh, Baldy?" He laughed and replied, "Well, it's a nickname! I named my dragon Balderdash because he was so wild and crazy, and it was the first thing that came to mind when I was told to name him, so they call me Baldy!" The three of them had a quick laugh and then Baldy continued, "Back to my message, Gatemaster, you've been requested to report to Grimhold Keep with your Lady and give them advice on this matter to judge whether this Arkadian who has been brought there is a true messenger from the town or a man of Brimstone."

Summer nodded and took the parchment, signing his name to it and handing it back, "Tell them we will report in two hours. There are a couple of things that I need to attend to here before we can come." His gaze shifted over to the two dragons much in need of grooming and the younger man laughed as he took an axe out of his belt, holding it out and disappearing as the blue glow spread from his axe, up his arm and engulfed him completely. "Well," said Gatemaster Summersong, turning to his mate, "What do you think of that? We've barely had breakfast and a walk, let alone started your training, and already we are called in to service. I'm afraid you will have to learn fast! Come, let's groom these two quickly and report to the armory so that you may claim your weapons. I want you to be able to transport at need without having to rely on another person to get you places."

"So," said Ruffian, the large, bearded, and burly Keeper standing behind the armory desk, "you have come at last to claim your weapons, eh?" He waved his hand expansively over the large room and she looked around at the many alcoves with walls covered in weapons of all types, then back to the man behind the desk as he continued. "All this is for choosing, so take that which suits you best."

She looked uncertainly at the man, and then up to Summersong at her side, "I've never handled a weapon of any kind before. I don't know how to choose." The men glanced at each other then back to her. "Most of the female Keepers have chosen the bow and arrow as their weapon of choice because they are a lighter weapon and allow the wielder some distance from battle. But we do have several women who have chosen the heavier style weapons. It really comes down to a matter of personal preference, both for what you're comfortable handling and which type of battle style you prefer, whether up close and personal or from a distance." Ruffian replied at length.

"Go ahead, walk around, and lift some down from the walls, hold them, swing them, feel their balance, aim at the target wall, and at the practice dummies, see how well you like the feel of each and as you walk around, think about how you would want to defend yourself if you had to fight. For instance, would you like to close with your enemy and fight hand to hand using a sword, battle hammer, or an axe, or would you rather stay at a distance and shoot an arrow, or throw a spear? Forgive me, but being someone smaller and slimmer in stature, you may wish to keep your distance to prevent being overpowered by an opponent's sheer weight and strength. We don't have to fight often, but it's best to be prepared, and you need a weapon that you can feel comfortable with if you want to fight well."

Summersong nodded at this suggestion, "We do not have much time before our meeting, but you must try. At the least you should choose a small knife or dagger, so that you are not weaponless when we attend this meeting. Keeper tradition requires that participants be armed. It's not that we fight each other, it's just always been done so. I also want you to be able to begin transporting on your own, and a knife will give you that ability, since your weapons will channel your dragon's magic. We can always come back later for you to choose your main weapon." Lady Thunderstroke hesitated, and then walked over to the nearest alcove, reaching out gingerly to touch the blade of a large two-headed battle-axe before moving further along and picking up a small crossbow to examine.

At length she picked up a small set of throwing daggers from the end wall of another alcove and balanced them one by one in her hands. Turning to the target wall at the opposite end of the cavern, she took aim and threw the three daggers so fast and so accurately that both men gasped in amazement at her precision. She walked across the room and removed the daggers from the center of the target before walking back to the desk and holding the set of daggers out towards Ruffian, "Will these do? I like these. I always did like to play darts." Summersong smiled and Ruffian said, "Those will do as your knife, but you still must choose your main battle weapon. You can come back later if you wish." Summer nodded, "That will have to do for the time being. It is best to choose your weapon carefully and I don't like pressing you to hurry, so we'll just go with these for now, but when the meeting is done, we will return here so that you can finish."

Thunderstroke nodded and then looked down at the small daggers, wondering how best to carry them. Both men chuckled and then the burly Armory Keeper reached behind to the shelves and took down a brown leather belt with many loops made for carrying knives and other small weapons; it looked almost like a tool belt Thunderstroke thought. "For now, use this, but we will see if you need a different style once your main weapon has been chosen." She buckled it around her waist and placed the daggers within three of the small sheaths, then looked to Summersong who said, "You shall now transport us to Grimhold Keep for our meeting, and I will see how well you remember your lesson!" "Okay!" she replied, "Let me just confirm with you before trying. I think of the place I want to go either by place name, image, or map coordinate, and then think of the power of my dragon. Correct?" Both men nodded in reply, and Summersong said, "Also, you should always transport to the common area of a Keep, and not into a sleeping room or map room. It's considered polite manners." She took one dagger out and held Summersong's hand with the other; picturing amethyst Thunderstroke's glowing horns, she thought "Grimhold Keep common area" and they glowed blue and were gone.

Chapter 9 - Tradition

"I'm keeping this councilor of theirs in one of the holding cells for now. He seems quite friendly and helpful, if you could call it that," Gatemaster Silverwing said to the small group, "but then that's just how he would appear if they wanted to trick us into believing their story." Gatemaster Summersong and Lady Thunderstroke had immediately been pulled into a small meeting room upon arriving at Grimhold Keep, to update them on the councilor that had been brought in. "I don't like the idea of having Lady Thunderstroke in there for him to see though," Silverwing continued, "he made mention to my Keeper, Nightfall, in Arkady about an escaped girl, and I wonder if he may be referring to Thunder. I wouldn't like them to know she's with us now, not too soon at least."

Summersong nodded and looked down at his Lady, "Are you willing to wait while we go in to interview this man? What are your feelings in this matter? You have just as much right as I do to be in there: Gatemasters and Ladies are equal in this world." She smiled gently at Summersong "I don't mind. You three go ahead and I will wait here until you call or finish. If you say it would be better that they don't know where I'm at, then you're probably right; I'm still learning!" Lady Evenflower chimed in, "Why don't you two men go ahead, and Lady Thunderstroke and I will wait for you together. That way the man won't feel overwhelmed with too many people, besides, those holding cells are small. You can tell us all about it when you're finished. The men nodded and left the room.

"You and I could pass the time by preparing a light snack for when the men are done, it will be a nice way to get to know each other better!" said Lady Evenflower to Thunderstroke, "You can call me Eva." The two women walked out of the meeting room and over to the kitchen area that was much the same as at Kingscannon Keep, except larger. They began preparing the food, talking happily together all the while. Lady Thunderstroke had felt an immediate liking for Lady Evenflower and

Gatemaster Silverwing of Grimhold Keep when she first met them at the meeting in Kingscannon the previous evening, and she was pleased to have some quiet time with the other woman instead of attending a meeting. "Thank you for waiting with me, Eva," she said to Lady Evenflower, "It really is nice to have some down time instead of going into yet another meeting. It's been so constant for me since coming here with lessons and meetings and hurried activity, all in such a short space of time. This is a nice change of pace!"

Lady Evenflower smiled in return and reached for a basket with tea leaves in it, choosing a selection and placing them in readiness upon a tray. "Oh, that's alright!" she said, "I get so tired of meetings too! I really enjoy Keep days, but meetings kind of mess those up even though they're a necessary part of our life, so it's nice to skip a meeting now and then. Once you get to know the rhythms of our world better, you'll find that the days you spend in the Keep cleaning it and preparing the evening meal are the days you'll look forward to; all of us Ladies think of them as days off!"

"Are the rock pillars which contain the Keeps and stables natural to this land, or were they built here? They seem to me almost like ancient, volcanic plugs." Lady Thunderstroke asked as she sliced a loaf of bread with a knife. Lady Evenflower replied, "The pillars were raised from the earth by the brown dragons, who hold the power of earth as their magical skill. The dragons raised the pillars, then hollowed out the centers for Keep and stable. After that, we Keepers put finishing touches to the interiors of our Keeps by building walls to separate the rooms, and the Smiths carved the bathing pools, water tunnels, and air vents." Lady Thunderstroke looked around the kitchen, "There are air vents in the Keeps? I wondered how the air could be so fresh in these enclosed places." Lady Evenflower nodded and pointed up to the ceiling over the kitchen stove, "Look there! The openings are small, and we designed them to be hidden, but they are all over the ceilings and the lower walls. We have several around the Keep, there's a small metal fan inside each one which is moved by the air that passes through, and the Smiths placed a raised metal sheet over the top of each upper vent to prevent rain from coming in."

Lady Thunderstroke put her bread knife down and walked over to stand by the stove and look up, there high above her head was a deep chute in the rock with a fan blade at the top. She gazed at it for a little bit and then returned to the counter and picked up her knife again as Lady Evenflower continued, "Some of our Keeps have stone shelves carved into the walls, mostly those are the older Keeps, and some of our Keeps have wood shelves, while a few have a combination of both wood and rock. When all of the rock work was completed, our green dragons, which have the power of water, made two large pools of fresh water on the top of our Keeps, one hot and the other cool. Those pools enter the bathing room through a series of tunnels that the Smiths carved into the rock; the hot water fills the bathing pools from underneath, and the cool water falls down as waterfalls into each pool. There's another tunnel carved underneath of each pool that drains the water away and recirculates it into the pools on the top of the Keep."

Lady Thunderstroke stopped slicing the bread and looked up in amazement at the tall woman opposite her, "That is really neat work, but how does the water stay clean when it's recirculated, and how does the hot water stay hot?" Lady Evenflower said with a sassy toss of her long, white braid, "Magic! No, really, I don't understand it, but when the dragons put the water pools in, they also imbued it with magic that allows the water to stay at the proper temperature, to move back up the water tunnels to the top, and to remove impurities and dirt as it travels back up, as well as replenishing itself so that the pools never run dry." She shook her head and laughed, "We have a lot of magic in this world, and even after all this time here, I still don't understand it!"

The two women moved easily about the kitchen making sandwiches, heating the tea kettle, taking teacups and plates down from shelves, and enjoying the relaxed pace. "There!" they both exclaimed together as the last item was put on the trays. They smiled at each other and then turned as one when the men reappeared from a small hallway further down the wide, main hall. "Already!?" exclaimed Lady Evenflower, "That was a very short meeting." The two men shook their heads, motioned the women to follow, and then walked into the map room and over to one of the desks there. Gatemaster Silverwing pulled a rolled parchment out of one of the cubbyholes in the wall behind the desks and unrolled it, revealing a map.

The women brought the trays over as the men placed some small, squared, and polished rocks on the corners to hold the map in place and began poring over the map side by side in hurried concentration. The women set the trays down upon a nearby desk and then leaned over the map from the other side of the desk to see what the fuss was about. "Here," said Silverwing pointing to a small clearing in a wooded location on the map of Arkady before them, "This is where the man met with my Keepers." Summersong frowned and asked, "But how did he get there with this storm in progress? It's a good way into the wood at that point and no marked trail leads to that particular glade." The men frowned at the map and after a few minutes of thought, Silverwing replied, "I do not know, but I am inclined to believe what this councilor says. He must have been desperate to have come so far in the storm." Summersong shook his head quickly but said nothing.

Lady Thunderstroke reached out and touched the map where Silverwing had indicated, then let her finger travel over the map until she came to the little town of Greenfield to the east and south of the location. "But!" she softly exclaimed, leaning in further to look closely before running her finger back from Greenfield, through an area marked as farmland, on into the wooded area to the north until at last coming back to the little glade indicated. She looked up quickly, glancing at both men and Lady Evenflower in turn.

"Speak, Lady," said Summersong to her curiously. She tapped the glade, "If I am reading this map right, and if I'm remembering my escape clearly, this is the glade I found you in that night when the storm first came. I would not have found it without being led there by the owl, there was no path. I had an awful time stumbling over the undergrowth in sandals and getting my bare legs all scratched up from branches." Summersong's eyes widened, "Yes! That is the place! We have designated areas in Arkady hidden from view where we transport into and out of because the Arkadians are a bit unnerved by our method of travel, so we try not to do it in front of them. That is one of our transport glades." Silverwing straightened and looked serious, "So this is a plant then, you believe?" Lady Evenflower spoke up then, suggesting "Why don't we sit with tea and you two can tell us how the meeting went. Then we might be able to better assist you with this problem." All agreed and they pulled chairs up to the nearby desk where the trays had been placed and began to eat while talking.

"The matter stands thus," began Silverwing as he took a sandwich and bit into it, "this man claims to have been sent by the council in Greenfield to warn us of an escaped and dangerous traitor." He nodded towards Thunderstroke and continued, "He means you of course, and it is nonsense as we know of your movements from the day you first entered Arkady. But they are trying to put a different slant on things to suit their own ends, I think." He finished the sandwich and reached for another, "This man says he came straight to the glade to meet with a Keeper as he knew they were seen there often. We asked why he didn't just have the council call for a Keeper in the usual fashion instead of going so far in the storm, since it is council business he claims to be on, but he would not answer that. He also wouldn't answer us on how he knew of that glade, since it's one of our lonelier transport spots that we thought was secret only to us. Well, it isn't any longer. In fact, I doubt any of our secret places in Arkady are secret, now. We might as well do away with them, and transport directly to the places we need from now on."

Lady Evenflower said, "Why don't you mention that at our next leaders meeting, dear? I'll make a note of it, so we remember to discuss it. I've always thought those hidden transport areas were silly, and entailed a lot of walking for us when we're already so busy with the work we do." She got up and walked over to the wall shelves, where she took out a sheet of paper before returning to the desk, picking up one of the pens scattered on the desk, and dipping it into an ink bottle to write. Summersong nodded in agreement and interjected, "I agree, please bring it up for discussion and we'll take a vote. I do not trust this councilor for that reason alone. None of the council should have known about that glade, and it worries me that they do. Then you must also account for the fact that the Keeper who met with him said he was certain there were other Arkadians further away, he heard their footsteps in the undergrowth." He took another sandwich and chewed thoughtfully, then said, "I'm inclined to agree with you on the transport spots, Eva. I now believe that we Keepers have been watched for a long time as we've gone about our duties in Arkady, and we will have to be more careful in future." Silverwing nodded, "Yes there is that and I have already sent a message to Harold asking if the animals have continued watching that area of the woods. It would not be

185

good at all if the council had managed to track Lady Thunderstroke to the glade because then they would know she was with us."

Summersong shook his head and answered quickly, "No it is impossible for them to have tracked her, the path taken by this councilor was different than the one she was led on by the owl for one thing. Another reason is that the storm had washed out tracks that day, and certainly after this amount of time there would be no trace." Lady Evenflower asked, "Could they have somehow tracked Thunder down by that locket she carries? Does it give off any emanations that could be picked up by one who knows what to look for? If it's a Seed, then it could very well be sending out signals." Both men looked momentarily startled and glanced over at the map on the other desk once more, lost in thought.

Lady Thunderstroke looked confused and spoke up quietly, "I don't understand. Why is it a bad thing if they know where I'm at, and why do they want to find me again? Who exactly are these councilors? I remember Harold told me that Silenus was bad, and not to be trusted, but are they all bad?" Lady Evenflower answered her, "They are not good men but are Nevilem working for the evil Master of Brimstone, well, most of them are. Somehow, over time, they have quietly replaced the ordinary councilors with Nevilem in many, if not all, of the towns, in order to gain control of Arkady. They now know through Silenus that you carry the locket or did at the time of your disappearance. So, if they know where you are, they will try and wage war against the Keeper's world to gain that locket. It isn't you they want, so much as the locket, but they need you because nobody else can carry it, as you discovered in your first meeting with Silenus and related to us. That I think is the only reason Silenus did not lock you up immediately or kill you: He needed you to handle the locket and he had to wait for a response from his Master in Brimstone on what he should do about you. At any rate, we are unprepared for such a war currently when we are so busy repairing the broken Gate pillars, as well as trying to save the people out of Greenfield, in addition to our regular duties. It would not be good for them to know where the locket resides at this moment. They will find out soon enough."

Summersong nodded and said, "As long as you remain in the Keeper's world, you are hidden from them. You will not be able to remain hidden forever of course, since you will assume duties alongside the rest of us in time, but for the time being you are hidden to them. I would like to keep it that way at least until I'm certain that you're fully capable of handling both your dragon and your weapon and feel comfortable with transporting and have a few practiced places that you could reach without conscious effort if you needed to get away quickly." Silverwing cut in, "That is why I didn't want you to be seen by this councilor tonight, just in case he is proven to be false. We do not want word of your location going back to them just yet, even though they may suspect you're here. Perhaps," he broke off, swiveling toward Summersong with a sudden thought, "we might lay a false trail for them?"

Summersong mused, "We still have the shift she was wearing when she came here, it is not needed now of course. It could be torn to some degree, muddied, and placed in Arkady at a completely different location to make it look like she is still in Arkady. Harold would know of a person or two on our side willing to play the ruse at a farmhouse somewhere, to say that they had helped a girl and given her new clothing and food. Send them on a wild goose chase?" Silverwing nodded excitedly, "I like that, yes! We can send them towards Thornapple Center, that's a large town that will take them ages to search and would buy us some time. I'll ask Harold about this idea when he comes with the message on the trails." Summersong nodded and said, "I'll send Baldy over with the shift so that you can give it to Harold if he agrees with our idea. I think it was left at Jumpriver." They finished tea and said goodbyes. "Would you be willing to hold this man a little longer, to be safe, before releasing him?" Summersong asked of Silverwing and Evenflower as they were preparing to depart. "Yes of course! We will keep an eye on him for the moment. I will let you know as soon as I hear from Harold.

Goodnight!" Summersong took his sword out and clasping Thunderstroke's hand in his, they shimmered out in a shower of blue sparkles and were gone.

Thunderstroke gave a start of surprise as they materialized once more within the armory. "I told you we would return here after the meeting, didn't I?" Summersong questioned her with a smile on his face. She answered him with a question of her own, "Is the Armory part of a Keep, Summer?" Ruffian the Armory Keeper bustled out to the desk from a nearby room, "Ah! So good to see you again this soon! No indeed. We built the Amory as a standalone location for protection. We don't want all these weapons easily found if someone broke in from Brimstone, so the Armory is heavily protected and stands alone from other dwellings. It is, however, considered to belong to Jumpriver Keep, since I belong to that Keep and am in charge of this place. Have you returned to search for the perfect weapon, Lady Thunderstroke?"

He smiled congenially and set down a glass bottle of polish and another of tea seed oil on the desk, along with a thick cloth as she answered, "Yes" with a smile and wandered into one of the weapon alcoves to browse. Summersong leaned on the high desk "Would you like help with that, Ruff?" he asked, motioning to the handful of older, discolored knives laid out on the desk. "Well, if you'd like to pass the time, be my guest! I'll get another cloth!" replied Ruffian, or "Ruff" as he was commonly called, bustling out once more for another polishing cloth and returning shortly as Summer picked up the first cloth and applied some polish to it.

Thunderstroke listened idly to the conversation as she wandered the cavern, looking at weapons. She couldn't believe the amount and variety of weaponry in this place, yet nothing struck her fancy. She was beginning to wonder if she was meant to be a Keeper after all, if she had no desire for a fighting weapon, although she admired the swords a great deal. "So, the meeting this afternoon was a short one, eh?" asked Ruffian of

Summersong, breaking in on her thoughts. "Yes," replied Summersong, "the man was rather uncooperative, and we suspect he is a spy planted on purpose to sway us in our opinions and actions, and possibly also to see if we know of Thunderstroke's location – which we will, of course, not tell him. We must return him before night falls tomorrow in Arkady, I think or there will be suspicions aroused among the councils there, but we are waiting to hear back from Harold first to be certain. He's gathering some information for us."

Thunderstroke called out to them from the alcove across from the desk, "I suppose this is going to sound silly to the both of you, but why did we say 'goodnight' when we parted this day when it hasn't even got to suppertime?" The men both laughed and looked over at her as Summersong replied, "It is not a silly question. We usually only find time to gather between Keeps in the evenings or at night, so even when we do find time during the day, we still say goodnight." She smiled, "Oh, all right! It's a tradition." Ruffian looked at

Summersong and said, "Did you hear that? We have a tradition! And I thought I was the only one who thought that was an odd thing to say in the middle of the day!" The men laughed and returned to polishing knives as Thunderstroke continued her search.

Chapter 10 – Return To Arkady

Lady Thunderstroke stood frustrated, hands on her hips, glaring at the two men as they leaned on the desk and talking animatedly with each other about dragons. Three times the men had stopped her when she showed interest in swinging the heavy swords, cutlasses, and scimitars around. "You are too slight to handle such a weapon," they had told her gently, removing each weapon from her and guiding her towards the bows, spears, javelins, and other light weapons every time. "I can't help it that I'm short!" she had retorted after the third instance as Summersong went back to join Ruffian at the desk. Lady Thunderstroke was tired of looking at weapons, it was boring her to death and back. She was tired of trying to find something that "fit her battle style" as Ruff called it. The only things she found interest in beyond the small set of daggers that she already wore were the smaller knives, which she didn't need, and the swords. In truth, they really were too big for her. She was strong enough to handle them, but they were too long for her to swing comfortably without hitting the ground. As she stood near the target wall in the alcove opposite the desk, glaring at the men, the air next to the desk began to glow blue and she forgot her momentary frustration to walk forward and join the men as they turned to watch the new arrival.

It was Baldy bearing another message. "Hello! I come with news from Grimhold. I brought the shift to them, but Gatemaster Silverwing asks for your return at once. He says to tell you that we have a problem larger than at first expected, and he fears that lives are now at stake, and one is already lost." Summersong nodded to Ruffian and said gravely "Once again, my friend, we will have to postpone this search." Thunderstroke caught his agitation and immediately pulled one of the daggers from her belt, reaching for Summersong's hand with hers. He smiled and shouted as they began to glow "She catches on quickly!" and they were gone.

Baldy turned to the large Armory Keeper and said "How goes the weapon search, Ruff? Has she chosen yet? It's always exciting to find out what someone new chooses!" Ruffian shook his head and replied "She keeps going for the swords, but they are too big for her to swing comfortably! I wonder if we should be fighting her desire. It is not good to push an unwanted weapon on someone." Baldy agreed, answering, "You are right: If swords are what she leans to, then a smaller sword you should find. If I were you, I would contact the Smithy while those two are gone, to see if a smaller sword can be fashioned to fit her stature because there will be no time later, if my guess is correct." He took his axe in hand and disappeared in a blue glow, leaving Ruffian standing solemnly alone, stroking his rough brown beard, and nodding his head slowly. "Aye," he said softly at last, "I will contact Steele this very afternoon, it wouldn't hurt to have a few smaller size weapons in the inventory anyway." He walked off into the stock room still muttering.

Silverwing paced rapidly up and down the large common room as Lady Evenflower, Lady Thunderstroke, Summersong, Harold and a dripping wet Keeper named Nightfall watched him. "This is not good! This is simply not good! We must return the man, or they will be suspicious, but returning him may play into their hands! In fact, it will, since he is demanding we return him to the city center immediately. I think it's a trap, and we would do well to hold him as a bargaining chip." He stopped suddenly and looked over to his Keeper Nightfall, "Tell Summersong what you found?" Nightfall swallowed and said, "Well sir, as you ordered, I went to the transport glade this councilor was found in to check for activity in the area or leading to it since the councilor was brought here. There was a young woman lying on the ground there, dead. A note pinned to her which read "Keeper beware! Give us the girl with the locket or others will die." No other signs, no footprints, nothing. But the forest is now burned black, it was pouring rain heavily and the wind was fierce with damaged branches coming down all over. Footprints might easily have been destroyed by fire or washed away in the heavy rain. The woman was cold, she had been dead some time, I'm afraid, and there was nothing I could do for her."

Silverwing sighed heavily, "We have to get those townspeople out of that makeshift dungeon tonight, we cannot risk anyone else being killed, and they cannot wait any longer!" He looked at Summersong, waiting for his take on the situation. Summersong instead turned away from Silverwing and looked to Harold, asking, "You say the owl reported three councilors had disappeared into the wood with the one we have here and then returned without him?" Harold nodded quietly and Summersong continued, "We know then, that this was a plant. We just cannot completely fathom why they did it in such fashion. Normally the councilors would summon a Keeper to the front steps of the Hall of Images, that is the usual method. There must be some purpose to this. I wonder if it was simply to show us that they know where we enter Arkady, to make us afraid." Lady Evenflower said, "But why would they kill like that? Even if they are Brimstone folk, which we don't know for certain, there isn't any purpose in the murder." Summersong looked over at her and answered, "They're trying to scare us into giving

Thunder to them, and they also want to get the Keepers out of Arkady for good, so that Brimstone can have a free reign there."

Harold shifted his feet and then spoke "Gatemaster, if you heed my advice, you will get those townspeople out tonight. I can provide shelter for as many as are needed in my tunnel if you can free them. The storm at least has dampened the fires that were spreading across the forests, but they are heavily damaged, and the crop fields are destroyed. The council has been sending their sentries around to search all area buildings and destroy them by fire once searched. Hiding places have become few and far between. Those townsfolk that escaped the original rounding up came to me and I have kept them safely hidden in the tunnel under my dairy barn, but the barn has been destroyed so we must be careful entering and leaving. I've barricaded the town entrance of the tunnel and backfilled it with some dirt just in case. We now stay close to the entrance into the forest, but that entrance opens close to your transport glade, which we now know that the council is aware of, so it is no longer a safe entry point and I'm afraid we'll be discovered before much longer. Also, the town has changed: the white marble on the buildings has all turned to blood red and black marble; you know what that means."

They did indeed: Those were Brimstone's colors, and it signaled the beginning of war; the evil Master was taking over. No safety was to be had in Greenfield anymore because it had been turned into a center of the evil activity now spreading throughout Arkady. "I wish we had noticed things long before!" Silverwing growled in frustration, "We should have noticed a year ago when we Keepers were suddenly ordered to begin staying away from the towns and avoid interacting too much with the Arkadians." Summersong agreed, saying, "That is true, but we've been extremely busy with Gate activity, being so few in number, and it was simply one less thing for us to worry about."

Lady Evenflower glanced over to Thunderstroke to
see how she was taking the news and stepped back
a pace in surprise when she saw fierce anger on the
smaller woman's usually smiling, round face.
Silverwing glanced over to see why his Lady had
started, and followed her gaze, his blue eyes
widening in surprise, as did Nightfall and Harold,
followed lastly by Summersong. Thunderstroke
realized suddenly that everyone was staring at her.
"What is it? Why are you all staring at me?"
Silverwing looked to Summersong and told him
shortly, "She is ready, she can help this night also.
That purple dragon would be a great help to us. I
don't care what rules the town councilors have laid
down about not allowing dragons near to towns, or
Keepers not interacting with Arkadians. These are
no longer rules we will follow, since it is obvious
that they were put in place to prevent us finding
out what Brimstone was doing there. We will set
our own rules from now on, and we will not wait
for a meeting of all leaders to start."

Summersong nodded, "We must go immediately.
We will bring the councilor back to Arkady, even

though we may be walking into a trap. We will get those people out, somehow." He glanced between Lady Evenflower and Silverwing, "We cannot risk going in force or they will think we are declaring war. Even though war is coming, I do not wish it to be started by our side or the Brimstone men may begin killing off the Arkadians indiscriminately to try stopping us. Therefore, we cannot have too many in our group, yet we must be strong enough to repel and escape any trap they have prepared for us." Silverwing nodded as Summersong continued, "I will return this man to the city center myself, I am more than a match for him and any of his sentries; there shouldn't be more than a few sentries on duty at any given time. However, I would like to have some backup, all the same. Lady Evenflower, I would appreciate your bow at my back, but I want you to stay safely aboard your dragon and out of reach of any spears they may throw." She smiled and replied, "I will certainly come!" then she left the room to retrieve her weapon.

Summersong turned to Harold, "We will need your help, my friend. You will return to the tunnel and prepare your people there for a quick rescue. Have them gather any belongings they still own and be ready to exit the tunnel at a signal. We cannot transport into and out of a dirt tunnel with no location coordinates, so they will need to come into the open glade, but I don't want them out of shelter until Keepers are in place to help." Harold responded quickly, "I will go now!"

Summersong nodded and motioned to Nightfall, "Go with Harold, transport him to his hiding place and help him defend the Arkadians if you will, it would be good to have your sword at the ready, for safety's sake! Remain hidden in the tunnel with them until help arrives. I would ask you to start transporting them one by one, but I need a guard over them and don't want to risk you disappearing at intervals leaving them unprotected, so instead I'll ask you to wait until more Keepers arrive to aid you." Silverwing interjected, "I will send some more of my Keepers immediately to the transport glade to aid you in getting the people to safety,

Nightfall." He hesitated and took a good long look at his Keeper, "Uh, do you want to change into dry clothes first?" Nightfall grinned and shook his head, "I'll only get wet again! I'll warm up with a bath once this is done." he answered. Silverwing gave a short laugh and said, "Okay, go now and do as Gatemaster Summersong has requested."

Nightfall nodded acknowledgement, drew his sword, and touched Harold by the shoulder. They glowed blue and disappeared from the room, leaving Silverwing and Thunderstroke standing there with Summersong. Gatemaster Silverwing turned and shouted to a Keeper taking dishes off of a shelf in the kitchen area in preparation for setting the table for evening meal, "Rudy! You were listening?" The man nodded, setting the dishes on the counter, and coming forward. "Get Bluebell and transport down immediately to the forest end of Harold's tunnel. You know where that is, near our transport glade? Be wary, the forest is burned and there are Nevilem all over it, you won't find any hiding spots, so you'll probably have to come in fighting." Rudy nodded and unsheathed his sword, transporting away without a word. Silverwing turned back to the other two and said, "Three Keepers should be enough to get the people safely here."

Summersong nodded and looked at Eva as she returned with her bow and quiver, then he answered, "Get another archer and send him with your Lady; I do not want her unguarded this night. Make sure they both stay upon their dragons for safety. I hope your Keepers can get everyone safely away from the tunnel, it should be unwatched if they go while we are returning this man because their attention will be upon me. If there are too many people for your Keep to house, have your men transport some of them to Kingscannon, we have plenty of room. Also, I would ask you to come on your dragon but remain high, so they do not see you at first and be prepared to come in fast if the fight looks to be going against me. You will know what to do." Silverwing asked, "Do you want Silver to make you invisible?" He was referring to his dragon, who carried the power of invisibility. Summersong shook his head, "No, I need to keep the attention of the sentries on me so that you and Thunder can get the people out of the prison without being seen. I'll have to take my chances." Silverwing nodded and left with Eva, leaving Summer and Thunderstroke alone in the common area.

"Do you know what I am going to ask you to do?" he asked her quietly. "Yes," she replied, "You want Thunderstroke and me to fight the storm tonight. We can do that!" He nodded, "Good! But I do not want you to take part in the battle because you are still unarmed, for I do not count three small throwing daggers as a weapon! We cannot risk you being captured, and that locket places you in a precarious position. You will remain on Thunderstroke and make sure to keep her out of arrow range so neither of you get hurt. I don't think any of the sentries have arrows, but they could throw a spear up at you, so it's best to be safe. You were throwing some of the spears in the Armory earlier today, so you know that you'll need to keep a good twenty to thirty feet above the ground at minimum.

Hold the weather at bay as much as you can while the rest of us deal with what resistance we find. I will depend upon you and Silverwing to get the Arkadians out of the Craft Hall prison and to the Keeps once we have the councilors and their sentries under control. Many people can touch a dragon at once so you will be able to transport them all in one go between the two of you, I hope! For a location to bring them, I want you to transport them to Kingscannon stable since your dragon won't fit in the Keep above very well without damaging furniture and possibly people. You can then transport the people up to the Keep one or two at a time using one of your daggers, just think of the Kingscannon common room. Silver will transport his group to Grimhold stable." Thunderstroke nodded nervously, but Summersong said, "Don't worry! You're a confident person and you've already learned a good deal. I trust you to do this."

Chapter 11 – Battle In The Dark

The town was dark and forlorn in the stormy night. Not a light showed from any window, the homes were now abandoned, and the residents imprisoned in the Craft Hall. Not a sound was to be heard over the crashing thunder and howling wind. A group of about forty sentries stood before the Hall of Images, weapons out, looking around nervously and shivering with the wet and cold. Two other sentries stood before the Hall of Crafts, huddled against the closed doors for warmth as they guarded the entrance. The dark, black, and red buildings loomed ominously large upon the empty square. The sentries tensed, pointing their weapons towards the square and spreading out as a blue glow lit the area, signaling the arrival of a Keeper.

Summersong let go of the councilor's arm and pushed him towards the Hall of Images as he looked sternly at the sentries now beginning to encircle him, pointing their halberds and spears at the large Keeper's chest but remaining several yards away. "What manner of greeting is this?"

Summersong questioned them sharply, "I have done you no wrong, but am returning to you an errand runner that was sent to us." A few of the sentries chuckled and lowered their weapons, forgetting themselves as they watched the pompous councilor fume with anger at being called an errand runner. "You will die this night, warrior! Your kind will never set foot in Arkady again!" screamed the councilor to Summersong. He stormed past the nearest sentries and entered the Hall of Images, shaking the rain off his cloak as he entered.

Summersong stood silent in the pouring rain, continuing to watch the sentries as they stood uncertainly about him in a rough circle. "Well?" he asked them pointedly, "Have you any business to conduct with me or shall I go?" He could have transported safely away before they moved, but he knew that Silverwing and Thunderstroke were moving silently into position to get the townsfolk out of the Hall of Crafts, which had been converted into a prison. He wanted to hold the guards' attention upon himself while that work was completed.

"Oh!" gasped several of the sentries at once, as they all looked up. The rain had stopped suddenly and there was moonlight shining brightly down into the square, lighting it as if it were daylight. The sentries glanced nervously around the square and at each other before looking back to the large Keeper in their midst. "What did you just do, warrior?" asked one of the sentries, leveling his halberd at Summersong once more while his companions, more concerned with discomfort, were trying to wring water out of their hair and clothing. Summersong glanced up to look at the sky and noticed a single, small cloud in it, behind which a soft purple glow issued; he knew Thunderstroke was hiding there. He didn't see Silverwing and knew that the dragon must be invisible – he suddenly wished he'd asked Silver to make Thunderstroke invisible as well. He turned his attention back to the sentries, raised an eyebrow and answered "I? What did I do? I did nothing but return your errand boy. You just watched me do so. I have caused you no harm."

One of the sentries stammered, "B-but the weather! The rain has stopped!" Summersong chuckled and replied, "What in the world makes you think that I can control the weather? No man can do that. Now if you will excuse me, I have some work to do before I return to my home." He strode quickly through their ranks and out into the open, sword still in hand as he headed past the fountain and towards the Hall of History, which was across the town square from the Hall of Crafts. They stood astonished a moment, watching him depart, and then one of the sentries came to his senses enough to shout, "After him, or the chief elder will have our heads!" Two sentries threw their spears after the Keeper and several rushed him, but the spears were badly thrown and fell harmlessly to the ground in front of him. He turned and looked back at them with eyebrows raised, goading them to ensure their attention remained upon him, "Is that the best you can do?" He turned his back on them again and continued on his way,

walking further from the Hall of Crafts. The
sentries snarled in response to his tease, and the
remaining spear bearers threw their weapons; one
spear lodged between the cobblestones in front of
the Keeper so fast that Summersong tripped over
it. He went down on one knee but managed to turn
as he fell, swinging his sword to break the attack
of the running men in the front. Three halberds
broke on the first swing, and two men went down.
The third turned and ran away weaponless as more
came up behind, swinging wildly with their
halberds at the downed Keeper.

It was obvious that they had no formal training and
didn't know how to use the weapons properly, but
despite that lack, one of them managed to knock
Summersong's sword out of his hand with a lucky
strike against the back of the Keeper's hand,
sending the sword clanging to the ground just out
of his reach. Summersong ignored the slash on his
hand and drew his small knife, then yanked the
halberds out of the nearest sentries' hands as they
swung, before continuing the fight with fist and
knife, unable to rise to his feet with men so close

about him. Sharp hissing filled the air as arrows began to fly in, unerringly hitting the mark and taking down sentry after sentry. Still there were eight men left too close to the downed Keeper and the arrows had stopped as quickly as they had begun.

Suddenly an earsplitting roar shook the air and made the men jump in terror. A woman landed in their midst, seemingly from thin air, and snatched up the fallen sword. She swung with deadly precision at the group. Three men were down. Four. Five. The remaining three sentries turned and fled in terror as Thunderstroke walked over to help Summersong to his feet. "Didn't I tell you to stay out of the battle tonight?" he yelled half-heartedly at her, taking her hand, and getting up, then taking his sword back and wiping it clean on the shirt of one of the dead sentries lying at his feet before sheathing it. She tore a strip off the bottom of her cotton shirt, wrapping it around his injured hand as she answered, "The archers had to transport out, a large group of sentries is coming up the road behind them and they were exposed

and in weapon range, they've gone to aid the
people in the woods. Quickly! We must get those
people out! Thunder!" she shouted up into the air
and the large amethyst dragon settled down to the
cobbled pavement. She helped Summersong, who
was still slightly shaken and held his injured hand
close, onto the dragon's back and then climbed on
herself as the purple dragon spread her wings and
pushed off the ground with her powerful haunches,
then hovered over the town.

"Look there!" Lady Thunderstroke pointed to a
large contingent of men marching up the road to
the town. They were not sentries but some other
sort of men, large and well-armed, dressed in
black, with spiked helmets covering their heads
and faces. "Those are not ceremonial council
sentries!" whispered Summersong in her ear,
"Those are Nevilem, seasoned warriors of
Brimstone! Where is Silverwing?" She looked
back at him nervously, "He couldn't make it, there
was a problem. I'll explain later. Can we get the
people out? We have a few minutes yet before they
reach the town!" He looked concerned for

Silverwing but replied sadly, "I don't know how, there's no way to get them all out of the building and grouped around Thunderstroke before those men arrive. That front door is exposed, and they'll be here in a couple minutes. We just don't have time."

She looked at her dragon's head, which was turned upside down to watch them, and said softly "Thunder, is there anything can you do sweetheart?" The dragon rumbled, angled her wings, and came to hover over the prison, and then struck one paw out fiercely; a thick stroke of lightning shot down out of the sky and hit the back wall of the Hall of Crafts. The wall cracked and fell in a shower of dust which was then blown away by a strong gust of wind summoned by the dragon, and the entire back end of the building was open to the night air. The dragon landed softly near the scorched opening and waited as Lady Thunderstroke jumped down and strode into the building, calling to the frightened people inside "Over here, quickly!"

The last of the townsfolk were finally settled in, forty in Kingscannon Keep and fifty-two in Grimhold Keep, and the Keepers had all returned to their home Keeps for the night. The amethyst dragon Thunderstroke had been groomed and fussed over to her satisfaction by both Lady Thunderstroke and Gatemaster Summersong. They had both been loud in their praises of her, and she was left purring and snuggled against her great golden mate as the two humans left the stable, Thunderstroke transporting them to Windspeak Keep. Gatemaster Stormchaser hurried forward to meet them and said with worry in his voice, "What happened?" as they arrived in the Windspeak common area. "Summer got hurt!" Lady Thunderstroke replied, pointing to Summersong's bandaged hand; the blood had soaked through the cotton wrap she'd put around it and was dripping down his arm and onto his shirt as he held it against his chest. "Oh dear!" Lady Rainsong, a tall woman with dark brown skin and thick, curly black hair said quickly, "I'll get Tabitha, follow me!" Summersong protested, "I'm fine, Thunder! You were supposed to transport us up to our own Keep, not here! I'm fine!" Stormchaser grinned and pushed Summersong on the shoulder, "Come on, you look like you need help, your Lady has good instincts. It'll be a quick fix. I'll do it myself if you're too embarrassed to have Tabitha care for it." He walked beside Summersong and Thunderstroke down the wide hallway and then turned left at the end of it, "The infirmary is over here. We had the Smiths place it opposite the bathing room." He said, leading them in through a wide door. Healer Tabitha bustled forward and immediately said, "Out! All of you, out! He's my patient now. Go on!" and made shooing motions toward Stormchaser, Rainsong, and Thunderstroke. "Best not to argue with Tabitha," Stormchaser said, "she can be a bit fierce! Come out to the common area and tell us what happened." The three Keepers left the infirmary and walked down the hall to the common area. Keepers were bustling about the kitchen, setting the table, and putting finishing touches on the evening meal, but several were sitting in the common room polishing weapons and talking. Lady Rainsong led them over to an unoccupied group of chairs and they sat down. By the time Thunderstroke had finished her tale, Summersong had reappeared in the common room, his hand now stitched and bandaged with a clean, proper bandage, and Tabitha was following him. "That hand was cut right to the bone, and one of the tendons was sliced badly. It's a good thing you got him here as quickly as you did, or he could have lost some use of that hand." The short, stout Healer announced tartly. Summersong said, "See? I told you it wasn't a big deal!" He looked at Thunder with a sheepish grin as she stood to her feet and thanked Tabitha. "Well," Summer said at last, after he had confirmed Thunderstroke's story, "I suppose we'd better report to Grimhold one last time." The two of them said goodnight and left Windspeak Keep.

"What happened, Sliver?" Summersong asked as soon as they had arrived. Silverwing shook his head ruefully, brushed a stray lock of his wavy brown hair out of his eyes and replied, "I am sorry, my friend! Just as your Lady and I were readying our dragons to depart, a Messenger came with news from my Keepers in the glade that there was fierce fighting with a contingent of heavily armed evil warriors that had been waiting near the glade at Harold's tunnel exit. Apparently, they expected us to arrive there with the councilor and possibly with the woman they seek. Your Lady agreed to continue with the plan while I split off to aid the men in the woods. There was no time to call for backups." Summersong hugged Thunderstroke as she leaned back against him and said proudly "You should have seen her, Silver! She must have jumped from twenty feet up in the air to join the battle and did amazingly well for a first timer with an overlarge sword! And her dragon!" he was speechless for a moment, as he remembered the way the dragon had totaled the back of the large marble building, then he related the tale to Silver and Eva. "What happened to your hand?" Lady Evenflower asked when the tale was finished. Summer grimaced and answered, "Lucky strike from one of the sentries." At last, they said their goodbyes and left for the night, all were very tired and in need of rest after the night's labors.

"Well Lady" Summersong said to Thunderstroke as they changed into dry clothes in their private sleeping room, "You have proven once again this night that you have Keeper's blood in you." He pulled his long ponytail loose and began to towel the dripping black hair as she smiled warmly at him and straightened the white cotton shirt she had just put on. "Does your hand still hurt?" She asked as she pulled the ribbon from her braid and quickly unwove it in preparation for toweling it dry as Summer brushed his own hair straight once more, answering as he did so, "No, Tabitha put some dragonbalm on it. That's a soothing salve we use here that numbs things completely. I might be a little clumsy using my hand tonight because I can't feel it, but I'll be fine." She began to towel her long wet hair, and then dropped the towel over the back of the chair before grabbing the brush he had just set down. Summersong pulled a fresh shirt over his head and then walked back to the table, taking the brush from Thunder's hand, and gently running it through her tangles, "I apologize to you this night" he said softly. Her brown eyes widened in surprise, "Whatever for?" she asked him as he brushed her hair out. "Because I should not have tried to make you go against your instincts earlier this day. You can indeed handle a sword, and one shall be found to suit you. We shall return to the armory tomorrow straight after breakfast and I will ask Ruff to order one from the Smithy to fit your stature." He put the brush down and she snuggled against him for a short while. "Come" he said at last, "We have a Keep full of men and visitors awaiting us at a very late supper table!" She laughed as he led her out of the room.

"Welcome, guests from Arkady!" Summersong and Thunderstroke both greeted the townsfolk gathered around the long supper table beside the company of Keepers as they sat to take their places. "We will have a busy day ahead tomorrow," continued Summersong, "but for tonight we will rest. We can discuss the recent turn of events in Arkady and will try to answer any questions you have. Then tomorrow the real work will begin." Things were quiet to start out and the Keepers held their usual talk to a minimum as they waited for the Arkadians to ask questions, but the people were still dazed and uncertain after their strange rescues from Hall and tunnel and sat quietly, not even eating. The silence was becoming uncomfortable when Thunderstroke finally spoke up and said, "You know, I hope this doesn't sound dumb, but I feel like I've been the cause of all this trouble. It seemed to start when I was killed in the living world and brought into Arkady?" The townsfolk relaxed visibly, seeing at last that the Keepers weren't a superior type of person, but people just like them. One of them spoke up and said, "I've been in Arkady a long time, longer than I was ever alive, and I've seen this sort of thing happen before, but never to this degree. I don't think you caused it, Miss." The other townsfolk and the Keepers nodded in agreement and Summersong said gently to her, "No you have not caused it although it is true that this coincided with your arrival. It is not your fault. Do not fear for that."

Another of the townsfolk ventured a question then, "What will happen now, sir, will we have to stay here forever?" Summersong shook his head, "No, of course not, but you will remain with us for a little while until we find a safe place for you in Arkady. We do not want any of you to be captured by the Nevilem again, and possibly tortured or killed the next time, so it's best if you remain with us a little while in our world. It is true that if some of you are willing to remain longer, we would be grateful for it. We need some serious help from any who will lend a hand." A woman from the town shyly asked, "How can the Keepers need our help? We're just ordinary folk." Baldy spoke up this time, "So are we, lady, so are we! Ours is a job just like any other in Arkady and while we have the extra duty now of protecting Arkady from this evil invasion, we also still must attend to our regular duties. We need people willing to lend a hand in ordinary tasks here so that we can put more Keepers on the Gates and at the battle front." Another Keeper by name Sundowner broke in, "Also we need Cartographers, Healers, Tailors, Farmers, and other Craft folk who know specialized trades, for as you know the Keepers world has only the basic needs supplied such as food for our dragons, and ingredients we gather from our land for medicines. We are lacking in many things, like those that we acquire in trade from Arkady. Now with the problems besetting the land, it will be next to impossible to get those

223

items, and we would like to make this world more self-sustaining, but we need Crafters like you folk to help us do that." Raindance said, "That's right, and we could even set up some villages in this land for you to live, if enough of your folk choose to remain here." Summersong nodded approvingly, making a mental note to suggest the village idea to Silverwing in the morning.

A general babble of voices began around the table, rising and falling gently as multiple conversations between Keepers and Arkadians began, and people started to eat at last. Summersong turned quietly to Thunderstroke and asked her softly, "Are you really worried that you began this?" She shook her head in return, "No, but I wanted them to feel at ease and I know how I first felt on arriving." He smiled and then leaned over and kissed her gently "Well done, Thunder!" he said, reaching for some meat from a nearby platter.

Chapter 12 – A New Day

The next morning before the sun was high, Baldy was sent with Summer's message about villages to Silverwing and once the Messenger returned, all the Keepers met in the stables extra early to feed and groom their dragons while talking about the day ahead. They wanted to finalize plans before the townsfolk woke from sleep. Summersong spoke loudly as he worked a comb through his dragon's plush golden fur so that all might hear him throughout the cave, "This day there will be a general meeting of all Keeps, not just our local four in the East. The meeting will take place in the Gathering glade here in the Keeper's world at noon and I expect all my people to be in attendance. I ask each of you to lock the Gate you are attending this day before leaving for the meeting and make sure to secure the locks with your weapons so that they cannot be broken, as you do in the evenings, because the Gates will have to be untended for a goodly while." Thunderstroke looked up in concern, "But Summer, what if someone in the living world dies? How will they come through?"

The men smiled at her, and Summer answered "Do not worry, no one will die while the Gates are locked. Remember, time passes differently between all the worlds. Securing the locks with power from our weapons will ensure that all will be well. I cannot explain the magic thoroughly now but trust me on this." Keeper Raindance spoke up, "A Dragon Gate may still occur, as those can happen at any time of the day or night, and if one happens, one of us will attend to it. Our dragons can sense those and will let us know. But the ordinary Gates are a bit more ordered, this will work just like it does in the evenings, when we finish work and lock down. Remember, the ordinary Gates are for people who are dying in their proper time: Locking them with the magic of our weapons slows that process for brief periods of time, so that anyone scheduled to come through that Gate will instead stay in the living world just a little bit longer. Perhaps in the living world they die in the morning rather than at night, or if someone is ill, it may be that they hold on for another week before dying. Time varies between worlds, and we cannot change that, but we can in some small part control when people enter Arkady.

You'll never see us going out at night to tend ordinary Gates, Lady." Summersong nodded and added, "Yes, Rainy is right. We can't stop death, or stop time, but we can alter in some small part when people enter Arkady at the ordinary Gates. Don't worry about it, everything will be fine." Thunderstroke nodded and returned to straightening a bent feather on the amethyst dragon's wing with her preening tool as Sundowner stopped polishing his great orange dragon's horns, and looked down from the stepladder he was standing on to ask "What about the three broken Dragon Gate pillars, Gatemaster? Surely, they will not be left untended this day?"

"None of the Dragon Gate pillars, broken or unbroken, will be left untended at any time from this point out until the war is over." Summersong replied swiftly, "Those men who have been guarding and repairing the pillars, as well as the ones traveling to and from the Deep Mines with supplies, have all been met with individually during this past night by Gatemaster Moonshadow and Gatemaster Sharptooth and informed of everything that is happening. All of them have agreed to remain on guard. There will be a few from Stonyvale and Redrock Keeps missing from this meeting, but most people will be there. I will be going around to the three broken Dragon Gate pillars this morning to check on repair progress in order to report on the repair at the meeting."

Baldy looked up from working a preening tool through his green dragon's feathered mane and reported "The last message I delivered before supper yesterday was to Jeweldance Keep in the south. The reception is usually a cold one from them, but this time no one was there at all, and there was dust all over the Keep, as if they hadn't cleaned it for a good month! I couldn't find any of them out working the land, either here or in Arkady. We may be one Keep short, Captain." Summersong nodded grimly and said, "They always have been a stubborn people, they give all Keepers a bad name. Is it any wonder that the townsfolk were so frightened of us last night with Keepers like the ones at Jeweldance to represent us? If they do not show, then they do not show.

There is no time for speculation on that matter now, but we will have to deal with them strictly when all is done. What was Farhaven's response to your message, Baldy?"

The Messenger struggled for a moment before answering, trying to both remain on his stepladder and escape his happy dragon's large, rough tongue as he licked his Rider thoroughly, "Gatemaster Blackwing gave me a rather stiff reception, but he did agree to attend. At least they will come, whether they will cooperate with us or not is another matter. Ever they have been stiff-necked and demanding in terms when asked to join forces." Summersong nodded again as he slapped his tawny golden dragon's flank affectionately and walked to the tack room to put away his basket full of grooming tools, just as Thunderstroke, who had finished with her dragon a minute ahead of him, exited the room.

Last touches were put on the grooming by the remainder of the men and one by one they returned supplies and ladders to wall hooks, shelves, and bins in the tack rooms, and then went to the food storerooms to fetch their dragons' favorite fruits and berries for breakfast. They worked quickly, lovingly choosing their dragons' favorite fruits from barrels and bins along the walls as they filled large, two-handled flat baskets. The larger fruits varied from apple-sized to football-sized, while the smaller berries were all the size of golf balls. Some fruits were bumpy, some were smooth-skinned, and all were different shapes and colors. All of these fruits and berries grew on trees in the Keeper's world and were gathered in by the Keepers using large baskets slung over their dragons' backs, then sorted into bins and barrels in the storage rooms according to color and size. Even though some of the fruits were berries, they were all referred to as "dragon fruits" and all grew on trees. The Keepers put the food out before their dragons, speaking quiet words to each and stroking their soft noses before meeting in the middle of the stable to listen to Summersong's final words while preparing to transport back to the Keep.

"As you know, Thunderstroke has yet to claim her weapon, so she and I will be reporting to the Armory directly after breakfast to request a special sword to be made for her: She has proven herself a swordsman of skill as you heard last night, although she will need training to hone that skill; and of course, the Armory weapons are all too long for her to use due to her short stature. Once that is done, we shall return and all of us will go about our daily duties until it is time to report to the meeting in the Gathering glade. I must supervise the work on the three broken Dragon Gate pillars this morning as I have already said, but I would like Thunder to have a taste of Gate work so that she understands better the things that will be discussed during this meeting. Which of you will volunteer to have her tag along with you today and observe? I do not want her doing the actual work of the Gates until she is properly equipped and trained on her weapon, I only want her to gain an understanding of what our work entails."

Hands shot up all around the circle as every Keeper tending a Gate that morning volunteered.

Summersong smiled and said "Rainy, you are my most experienced Keeper. I will ask you to take Thunder this time." Raindance smiled and replied, "Delighted!" then glanced over at Thunderstroke, who returned the older man's smile warmly. "Rainy," Summer added after a moment's thought, "I think I'll also put you in charge of Thunder's training. She's a quick learner, so I don't think it will take you long! Teach her how to use her sword once she has it, and all about our work and duties." Raindance nodded cheerfully.

Summersong continued "Those of you attending Gates this day near Greenfield do not forget that anyone brought in must now be brought to Lindentree Town further to the north, as Greenfield is now off limits and considered dangerous. It will be a longer journey and you will have to work fast this morning to make up the distance and still get all of your Gate calls in. Those of you at the farthest Gates, use your dragons to speed the task, but take care that you do not frighten anyone. I'm no longer concerned with keeping the dragons out of sight of Arkadians, that is no longer a rule we will follow, but I do not wish for anyone to be frightened. Are there any further questions?" Summersong asked his men. There were no questions, and everyone collected the now empty baskets sitting in front of their dragons and replaced them in the storerooms, then drew weapons and transported back up to the Keep for their own breakfast.

Chapter 13 – Lady Thunderstroke's Sword

Thunderstroke stood before the Armory desk once more, holding a gleaming sword in her hands and admiring it with shining eyes and a large smile on her face. The black hilt was set with small, fiery purple gems and fit her grip perfectly. The polished steel blade was wrought with Keeper's runes made of purple crystal, which were laced throughout the length of the blade. The edges of the blade glinted brightly as she turned it around in her hands, marveling at the exquisite workmanship. She placed it in the sheath on her belt at last and rushed forward to hug the large Armory Keeper in delight. "How did you know, my friend?" Summersong asked him as she stepped back and walked over to stand by his side.

"Ah, that was Baldy's doing," Ruffian replied, "He reminded me yesterday after you left that it wasn't wise to fight a warrior's desire. So, I contacted the Smithy and told them what I wanted and who it was for. Steele did the rest, he's the one to thank!" Summersong nodded and answered, "We will find him at the meeting this day and give our thanks. Thank you also for I did not expect we would be able to equip her this quickly. It is well. You will be at the meeting today?" Ruffian nodded as he put some new arrows on display, "Yes, I will be there! Let your Lady transport the two of you out: I wish to see the effect. The Smithy added a different touch to her weapon and said it could easily be added to all weapons, even those currently in use." Summersong cocked his head curiously, "What touch is that Ruff?" The large Armory Keeper smiled widely, "You will see! Steele will explain at the meeting, he's come up with a capital idea for us that may be of aid in the coming war, but he wants to spring the news himself so I will say no more." Summer grinned back, "Very well then. Lady, let us go home and get this day underway!" Thunderstroke drew her new sword and held it out as they disappeared in a shimmering fall of purple sparkles.

A moment later they reappeared in the common area of Kingscannon Keep amid a shower of falling purple sparkles and all the men exclaimed excitedly, "Oh, wow! How did you do that! You didn't even glow!" gathering around and admiring Thunderstroke's new weapon as she held it out. Summersong grinned in delight and said, "We are in for a surprise at this meeting! Steele tried a new technique with Thunder's weapon and Ruff said they can add this special technique to all of our weapons. It may prove useful for identification purposes." They separated, those tending Gates transporting out first, then the remaining men detailed to help the Arkadians this day each took one of their guests and transported with them to Grimhold Keep where an early meeting was scheduled for the Arkadians to come together and discuss what part each would like to take in the coming days, whether to remain in the Keeper's world or to return eventually to Arkady. Summersong left last of all, making sure all of his people were safely away before transporting to the first damaged Dragon Gate pillar.

Chapter 14 – Keeper Duties

Lady Thunderstroke waited nervously on the back of a large, chocolate brown dragon who was crouched on the ground as Keeper Raindance walked with an easy, measured pace over to the Gate. Rainy was a tall, muscled but lightly built older man with short white hair that still held a hint of strawberry blonde. He wore a sleeveless leather vest over his long-sleeved and lightweight white cotton shirt, and Lady Thunderstroke wondered how he wasn't shivering with cold on this wet day. She was not so much nervous of the Gate as she was of being in Arkady after the previous night's happenings, and she was very tired of the rain; she pulled her soft, brushed leather jacket closer and hugged her arms around herself to stay warm. They were in a secluded area, attending one of the farthest Gates from any populated areas, yet still she looked around nervously for any signs of the evil warriors.

Rain poured down and thunder rolled constantly in the background, accompanied by flashes of lightning further away to the south. She wished that she'd been allowed to bring Thunderstroke to control the weather, they were soaked through to the skin, but Summersong's orders had been that the purple dragon was to be used only at need in these first few days in order to keep surprise on their side for as long as possible. Thunderstroke brought her mind back to her present situation as the brown dragon underneath of her shifted gently. He was twitching his pointed ears around; listening to the surroundings as he calmly watched his Rider work the Gate.

Rainy systematically touched the point of his sword to the runes engraved in the stone pillars in a measured rhythm, walking back and forth between the two pillars to complete the sequence. The runes on the red rock of the pillars began to glow brightly blue as he touched the last one, and suddenly the space between the pillars began to glow blue as well. Lady Thunderstroke watched closely as Rainy reached a hand through and grasped another hand, then the glowing stopped, she could see through the Gate once more to the wooded hill beyond, and a middle-aged man stood there blinking and staring at Raindance. "Greetings, Michael" Rainy said to him, "Awful weather we're having today, isn't it? Welcome to Arkady!" The man named Michael smiled and replied, "Yes, it is rather wet, isn't it? But better than the blizzard we have on the other side."

Thunderstroke shook her head in confusion; this man seemed perfectly at ease with being dead and understanding what was going on, unlike what she had gone through. It was the fifth time she had seen this enacted today and it still amazed her that none of the people who came through were surprised. Rainy introduced the man to his dragon and allowed him to stroke the soft fur as the dragon purred encouragingly, then Rainy helped Michael up onto the dragon's back as Thunderstroke reached a hand down to him to lend aid. The great dragon took flight as Rainy settled in behind and Thunderstroke asked curiously, "Rainy, how do you know what everyone's name is when they come through the Gate?" The man named Michael said, "I was wondering that, too!"

Raindance laughed and said, "It's part of the Gate magic, I learn the name as I reach through to grasp the hand of the person I'm helping. I can't explain it, it just happens!" Within minutes the brown dragon had guided them to Lindentree Town twelve miles away. "Stay here, Lady Thunderstroke, while I escort the man." Rainy said, dropping to the ground as the newcomer clambered off behind him. Thunderstroke watched as the two men walked to a white marble Hall similar to the building she had been led to and heard the familiar shout from the two sentries there, "Keeper! You have brought him?" followed by Rainy's response "Yes, it is I, and this is he." She grinned suddenly, remembering Lady Songbird's words to her. "Tradition!" she whispered to herself.

Thunderstroke watched as Raindance walked back over and climbed up onto his dragon's back, settling in behind her once more. "You know, Rainy," She said gently, "there's no need to be so formal with me. It's well, it's rather uncomfortable to be called Lady all the time, I'm not that sort of person." Raindance laughed and said, "You're Summersong's mate, and are just as much in command of our Keep as he is. That's what the title is! We have a Gatemaster and a Lady of each Keep." He hesitated, and then added after a moment's thought, "Well, until you came along, our Keep didn't have a Lady, but it does now, and we're all very glad of that. I think Farhaven is now the only Keep without a Lady. And, I'm not being formal, it's simply a title of respect." She twisted around to face him, looking up into his smiling face, "I know it's a title, but you don't have to use it every time, and I'm still learning, I don't feel like I'm ready to be in charge of anything yet!" She grinned at him to take any sting out of the words, and he laughed again, "Very well, Thunder, let's head back to our Gate." Soon the brown dragon took flight once more, heading back to the Gate.

Chapter 15 – Broken Gates And Busy People

Summersong cast a critical eye over the single massive pillar that powered the Dragon Gates, four feet in diameter and twice as high as the length of his dragon, the work was almost completed and the Smiths repairing it had stepped back to allow the inspection. He crouched down and ran his uninjured hand over the lowest rune, glowing faintly blue against the red slate surface, "This rune needs some smoothing. Do you see how the glow is dim yet at the tip of the rune?" One of the men came forward and looked closely, reaching a finger in to feel alongside the rune, he nodded quickly, "Aye! I'll fix it myself while the rest of the men continue with the crownpiece," he replied, casting a glance up at the top of the unfinished pillar, "I'll add a bit more crushed diamond to the rune surface after I've smoothed it as well, just to be safe." Summer nodded and stood up, "Good work, men! You're making excellent progress!"

The man agreed answering "It's a good thing that the pillars for the Dragon Gates are located in the Keeper's world or we'd never have peace to work on them!" Summersong asked, "Do you have enough men guarding all of the pillars here, not just the broken ones? I can lend you some of my Keepers for guard if you need them." The Smith at the base of the pillar replied, "Yes, Gatemaster! We've been running triple contingents lately just to be safe. It might be well, though, to have Keepers from all Keeps on guard, to prevent any particular Keep from being too depleted of help." Summer clapped the man on the shoulder, "I'll see to it and bring that up at the meeting today." He moved towards the tawny golden dragon waiting patiently for him. A rumble shook the ground as the men went back to their work cheerfully and Summersong and his dragon prepared to fly to the next damaged pillar. Everyone stopped and looked around, and the golden dragon began to growl.

Grimhold Keep was a bustle of activity with all the rescued Arkadians gathered about a large, circular table in one of the conference rooms. Parchments detailing the immediate needs of both Arkady and the Keeper's world lay scattered across the table before them and two large maps - one of Arkady and the other of the Keeper's world - were spread out in the middle of the table. Daisy Mae stood to one side with a handful of brightly painted wooden markers, placing them on the map as decisions were made. Maximilian the Cartographer from Greenfield stood next to Daisy Mae, he had been rescued from the Hall prison along with the rest of the people but had already chosen to remain with his young protégé and help. He stood with pencil and parchment and noted down all the details for each marker, proudly watching his young student with her new job.

Messengers from several of the Keeps hurried in and out of the room, taking those people who had made their decisions to the places they needed to go, while other Keepers were giving advice and answering questions when requested, and generally keeping the meeting going in full swing by helping people choose where they wanted to go and what parts they wished to play in the days ahead, whether the decision was to stay in the Keepers world and help or merely to resume their lives in a new town in Arkady. Smiths from Stonyvale and Redrock Keeps were also bustling in and out of the room, taking orders for new buildings and rushing off again to gather supplies and begin work on Craft buildings and homes in a designated central area of the Keeper's world to make a village for the new people to live and work in.

Meanwhile, Tabitha, Caroline and the Keepers at Windspeak Keep were putting the finishing touches on the new infirmary room that had been added a week previously in their Keep. The room was furnished with many beds for sick and wounded people, a small set of shelves that would be used as a library, and which the Loremasters and Historians were busy filling with parchments and scrolls containing remedies, healing advice and potion recipes. A long, low table with short, three-legged stools pushed underneath of it was positioned along the short wall at the far end of the room, ready for mixing medicines and salves. More shelves were carved into the wall behind the table, and already held bottles of healing potions and herbs, bandages, mortars and pestles, knives, and other necessities. Above the table were long, wooden beams hung with a series of rope loops and hooks that would be used for dried herbs. The Healers had everything prepared for human aid except for gathering more herbal ingredients, which could only be done as the various wild herbs and plants came into season, and they were now working hard at the long table mixing up medicines and salves to be placed in the large Healers stable specially prepared for dealing with and caring for any injured or sick dragons. The Healer stable was built next door to the regular Windspeak stable, and could be reached by transport, or by the front cave entrance, which opened onto the same area as the regular stable.

Chapter 16 – The Gathering glade

Weaponsmith Steele was an extremely tall, heavily muscled man of Spanish heritage with short, curly black hair and a long curly black beard. His dark eyes missed little, and when he arrived early at the Gathering glade along with some of his men, he noted an old, dead pine tree to one side of the clearing. "We'll set up there," he grunted, directing his men over towards the tree, "I have a plan for that tree." Steele and his men belonged to Stonyvale Keep, but worked to supply all the Keeps with weapons, tools, furniture, and stonework just as Ruffian belonged to Jumpriver Keep yet served all the Keeps as Armory Keeper. The Smithcraft cavern was associated with Stonyvale Keep, but Smiths from Redrock also worked in the Smithy alongside their Stonyvale counterparts. The Deep Mines were associated with Redrock Keep, since most of the Miners called Redrock their home.

The Smiths were hard at work setting up forge, anvils, and other equipment at the edge of the meeting area in front of the dead pine tree, and Steele was just lining up a row of clear glass bottles on a table, which contained various powdered gems and metals, when he caught a light out of the corner of his eye. He looked up to see who was first to arrive and watched with satisfaction as a shower of purple sparkles appeared, signaling his newest created weapon and its wielder, Thunderstroke. With her came Keeper Raindance who had wanted to experience her sword in action. Steele waved them over and they smiled, returning the wave as they walked to the edge of the glade.

"You arrive early!" Steele shouted as they approached. "Yes Steele," Rainy replied, "we finished our work, took care of my dragon and then decided to come here since it will soon be time for the meeting." Thunderstroke spoke next, "Thank you for my sword, Steele! It's simply perfect and I love the purple touch." Steele smiled in response and questioned, "Have you discovered what special trick you can do with it? I'm going to ask you to demonstrate for everyone when the time comes for me to speak at the meeting." She shook her head curiously, "No, I didn't know I could do anything special. Do you mean it's more than a sword?" Rainy also looked curious. "You will see," the Weaponsmith replied, "You will know what to do when the time comes."

A blue glow in the center of the glade signaled more arrivals and as the glow faded, the new arrivals walked over and gathered about the portable Smithy setup; it was the entire company from Kingscannon Keep, minus Summersong. The men greeted the small gathering; "We thought we'd find you here!" Baldy said cheerfully. "Have any of you seen Summer yet? I thought he might be first to arrive here." Thunderstroke felt a twinge of anxiety, although she couldn't place just why. The other men shook their heads, "No, it's unusual though that he would be last of us to show." Thunder glanced quickly up at Rainy, and he gave her a reassuring smile, whispering to her, "Do not worry. Summersong is the best of our company and knows well how to take care of himself and others. That is why we elected him as Gatemaster."

She nodded but felt no reassurance. Something wasn't right.

Before long all had gathered in the Glade and were seating themselves in their designated areas around a large, flat central stone platform. They arranged themselves by compass points. Kingscannon, Jumpriver and Grimhold were the eastern Keeps, along with Windspeak Keep which, though centrally located, was grouped with the eastern Keeps. They sat in the eastern section of the circle. In the western section sat the people from the western Keeps of Greyweather, Meadowbrook and Plainsrunner. The north had only two Keeps, those of Stonyvale and Redrock, but they were larger Keeps which housed Smiths and Miners in addition to the Keepers, and the two Keeps as many people associated with them as the four eastern Keeps together. The southern section of the circle held a sparse showing: of the two southern Keeps, Farhaven and Jeweldance, only Farhaven had bothered to come. Farhaven Keep was smaller in number, with only fifteen men, they had no women. Everyone sat quietly whispering among themselves, waiting for Gatemaster Summersong to arrive and start the meeting, as designated leader of all the Keeps during this time. The whispers were tense, it was unusual to have a leader be late.

Gatemaster Silverwing was just getting to his feet to begin the meeting when a blue glow signaled Summersong's arrival. Summersong hurried through the waiting crowd to the central platform, apologizing, "I'm very sorry to keep you all waiting! As you know, I was inspecting the progress on our damaged Dragon Gate pillars today. One of the pillars was attacked by Nevilem while inspection was in progress, and we had an unexpected battle on our hands. We managed to push them back and close the rift, but we are now in greater peril than we have been in for many long years, because a way has been forced into the Keeper's world directly from the evil world of Brimstone once more."

There was a collective gasp from the crowd and Summersong continued, "We have doubled the number of guards on all Dragon Gate pillars in this world, pulling a few of the extra men off the Gate work in Arkady to do so. Our original plans must now change, and the first need will be the protection of the Keeper's world, for if we fall, all of Arkady will fall. We will need to rotate Keepers from all Keeps to help protect and guard the pillars until a solution to this has been found, I do not want any of the pillars left unwatched from this point forward, and I also do not want any Keep too depleted of people to do their regular work duties. We must all share in this burden." There was stunned silence for a moment after Summersong's words, and then a babble of voices broke out around the circle, discussing this latest danger. Summersong let it continue for a space as people worked off tension, and then held his hands up for silence. "Thank you all for coming today," he said, turning around to view the entire circle of Keeps and noting the empty place where Jeweldance Keep should have been, "Let's get down to business."

Chapter 17 – The Smith's New Trick

The meeting was winding down, plans had been made and duties assigned. Steele the Weaponsmith now stood before the assembled group with Thunderstroke at his side. "I know that you're all in a hurry to get to your home Keeps, it's been a long, hard day for all of us, but I would like to take a few moments to tell everyone that we've had a breakthrough in weapon manufacture at the Smithy over the last couple of days. An ancient scroll was found tucked away in a forgotten drawer of one of our workbenches. I started looking over the scroll and discovered it held a technique for transferring dragon power to the weapon of each wielder."

The crowd laughed softly in disbelief as Steele continued, unheeding, "This lady here has an amethyst dragon." Several of the further Keeps stopped laughing and paid attention then, but Gatemaster Blackwing from Farhaven shouted scornfully, "The purple dragons are untamable, and everyone knows that!" Steele answered, "Nevertheless, she has done it!" Gatemaster

Blackwing argued, "Even if it were true, what does this have to do with your weapon-making skills?" Steele addressed the entire crowd in reply as Thunderstroke shifted nervously on her feet, "The new technique can be added to existing weapons and hers is the first it has been completed on. I am going to ask you to witness because the effect is twofold." He turned to Thunderstroke, "Go get your dragon, that will silence the unbelief and show the first effect. Then we will continue."

Thunderstroke looked over to Summersong and he nodded confirmation. She drew her sword and transported out in a cascade of falling purple sparkles as the crowd gasped. Moments later the sky above the crowd shimmered purple, signaling her return. The crowd looked up and went silent at the sight of the purple dragon above them. "Very good!" shouted Steele, "Now come and demonstrate the power of your weapon so that all might see what can be achieved with this new technique." Thunderstroke guided the amethyst dragon swiftly down behind the men of

Kingscannon Keep and walked through their ranks to reach the center platform once more.

"Now everyone listen to me carefully: The purple dragons control the weather, both making and breaking it; this was discovered by the four eastern Keeps on the night Lady Thunderstroke paired with that one. Her sword holds the same power but to a lesser degree as her dragon holds. Watch this." Steele turned to Thunderstroke, who was as much amazed by this news as the rest of the crowd, and pointed over to his Smithy setup on the side, "Do you see the dead tree behind my setup, standing alone?" She nodded, waiting. "Point your sword tip at that tree and think of the power of your dragon. Hold steady!" Lady Thunderstroke drew her sword once more and faced the tree, held the sword out and leveled its tip at the pine tree. A streak of white-hot lightning shot out from her sword and struck the tree, consuming it with fire.

She almost dropped the sword in her surprise and the crowd yelled and jumped to their feet amazed.

She sheathed her sword quickly to prevent herself from dropping it and turned to Steele as he held his hands up for silence. The crowd gradually quieted but remained standing as he spoke, "This power of each Rider's Ride, be it invisibility, fire, ice, growth, all the powers of all the dragons, can be added to your existing weapons. Each of your weapons will carry the distinctive glow of your dragon's color, and you will be able to light small areas with the weapon's glow, just like the dragons can light entire stables. Also, your weapon will hold a power like that of your dragon, though it will not be as strong as the dragon."

Summersong shouted out then, "This is a great battle advantage Steele is offering us and I advise all to take advantage of it at the earliest opportunity. It will aid us greatly in coming days!" Gatemaster Silverwing shouted, "She didn't glow when she transported, she sparkled. Is that also part of this new technique?" Steele spoke once more "The sparkles are indeed part of the new technique, and the transport happens quicker with the new method, although I don't fully understand why it should do so. However, that will be an aid in identification purposes, and a help in its own way. I have all of the equipment and supplies with me here and my Smiths and I can do this today, for any who desire." Steele motioned Thunder to her Keep's designated area, and she jumped down from the platform to return to Summersong's side as the Smith moved over to his little area and he and his men prepared for the people already streaming over and lining up, weapons out as they glanced up at the still burning tree.

Chapter 18 – Danger In The Night

Thunderstroke sat alone in a chair in the Keep, gazing into the soft red glow from the wood stove over in the corner of the common area that was always lit. She couldn't sleep. The day had been a long one, with Kingscannon Keep the last to leave the Gathering glade long after evening had begun. Summersong had felt his men should wait until last while all of the other Keeps had their weapons altered by the Smiths and his men willingly agreed, then helped the Smiths pack up their tools and supplies. While they waited, they had gone around the Glade talking to people from the other Keeps and answering questions, the men and Thunder representing Summersong since he couldn't be everywhere at once. There were many questions about Summer's bandaged hand and Thunderstroke had been extremely tired of repeating the story by the time the night ended. Returning home at last, they had all been so exhausted that they simply skipped supper and went straight to their beds.

All except Summersong, who had grabbed an apple and a strip of dried jerky from the kitchen baskets and eaten hungrily, standing at the counter. Thunderstroke had offered to make something more fulfilling, but he said "No, you get some sleep. I must report to duty on those pillars. Our Keepers need a break, they have been on guard all day long, and the Gatemasters of each Keep are filling in to allow our people to rest." He rolled his eyes and huffed, then continued, "Well, except Farhaven and Jeweldance Keeps. But we other eight Gatemasters are filling in for a turn, along with our dragons. Go to bed, Thunder, I'll see you tomorrow night. Everything will be fine." Then he shimmered out in a warm yellow cascade of sparkles and was gone, leaving her standing all alone.

Thunderstroke was worried about him, knowing he was exhausted from leading the meeting today as well as working all morning and fighting an unexpected battle with an already serious injury to his sword hand. She didn't like the thought of him being out there at night and all the following day, tired and exhausted. "I'm going to find him and help!" she declared resolutely to the empty room, standing up. She would go first to the stables and get her dragon, and then search for Summersong if it meant flying all night over the land. She had no idea where the pillars were but was certain her dragon would know.

She shimmered into the stables and stood surprised for a moment when she saw all the dragons awake and their lights flickering. "What is it?" she asked them, "Why are you all awake in the middle of the night?" The dragons immediately rushed to her and started chirping, grunting, barking, and mewing at once, agitated. They felt something, an evil presence that didn't belong in the Keeper's world. She felt herself grow cold all over and her heart pounded in her ears, "Wait here! I'm getting your Riders now and we're all coming to help!" She disappeared while still talking and hit the floor of the Keep common area running, rushing down the hall and banging open the first common sleeping room door to shout.

The men jumped half asleep from their beds and started shouting incoherently "What?" "Who's there?" "What's wrong?" "Oh, it's Thunder!" They sat up and looked at her, surprised. "The dragons feel an evil presence in this world and they're waiting for us to come!" She was gone again with no other explanation, heading for the next sleeping room. The men jumped out of beds and hurried into their clothes before buckling weapon belts on, suddenly wide wake.

One by one everyone shimmered out and reappeared moments later in the stable where they found their dragons hopping with excitement and agitation. They mounted swiftly without talk and then as the dragons formed a circle in the center of the stable, Baldy turned to Thunder from atop his bright green dragon and said, "Where to, and how did you discover this?" Thunder shook her head "I don't know where to go, hopefully the dragons do; and I discovered this because I couldn't sleep. I've had a bad feeling on me all evening and night, so I decided to head out and see if I could find Summer at one of the pillars and help him. Instead, I found

all the dragons awake and waiting. They told me
they felt an evil presence in our world, so I came
back for you!" Everyone looked around at
everyone else for a moment in silence, then drew
their weapons, ready for battle upon arrival. The
men looked over to Thunder and waited. "You are
the leader, Lady Thunderstroke, since you have
felt this, we will follow!" announced Raindance.
Thunder took a deep breath and let it out slowly,
mustering her courage, then she announced, "Let's
go to the nearest Dragon Gate pillar first." The
dragons and Riders shimmered out in a
multicolored rainbow and disappeared, leaving the
stable empty.

Shards of diamonds lay strewn about the field
among heavier chunks of broken red slate rock,
and everything was coated in glittering diamond
dust. The enormous Dragon Gate pillar had been
shattered with the forced entry of the evil warrior
band to the Keeper's world. The grass was
scorched black, and blood was everywhere:
Keeper's blood mixed with that of dragons. The
small band of eight Keepers and their dragons lay

upon the debris strewn field, five Keepers struggling to rise and reach their weapons to continue fighting despite grievous injuries, two unconscious and one left kneeling, still holding his sword with a bandaged hand but not fighting. He was gasping for breath, staring in disbelief at the band of Nevilem dressed in the black, red, and silver uniforms of Brimstone as ribbons of smoke twisted about them.

The leader of that evil band addressed him, laughing cruelly, "Ha! You will never win! Your defeat is certain; you cannot touch us in your world! Look how you have tried already and failed, though we can touch you! We will triumph this night and your world will be ours!" He threw his head back to laugh again as the sky split open with a crashing blast of lightning. Summersong hung his head in defeat and lowered his sword, grabbing his injured hand reflexively with his good hand. He looked up quickly, however, as the evil leader's laugh turned to a high-pitched scream and he fell smoking to the ground, dead. A large band of dragons had materialized in the night sky above and the amethyst dragon in the lead sent down another bolt of lightning, striking two more of the evil men dead. Another bolt and another rained down and within minutes it was over. The dragons landed and their Riders leaped off, rushing to help the downed men as their dragons hurried to the eight injured dragons on the field, which lay silent and unmoving.

"Thunder!" he gasped out as she rushed over, "But how did you know?" She knelt and put her arms around him, gently taking the sword out of his injured hand, "The dragons told me. Hush! You are hurt. Baldy went to Windspeak Keep to summon the Healers. How are you all here at this pillar? The others were undefended." Summersong gasped, "Silver called for help, and we came here, leaving our own guard to aid him." Thunderstroke said, "Alright, everything will be okay. Rest now until the Healers come." She kissed him and held him tightly as he nodded and collapsed into unconsciousness. She looked up after making certain he was still breathing and yelled out, "How are the others? Are they alive?" One by one the answer came back, "Yes, this one's alive!" The other five Gatemasters who had been struggling to rise had by this time also lapsed into unconsciousness.

All eight Gatemasters still alive, help on the way, but - Lady Thunderstroke looked around for her Ride and saw her not too far away nuzzling frantically at her mate as the great tawny gold dragon lay breathing shallowly. "Thunder? Is he going to make it?" The amethyst dragon gave voice to a pitiful squeak and draped herself on top of the golden dragon to keep him warm with her body heat. Green Balderdash, waiting for his Rider to return, barked at the other dragons, and then walked over to the golden dragon to help keep him warm; the other dragons copied him, warming the remaining downed dragons as best they could by covering and surrounding them with their own bodies. The air sparkled in a rainbow of colors just then as more dragons and Keepers materialized led by Lady Rainsong, help had arrived from Windspeak Keep. They worked quickly, several Healers and Keepers to each man and beast as the

Keepers and dragons of Kingscannon stepped back to allow them room to work. Lady Thunderstroke held the hilt of Summersong's sword tightly, twisting her hands around the hilt as she stepped back to let the Healers do their work.

"Rainy," she said quietly to the older man standing nearby as they watched the process, "what are we going to do about this pillar?" Raindance turned and looked at the deep, blackened hole where the pillar had once stood, then sighed heavily. "We will have to call Steele and his men to help rebuild it; only a Smith has the tools and powers necessary to begin a pillar build, though all Keepers can mend them. I sent Baldy to Stonyvale Keep with the news after he returned with the Windspeak folk." Thunderstroke nodded, "In the meantime?" she asked fearfully, "Is this an open rift in our world?" Rainy nodded solemnly, "These pillars power the Dragon Gates in Arkady, but if one is destroyed, then yes, it leaves an entrance wide open to our world for any who know how to find it." She stared at him, aghast, "How do we seal it then, like they did earlier today?" "We cannot." Rainy replied shortly.

Her eyes widened and he clarified for her, "The pillar is the seal. We will have to station a large body of men here until work is finished. It's a good thing the other two damaged pillars were completed today. If this one hadn't needed a rework on one of the runes, it too would have been complete and withstood the attack." She glanced around the field, taking in the extensive damage and noting how far the heavy rock pieces had been thrown in the breakthrough, gouging the landscape in the process; she wondered how many of those heavy rocks and jagged diamond shards had hit the dragons. The Windspeak Healers and Keepers gradually left the field, returning with the injured men and dragons to Windspeak once they had each been stabilized for transport. Lady Thunderstroke handed Summersong's sword to one of the Healers as he was lifted for transport, then watched with her heart in her mouth as he was taken away. Soon none were left except the thirty-seven men from

Kingscannon Keep who gathered now about the pillar hole and Lady Thunderstroke.

"You will have to lead us, Thunder, until Summersong our Gatemaster is fit for duty again." Rainy told her gently, "Though you are new to this world and still must learn so much, you are our Keep Lady and we hold you our leader in his absence." The other Kingscannon men standing around immediately consented to this and added their voices as she looked grimly around at them, not at all liking this new position. Finally, she spoke, "If you will all guide me, I will do my best to lead. First, I think we must remain here until others arrive to help guard this open rift." Everyone agreed and some men spread out to watch the area while others began moving the heavy pieces of red slate off to the side and pulling the glittering gem shards out of the ground to toss into the pile of rubble as they prepared the way for the Smithy and his men.

Baldy arrived a short time later, followed almost immediately by Steele and his Smiths, who were all still rubbing sleep out of their eyes. They had endured a long day as well, altering everyone's weapons. Baldy walked over to Thunderstroke and reported, "The Smiths will work through the remainder of this night and Steele says they should be able to have the magical properties woven into the placer hole shortly after daybreak, after which they can begin the build. He sent word to Redrock Keep and they're sending Miners to the Deep Mines for the extra materials he'll need, and they should arrive with the first load of red slate and diamonds just in time for it to be shaped and placed."

Thunderstroke smiled at the Messenger and said "Thank you Baldy! I don't know what I'd do without all your help." Raindance filled Baldy in on their decision to make Thunderstroke leader in Summersong's absence, and Baldy readily acquiesced. Thunderstroke asked, "Is Balderdash tired or could he fly further for you? I'd like you to go around to the other Keeps and let everyone know what's happened here, so that they can be more prepared in case of another attempt. We also need some Keepers to guard the other pillars which are currently unwatched. I'll send a few of our men to them now but see if you can get some others to help, too. We're a pretty small Keep." Baldy reassured her, "Oh he can fly all night, he loves it! We'll go now and I'll report back once I've been to all of the Keeps." He ran off to his dragon and disappeared in a green shimmer.

Chapter 19 – Reports And Revelations

Thunderstroke arrived in Windspeak Keep two days later accompanied by a tall man with a ruddy complexion, green eyes and long, straight, sandy brown hair. This was Gatemaster Blackwing of Farhaven Keep. Lady Rainsong came forward to greet them, "It is good that you've arrived! The men are chafing for news and have many questions, and Tabitha of course will not allow them to leave the infirmary!" She winked at Blackwing and then whispered to Thunder, "You're still new here, but you'll soon learn that nobody argues with Tabitha!" The three of them laughed, and Rainsong said, "Come, I'll show you through to them; they've been anxiously awaiting your arrival ever since we told them this morning that you would come." The threesome walked down the long hall leading off the common area and turned left down another short hall until they reached a doorway, where they entered the infirmary. All eight men were sitting up in chairs in the near corner, watching the door attentively. "Do not rise or I will send you back to bed, all of you!" Healer Caroline announced sternly from another part of the room as they entered. The men remained seated, but it was easy to see that they were not happy to do so. Thunderstroke went straight to Summersong and leaned over to kiss him, then straightened and greeted the others formally.

"Gatemasters, I come with a report for you as requested!" The men returned the greeting and then stared at the tall Gatemaster standing quietly next to Thunderstroke. They had not expected Blackwing. Lady Rainsong pushed two more chairs over to the circle, saying "Sit here and talk, I have work to deal with about the Keep, but Caroline over there will help if you have need of anything!" then she left the room quickly. Around the circle of chairs sat the Gatemasters from eight of the Keeps who had been injured in the attack. Summersong from Kingscannon Keep, Silverwing from Grimhold Keep, Firestorm from Jumpriver Keep, Zephyr from Plainsrunner Keep, Moonshadow from Stonyvale Keep, Jasmine from Meadowbrook Keep, Sharptooth from Redrock Keep and Stormchaser, who wore a chagrined look on his face at being a patient in the infirmary of his own Keep.

Summersong addressed Blackwing abruptly, "Why have you come this day? I had thought Farhaven Keep did not wish to take part in this war but were simply going to continue their ordinary Gate duties?" Gatemaster Blackwing looked somewhat embarrassed as he replied, "Well, we heard news of the attack when your Messenger Baldy came to us to report. He said Lady Thunderstroke has been organizing the repair work as well as keeping everyone going about their regular duties in the absence of eight Gatemasters, along with the help of the other Ladies, and that is not an easy feat! He said he was asking for help from all of the Keeps. We were shocked to hear of the attack, but even more surprised to hear that a woman would be willing to work so hard at this, especially a newcomer to our world."

He glanced apologetically at Thunderstroke and then continued, "We in Farhaven don't have any women among us and know only the women of Jeweldance Keep. As you know, they are a haughty and proud people, men, and women alike, who refuse to work. We few in Farhaven have been minding the Gates for Jeweldance as well as our own over the past year, it has gotten that bad. But we came to witness the work and saw the devastation of the attack. It is indeed going well with your mate at the helm! All fifteen of us offered our services on the spot, and when I learned that Thunderstroke was coming here to update all of you today, I asked if I might accompany her. I now ask your forgiveness for our Keep's distance in the past and tell you that we are ready to do everything that we can to lend aid in this war. My men are currently working alongside all of yours this very moment, we locked down our Gates so that we could lend a hand, but Thunder has since reassigned some men from other Keeps to tend them for us." The eight recovering Gatemasters looked at each other and then as one accepted Gatemaster Blackwing's offer of help. "It is good to have you with us!" Summersong said.

He then turned to Thunderstroke and asked, "Lady, what news to report?" Thunderstroke and Blackwing took their seats, and then she began. "The destroyed dragon pillar has been completely rebuilt and is fully operational once more; the other two pillars that took damage were inspected and repaired immediately by Steele and his men to insure soundness. The Smiths then went to each of the remaining pillars in turn and applied warding glyphs to them, hoping to prevent future breakthroughs of the kind we witnessed the other night. Gate duties have been resumed and are in full operation, and two guards are posted at each of the dragon pillars, with a Messenger stationed at each to go for help at need. We're using Grimhold Keep as the check-in location; all Keeps have currently got a Messenger checking with Grimhold several times a day for news, and the Messengers stationed at each pillar alongside the Keepers on guard will report to Grimhold at regular intervals, to speed the passing of information to all."

Gatemaster Stormchaser cut in then, "Lady, two guards at each pillar are not enough. The eight of us and our dragons was not enough." She paused and traded a glance with Blackwing before continuing, "We discovered a curious thing when trying to clean the damaged area. We wanted to remove the bodies of the Nevilem, but none could touch them except me." The men straightened in their chairs and looked at her in surprise and Summersong said, "Neither could we touch them, yet they could touch us. How are you able to touch them? And I assume your dragon also since she is the one who blasted them?" Thunderstroke answered quickly, "Because I carry the artifact. Do you remember the strange piece of crystal wrapped in a cloth that I brought here? We have finally discovered what it does. It allows someone to touch something in another plane of existence. You can fight with and touch those evil men in Arkady or the living world because they and you have both come from other planes and met in the middle, so to speak. But when they linked directly from Brimstone into the Keeper's world, it afforded them a protection. I could touch them, and my dragon also could while I was on her, because I held the crystal in my pocket. So that means if another breakthrough occurs, I will have to go meet it, since I can touch them."

Summersong looked grave at this news; he did not like the thought of her facing such invasions on her own, but she was right, she was the only one who could touch the Nevilem.

Silverwing spoke next, "But how were they able to touch us?" Thunderstroke shrugged, "We do not know. I searched each of the bodies very carefully to check for any sort of artifacts or crystals like mine that would allow them contact. They carried nothing. I gave my crystal into Steele's hands so that he could also check, and he produced nothing in his search as well. There is a hunt going on now for answers at all Keeps. Lady Evenflower has the Loremasters searching through all the old records trying to find out information on the artifacts, as well as information on contact between planes in the past. Also, there are searches being conducted in Arkady for any information. That search is being done quietly of course, so that we are not found out by any watching Nevilem. Eva has the Historians undertaking that task since they can blend in better with the Arkadians, having lived in

Arkady long ago. They also know what to look for within the Halls of History and can read all sorts of writing and symbols."

Blackwing spoke up then, "How long will you be off duty? Your people are worried about you." Thunderstroke nodded, wanting an answer as well. Caroline flung an answer out as she walked past the small group with her arms full of clean, folded bedding that she had just collected from the bathing room where the sheets had been washed and hung to dry over steam vents, "They will be released in two or three days, depending upon the review by Healer Tabitha. She will be by to check on them later. Currently, she's in the stable tending their dragons, which took a greater hit than the men and may not be ready to leave at the same time as their Riders." She bustled off to freshen the bedding for the men.

Chapter 20 – The Ladies' Discovery

Thunderstroke sat quietly in the stable, curled up against her dragon's warm side and slowly turning a fist-sized, elongated crystal in her hands. She noted the intricately carved runes which were not on the outer surface but somehow within the crystal. "What is this thing, Thunder?" she asked her dragon softly, "They call it the artifact, this crystal that the women in the Craft Hall gave me before I ran away that day, but what is it, really?" The great amethyst dragon rumbled deep in her throat to show that she was thinking. "It must be something magical to allow me to touch someone from another plane here in the Keeper's world. But how did they touch someone here without a similar object?"

She leaned back and snuggled into the warm, furry dragon, closing her eyes to think. It was now two days after her meeting with the Gatemasters in Windspeak Keep infirmary, and chores had been finished for the day. All had returned to their Keeps except for those on guard duty.

Thunderstroke couldn't sleep and returned to the Kingscannon stable after seeing the men of the Keep all settled for the night and suppers delivered to all the Keepers on guard at the pillars. She had found her dragon awake and restless without her golden mate, and the two took comfort in each other's closeness. When she couldn't drift off to sleep even here, she had pulled the artifact from her pocket and inspected it. She was growing sleepy now, yet the puzzle of this odd crystal held her thoughts.

The dragon chirped suddenly to get her rider's attention. "What is it, sweetheart?" Thunderstroke asked her. A short series of rapid chirps and barks told the story: there were crystal shards all over the field that the men had picked up and thrown into the rubble pile. Were they all from the destroyed pillar? Or did some belong to the Nevilem, flung out when they were struck down? Were there artifacts like this one mixed in with the rubble? "Oh, Thunder! What a good thought! I bet you're right! We'll go there first thing in the morning, it's too dark to look now." With that decided, both Ride and Rider were settled enough to sleep, and they drifted off.

The following morning saw eight women sifting through the rubble pile that was once a Dragon Gate pillar. Lady Thunderstroke had gone to Grimhold Keep to send a message to the other Keeps that were missing their Gatemasters, to ask the other Ladies to meet with her. Lady Songbird from Jumpriver Keep was the first to arrive. "I'm so glad you've got a task for us to do because I'm going crazy without Firestorm around!" Birdie had said upon arriving. Lady Evenflower of Grimhold Keep was of course already there and agreed with Birdie, "I'm excited to find out what this is about. Thunder said it was possibly important and something we can surprise our men folk with!" The three women giggled like kids as they waited for the other women to arrive. At last Lady Rainsong of Windspeak, Lady Rose of Redrock

Keep, Lady Shimmerwing of Stonyvale Keep, Lady Jubilee of Greyweather Keep and Lady Sundancer of Meadowbrook Keep arrived. Thunderstroke passed the artifact around for all the women to inspect and then filled them in on her dragon's suggestion for the crystal shards. All thought it was an idea worth following through, so they collected their dragons and transported without further delay to the area.

By midday when the sun was high in the clear blue sky, they had already amassed a great collection of crystal fragments and shards. Their dragons helped the women by moving the heavier red slate stones out of the way when requested. When afternoon rolled around, the women were seated on the grass around an enormous pile of jagged diamond and quartz shards and sorting through them, talking animatedly the entire time. "This looks different," Lady Shimmerwing said suddenly, holding up a crystal with runes carved inside. The other women looked over and agreed, then returned to the pile with intent, knowing for certain they were on to something.

That evening the ladies were once more back in Grimhold Keep, with their men and the Keepers from several of the area Keeps, Steele the Smithy among them. Twenty-three fist-sized, elongated crystals were laid upon the large round planning table in front of them. "Now that we know how the Nevilem managed to touch us in this world, the next question is how many of these crystal artifacts are there in all the worlds? Are there more to be found, and does Brimstone hold them all?" It was Silverwing who spoke, voicing the concern of all.

"With these twenty-three crystals, plus the one carried by Lady Thunderstroke, we can put twenty-four men into positive action against any further breakthrough." Steele said as he examined one of the crystals, "That will give us some breathing space. Furthermore, if you will allow me to take one of these back to my workshop to allow Ajax, our Crystal Smith, to inspect it with probes and tools, we may perhaps discover the properties and be able to make more of these so that we can arm each of our Keepers with one." The others nodded quick assent and Lady Thunderstroke took her artifact out of her pocket and handed it to Steele, saying, "Perhaps take mine as well, Steele, so that we can determine if it is indeed the same type as the others? The runes in it are different than the rest of these crystals."

Steele nodded, taking the crystal from her, then he looked up as Gatemaster Sharptooth said, "I have one more suggestion to make, namely, that we should build some guardian pillars in this world specifically for protecting us here. That way, if another Dragon Gate pillar is broken again, it will not be an open rift into our world. The Dragon Gate pillars from this point onward should only be used to power the Dragon Gates. We can place one guardian pillar among each group of Dragon Gate Pillars, then also put some in separate places for added protection, in front of each Keep and at each of the new Craft villages, for instance." Everyone agreed, and Gatemaster Moonshadow granted his Smith permission to build some guardian pillars. "I still have plenty of diamond available, but we'll need some more red slate." Steele said, accepting the task. "I'll get the Miners on it tomorrow morning and have them deliver it to the various places. Send me word where you want to start your build, and I'll have them deliver to that location first." Sharptooth answered. Summersong spoke up then, saying, "I agree that you should take Thunder's crystal to examine as well as one of these others, and we will use the remaining twenty-two crystals to arm the Keepers on guard at each of the Dragon Gate pillars, to be traded off as guards change. This is a great advantage to us, and it gives us a hope we didn't previously have."

Gatemaster Silverwing repeated his previous question, "Do any of us know just how many artifacts there are in the world? I have heard of such things before, of course, but I had originally thought that all were lost or destroyed centuries ago and that Thunderstroke's crystal was one of very few remaining, if not the only one. Yet here we hold twenty-four together, and if the enemy has more," He left the rest unspoken and the gathering around the table grew silent as they thought about the implications. "I think you will need to ask the

Loremasters about that one, Silver." Jasmine said at last, and Lady Evenflower offered, "I will ask the Loremasters to check for answers on the crystals." Everyone was silent once more, looking at the crystals.

Lady Thunderstroke spoke into the silence, "I've just had a thought! We can plant the seed in my locket now. If someone holds an artifact then they can touch the living world to dig a hole in the ground and plant the seed." An excited babble of voices rolled around the table as her words hit home – a solution to their problem! Perhaps war could be avoided if the seed could be planted by stealth, which would weaken the Nevilem; they now had the means to plant. "Snowmelt Wood is heavily infiltrated already by the enemy, and it will take some planning to get there. I don't know that we can reach the living world location unless we start at Snowmelt Wood's planting glade, it's difficult to reach." Summersong announced into the excited babble of voices. The company grew silent once more.

Finally, Lady Songbird spoke up saying, "We should call another meeting of all Keeps in the Gathering glade, both to draw up plans for advancing on the wood and to see if there are any ideas or suggestions to aid us in this matter. Also, we can let everyone know what we have now discovered about these crystals, and if we give it a couple of days before the meeting time, perhaps Steele and Ajax will be able to learn the properties of these crystals and make more." Everyone agreed to this, and the meeting broke up at last, with people saying goodnight and returning to their home Keeps to settle dragons in to stables and have supper.

Chapter 21 – Emergency Meeting

"We've got problems." Summersong looked up from the map he was studying in the Kingscannon map room after breakfast two days after the leaders' meeting to see who had transported in and was now addressing him. It was Gatemaster Blackwing from Farhaven Keep. "What is it, Blackie? What sort of problems?" Blackwing played silently with a stack of the small, polished square stone weights used to hold scrolls in place and then shook his head in disgust, saying, "Can you call a meeting of all Keeps? It's a big problem."

Summersong waited a moment to see if any more was forthcoming, and when it became apparent that Blackwing would say no more, he replied, "We have a meeting tomorrow." Blackwing tossed his sandy brown hair back from his shoulders and said curtly, "Not soon enough, we need one today." Summersong nodded, "I'll call one at once. I will summon all Keeps to the Gathering glade immediately." Blackwing nodded and transported without another word. Summersong stood silent a few moments before rolling the map of Snowmelt Wood and putting it away.

An hour later, all the Keeps were assembled in the Gathering glade once again. Blackwing walked to the central platform and turned slowly around to survey the assembled gathering. He held up his hands for silence and began, "Thank you all for coming on such short notice! It is never an easy task to lock the Gates down early and come away before the day has truly begun. As you can see," he gestured to the empty place where Jeweldance Keep should have been, "we have a missing Keep once more. The news I bring to you this day concerns Jeweldance and is grave indeed." Murmurs began to circulate throughout the crowd as everyone wondered aloud what the problem was. "As most of you know, the people of Jeweldance have long held themselves to be better than all the rest of us and over the past year have refused to watch any Gates, holding themselves too important for such work and leaving the extra Gates to the men of Farhaven. Unfortunately, it was not until early this morning that we at Farhaven Keep discovered exactly how far they have fallen from Keeper duties."

Blackwing shifted his balance and took a deep breath before continuing, "This morning two of my men were attacked by a rogue dragon in the southern jungle while they searched for any attempted breakthroughs from Brimstone." The crowd gasped and some sprang to their feet at the news. "How did this happen?" "Did this dragon belong to someone?" "Are the men alright?" "Surely, there are no wild dragons left in these days?" "Have you captured the dragon?" The questions flew out from the audience helter-skelter. Blackwing held his hands up over his head for silence once more and the crowd gradually settled and sat down. "My men managed to transport out of the situation and back to Farhaven, where they reported to me, unfortunately as you are all aware, dragon attacks, though rare, are vicious, and both men died a short time after reporting the incident and before we could fetch the Healers. So, we are now a company of thirteen at Farhaven, and we would appreciate some more people if any of the other Keeps have folks who would be willing to move, even temporarily. But for the moment let us concentrate on the most serious issue: the dragon was one belonging to Jeweldance."

He looked grimly around at the gathered Keepers, "I transported to the location with one of my men, Sandy, who can speak to all animals, and we found the dragon after a short search. It did not wish to have anything to do with us and we had to transport out quickly. However, the dragon was communicating as it ran towards us in the jungle clearing; Sandy told me that it was angry because all of the dragons at Jeweldance had been abandoned by their Riders. We next transported to the stable of Jeweldance to confirm this and they are thoroughly destroyed. Something only dragons could do, I think. At least, I don't know what else could have destroyed the stable. Apparently Jeweldance has become so involved in their own selves that they have not only stopped feeding and grooming their dragons but have forgotten them entirely."

Angry talk rolled in waves around the audience; it was unthinkable to abandon your dragon – the other half of you – to forgetfulness and slow starvation. No wonder the dragons had left the stable to fend for themselves, and finally stopped returning at all. Summersong stood and spoke directly to Blackwing at last, "How many people does Jeweldance have?" Blackwing stood a moment in silence, counting from memory, "I believe they number fifty-two, but they used to number well over two hundred. Their numbers have dwindled of late years." Silverwing asked, "Did you transport in to Jeweldance Keep, or just to the stable area? Did you try talking with any of them?" Blackwing shook his head, "We don't go to Jeweldance Keep anymore. The last time I sent men there, they were attacked and beaten by the Jeweldance Keepers and told they weren't welcome, so I haven't allowed any of my men to even try talking with them for at least a year. We simply mind all the southern Gates as best we can,

which is why we've remained aloof from the rest
of you so long, because we're simply too
exhausted to do anything at the end of each day,
being so few." The crowd grew silent once more as
they thought over the implications: Not only were
there fifty-two rogue Keepers who didn't hold to
the standards and laws of their world, but there
were fifty-two abandoned dragons roaming free in
the southern jungles. Dragons that had been treated
so badly that they would now attack and kill the
very Keepers they were meant to pair with.

Eventually the crowd turned as one and looked at
Summersong sitting in front of the group from
Kingscannon Keep. They were looking to him for
an answer. Thunderstroke nudged him and said,
"Look! Everyone is waiting for you to speak!"
Summersong looked around in surprise at the other
Keepers, then jumped onto the platform and
walked to the center to stand next to Blackwing.
"Keepers, hear me!" he began, "We have a larger
problem than just a Keep with abandoned dragons.
As you know, the southern jungles are lined up
directly with Snowmelt Wood in Arkady, and that

is the source of all the evil. We all know that Brimstone has long sought to break through into Arkady and the Keeper's world, but it is clear to my eyes now that they broke through to our world over a year ago, which is why the other breakthroughs have been happening with more frequency. Their point of entrance is the same in both worlds – Snowmelt Wood, which few people travel because it is wild and takes so many days to cross, and Jeweldance Keep, who have long kept their distance from all other Keeps. We will go there this day with enough men to fend off any attack, but I doubt that we will find any left living there. My Messenger found the place deserted and dusty when he stopped there to request their presence at the Gathering glade for our previous meeting, and he could find nobody in the Keep, the stable, which was at that time intact and empty, or around the land."

Blackwing looked startled and gasped out, "Do you truly think they are all dead at Jeweldance?" Summersong turned to him and said, "Why else have you had to take over their Gates for so long? Can you really believe that even they would abandon their dragons, the pride and joy of every Keeper?" The crowd shifted uneasily at these words and looked uncertainly around at each other before returning their gaze to the central platform. Summersong turned to the crowd once more and continued, "This day will be a day of battle on many fronts. Keepers of Meadowbrook, Plainsrunner and Stonyvale, I ask you to try rounding up the rogue dragons, since it was your three Keeps that originally captured and tamed the wild ones for use as Keepers Rides. If they cannot be rounded up and tamed," he paused, "they will have to be killed. I will have no more men die in this manner." The people of the Keeps mentioned stood and nodded, preparing for travel to their various Keeps to get their dragons and the equipment necessary for the work.

Gatemaster Zephyr of Plainsrunner Keep spoke up, "To where shall we bring these dragons? Who has room in their stables for fifty-two unruly beasts?" Blackwing answered him, "We at Farhaven used to number well over one hundred, yet we are now down to thirteen men and fifteen dragons. You may bring them to our stables. We will move our few dragons out to another Keep stable in the meantime so that they are not influenced by the rogue ones." Zephyr nodded to Blackwing as Summersong once again assumed the lead, "Bring your dragons to Kingscannon, Blackie, we have plenty of room, for we number only forty."

He sighed and then said, "For the rest of you I ask everyone to decide who the twenty-four strongest and most seasoned warriors are; that will be the group sent to Jeweldance to check the situation there, and they will carry the crystal artifacts for protection in case any Nevilem are present. Also, I will ask Gatemaster Moonshadow and his Smiths to travel with that group so that any rift we find there may be sealed quickly. Moonshadow, Steele, be sure to carry as much equipment and supplies as you possibly can. Take a Messenger with you so that they can report to the Deep Mines for whatever else you need sent. Gatemaster Sharptooth, go to the mines now and ask the Miners to begin preparing as much red slate and diamonds as possible." A general discussion started as everyone began to discuss who should be the chosen twenty-four Keepers to enter Jeweldance. Sharptooth transported out on his errand, followed by Moonshadow and the Smiths who left to get their equipment ready.

Chapter 22 – Jeweldance Keep

Raindance looked around at the twenty-three men with him, "Everyone has their crystal?" Each man checked a pocket and confirmed the crystal he carried was in place. Raindance spoke again, "Alright, men, weapons out, we transport together. Steele and his men will follow shortly." Steele glanced around at his men as Rainy's group shimmered out in a cascade of multicolored sparkles. They would wait for one man of the twenty-four to transport back and report, before they themselves went.

A great moaning howl of fierce wind greeted the chosen twenty-four men as the arrived in Jeweldance Keep. "Stonyvale Now!" Rainy shouted as soon as they entered the Keep. The men needed no further urging. They all shimmered away once more, leaving behind a cold black nothingness, which was all that was left of Jeweldance Keep. Steele and his men started in surprise as all twenty-four men reappeared moments later at Stonyvale. "What happened, what did you find?" Steele asked as Rainy looked grimly towards the waiting Smith. The men were shivering with cold. "Easy, men," Rainy said to them, teeth chattering, "We will have to find another way." He shook his head at Steele and answered the Smith's question as he stomped his feet and slapped his arms to warm up, "There is nothing left. It is as if the world were torn right out of place inside that Keep. It is icy cold with a wind howling throughout, and pitch black, even the glow of our transport did not lessen the darkness. We could see nothing, but I doubt that anything is there to see. Nothing remains of Jeweldance or her people."

Steele spun around to the Crystal Smith, "Jax, get to the dragon hunt quickly and tell them what has happened to Jeweldance; it may help them calm the dragons; then to Grimhold Keep and report to the leaders waiting there. I must plan how best to forge a seal over this gaping hole in our world." Crystal Smith Ajax took a knife out of his belt and transported away in a shimmer of red sparkles. Steele turned back to Rainy and said, "Can you and your men help us?" Rainy nodded, "Yes, we will help."

Chapter 23 – A Busy Day

The abandoned dragons in the southern jungle roared and snarled, angry at being roped with magical golden catch lines that they could not break. They thrashed violently, breaking, and bending small trees and trampling the undergrowth as they fought to free themselves from the lines, which canceled their magic so that they couldn't use their special powers to fight. The paired dragons and their Keepers held the lines taut, letting the rogue dragons work their fury out until they were too tired to fight. The dragons would be transported to Farhaven Keep stables once they were too tired to resist further.

Not too far from the dragon hunt, Steele's group of men stood outside the Jeweldance Stable, looking at the shattered rubble that once was a magnificent cave. The gigantic rock pillar was shattered to pieces at the base and blackened as if by soot, and jagged cracks ran from the stable up the full height of the pillar. "This was no work of dragons," Steele announced to them all as he looked up at the

301

tall grey pillar of rock that stretched far up into the canopy of the jungle, "This was part of the breakthrough from Brimstone." Rainy agreed saying, "Only the brown dragons have power over the earth and could have done this, but they would not destroy their home. Probably the dragons had been returning after each day's search for food to shelter here, and when the breakthrough happened it closed off their shelter, that's what must have driven them to madness." A man holding a lantern crawled out from a small gap halfway up the pile of rubble just then and waved down to them, "There are fourteen dead dragons inside, buried in the rubble! They must have been home when this happened and not all made it out alive!" The men shook their heads sadly at the loss of such great beasts and then went about mapping the area in order to begin building a barrier against the new rift in their world.

Thunderstroke slapped her hands down on the map the leaders were studying in Grimhold Keep and shouted, "Stop!" They looked up at her in surprise and stopped their discussions, waiting for her to explain her strange outburst. "You keep planning ways into Snowmelt Wood to plant this seed, saying this is our next course of action." She said to them. "Yes of course! It must be planted, you said so yourself now that we have the crystals to aid us." Summersong answered her. She shook her head quickly, "I know, but not yet. It can't be planted yet, not if I understand all of this correctly." Firestorm answered her this time, "It must be planted, or this world will end in chaos. The chaos has already begun! The seed will stop the madness." She clenched her teeth and then said, "Look at this, I mean, we've been looking at it all day but not really seeing it because it's so familiar. Take another look, and really study it this time." They all looked down at the map on the table. Green lines were drawn to mark all paths into the wood that led to the Planting Glade at the center. Red markers set out on the map showed where owls scouting the forest had spied permanent encampments of Nevilem from Brimstone, and blue markers showed places where marching troops had been spotted passing through. The green paths were thoroughly covered over with red. The center Planting Glade was also ringed in red. blue markers were scattered evenly all over the map, even in the wooded and pathless areas. There was no entrance, even by stealth or by transporting directly into the glade.

The rogue dragons were at last rounded up and brought to Farhaven Stable. Once the dragons were inside, the magical golden lines were roped across the entrance of the stable, closely crossed together to prevent dragons from leaving yet allowing ample gaps for the humans to pass through. The Keepers had found only twenty-eight dragons. With the fourteen dead in the Jeweldance Stables that left ten still unaccounted for. Harold and a few of the other Tenders of Beasts were transported in from Lindentree Town in Arkady and they went around the exhausted dragons with the Keepers, setting baskets full of fruits and berries before the dragons and then they groomed the tangles and mats out of the dragons' fur and straightened their bent feathers before polishing the great, sweeping horns and hooked claws.

The animal handlers spoke softly and gently to each dragon in turn, reassuring them that there would be no more abandonment, but the dragons simply stretched out on the cave floor, unmoving, not responding to words, grooming or food. "Come," Harold said at last, "We have done all that we can for them. Now we must let them rest and hope they are still sensible enough to take in our words and actions once they return to strength." Gradually everyone left the stable to the dragons and stood together outside. "Did you notice?" Gatemaster Jasmine of Meadowbrook Keep said to them all as they prepared to transport, "There are no black or white dragons at all in this group, those are the ones that control darkness and light. If they have somehow landed in the hands of our enemies," he left the rest unspoken, not wanting to voice the dire consequences that could follow if the enemy had indeed managed to steal dragons. The group transported without another word.

Back in Grimhold Keep, the argument continued. "We cannot plant the seed, until we get rid of these evil men." Thunderstroke said to the group around the map table after they had given a solid look to the map. "We cannot get rid of them without planting the seed, they outnumber us by thousands." Summersong answered her, just as grimly. Everyone stared at the map once more as they thought through the situation. Finally, Thunderstroke asked, "Where is the Snowmelt Wood Planting Glade in relation to the living world? I know you said we have to reach it through Snowmelt Wood by opening a Gate there to reach it, but couldn't we open a Gate further away into the living world and then travel through that world to the planting glade, thus circumventing Snowmelt and the southern jungles entirely?" The room grew silent as everyone stared at her. The audacity to travel through the living world, where they did not belong, rather than opening a Gate directly at the planting glade! "Summon Maximillian, the Master Cartographer, quickly, and his apprentice Daisy Mae!" shouted Silverwing to one of his Keepers passing by the meeting room, "Tell them to bring a map of the living world and prepare for work!" The Keeper nodded and hurried off. Jasmine, Sundance,

Zephyr, Starmist, Talon and Jubilee transported into the common room just then and walked over to join the other leaders in their conference room. "Well," Talon announced, "the rogue dragons are rounded up and in Farhaven's stable. They're groomed, fed and quiet, but not happy." A cheer went around the table as the newly arrived leaders took their seats, and then Silverwing filled them in on what they were doing while they waited for the Cartographers to arrive with the map of the living world.

Chapter 24 – Surprise Attack

Thunderstroke looked up from the map of the living world and straightened in slow motion, standing as if in a daze. "Are you feeling alright, Thunder?" Summersong asked her in worried tones. She did not answer, didn't move. Summersong walked around the table to reach her, concerned, he shook her gently by the shoulder, "Thunder?" Now everyone was looking up from the map and watching; Summer put both hands on her shoulders and shook her again, "Thunder! Thunder!" No response came; she seemed to be completely unaware of her surroundings. Summersong turned to the others for help, "Stormy, can you heal her, what can be wrong?" Suddenly Thunderstroke screamed and jumped back, reaching for her sword, and yelling out, "Quickly! There is danger at the stables! All to your home stables! The dragons are in terrible danger!" and she was gone in a purple shimmer. The others stood in shock for a split second, looking at the space she had been, and then moved to action, drawing weapons, and transporting to home stables without a sound.

"Get up there! Get up you mangy beasts!" the harsh words rang out amid the cracking sizzle of electric whips and the angry roars and frightened squeals of dragons. Ten evil warriors stood at the entrance of the Kingscannon stable brandishing the crackling whips and striking the dragons with searing electrical shocks as the terrified, squealing group of dragons rushed further back into the cavern in a desperate attempt to get out of range. Suddenly a purple cascade of sparkles appeared in the stable cavern just ahead of the dragons and Thunderstroke stood there, sword in one hand, dagger in the other, "How dare you enter here and try to steal our dragons! How dare you!" She shouted at the Nevilem. Her fury led her into the battle, jagged bolts of lightning shot from her sword and dagger one after the other as she raced toward the group that now scattered with screams of terror upon seeing three of their men fall dead from the small woman's deadly strikes at such distance.

A yellow glow appeared behind the running Nevilem as Summersong transported into the cave entrance, his sword at the ready, and proceeded to take down the remaining seven men. Summersong watched as the last man in the cave, thinking the diminutive woman an easier target, turned, and charged Lady Thunderstroke, who tripped him as she jumped aside, then stepped on him with one foot and pointed her sword at his face. The man gulped and dropped the whip he was holding, staring at the bright point of the deadly sword held over his face. Summersong cried out "Hold! Keep him alive! We need answers." Lady Thunderstroke waited silently; anger written all over her usually smiling round face. Summersong walked over and opened his mouth to speak, but she shook her head, "No time for talk yet, the dragons are terrified because their powers were stolen by those whips."

She turned and went into the stables, sheathing her weapons as she walked off to comfort the scared beasts. Summersong reached down in silent rage and grabbed the man still lying on the dirt floor of the stable, yanking him roughly up and holding the smaller man high overhead. He snarled at the man, "What did you do to our dragons? What did you do?" Then Summersong threw him roughly toward the back of the cave where the man landed in a sprawl and tried vainly to regain his footing as he saw Summersong running forward. Summer got to him before he could rise and picked him up once more, tossing him further into the cave. He turned to Lady Thunderstroke, "Get a rope. I need to tie him so he cannot escape while we tend the dragons. We'll make sure he is weaponless, too, so he cannot transport." Thunderstroke changed direction and headed to a tack room for one of the magical golden catch lines stored within.

"Easy sweetheart, don't worry, I won't abandon you. No one is going to steal any of you!" Lady Thunderstroke rubbed her dragon's nose and cooed as the dragon whimpered and gradually quieted, gentled under her hands. Lady Thunderstroke had told all of the dragons to call their Riders to the stable, and now the other dragons were each calming down under their respective Keepers as the men returned to comfort the great beasts. Soft talk flowed around the cavern, reassuring the dragons as they sat huddled in a group at the back of the cave. "There, that's better! Can you make the sun come out now, dear heart?" Thunder cooed again to her dragon. The great amethyst dragon hung her head and whimpered. "No, you must try! Come, your power can't be gone for good. That was a temporary effect from those whips. Those things are no different than a magical catch line, except that they hurt."

She raised her voice so all the dragons would hear, "Trust me now, if they wanted to kidnap you, they would want your powers. The effect was temporary. Your lights are already returning, just look around the stable and see. Come, try using your powers!" Sapphire's large blue dragon turned towards an open space in the floor and breathed out. "Hey!" Sapphire yelped, jumping back, "Be careful there, you almost got my boots!" The dragons one and all started chirping, barking, and jumping as the floor iced over and frost filled the air above it. A red dragon stretched his neck out and breathed fire onto the ice, melting it into a puddle. "Wait! Whoa! Let's take this outside before you all start doing this!" Sapphire shouted, hopping from one foot to the other in the puddle, his soft leather boots now thoroughly soaked. The dragons rushed for the door in a group, nearly trampling their Riders in their excitement.

Lady Thunderstroke watched from the cave entrance as the sun broke through the clouds and shone down on them all, "Well, she's alright!" she said to Summersong standing next to her. "Yes, they all are. Look at Summersong now, the great goofball!" The large golden dragon had puffed his chest out and softly exhaled all around the dirt directly in front of the cave. The hard-packed dirt suddenly sprouted flowers of all colors in merry profusion and the golden dragon plopped down to begin rolling in the flowers. "So that's why you call him Summersong!" she exclaimed brightly. "Yes," he answered, "The golden ones have the power to make things grow. I thought you knew all the dragon powers?" He looked down at her curiously as she shook her head, "Only the colors of the dragons in Jumpriver stable where I first met my Ride. There were no yellow dragons in there." At last, the dragons were satisfied of their abilities once more and calmed enough to allow their Riders to mount. "Come all" Summersong announced, "Let's go to the other Keep stables to see if they need help, we will split up." One by one they transported away in groups until the stable was left empty save for a single lone man shouting obscenities into the cave opening and tied tightly with magical golden catch lines that he could not break.

Chapter 25 – Escape Of Argos

That evening found all of the Keepers and their dragons together once more in the Gathering glade, which was the only place big enough to hold them all together. The Nevilem who had been captured at Kingscannon was held fast between two large Keepers on the center platform. Summersong held his hands for silence after allowing all to have a good look at the man standing and snarling at the crowd through his helmet. "Ladies and gentlemen, Keepers all, we have come through some unexpected battles this day and emerge relatively unscathed. The injuries sustained by some were treated and are minor enough to enable the Keepers to be here with us tonight, and all of the Nevilem except for this man have been killed."

The crowd cheered, feeling they had somehow won a great victory. "As many of you may have noticed this day, some of the evil warriors who invaded our world and tried to capture our dragons were familiar, former Keepers from Jeweldance Keep." Summersong turned suddenly to the man held fast on the platform and grabbed his Brimstone helmet by the top spike, pulling it up and off in one smooth motion. "Here is the main perpetrator of this horrible crime – behold! Argos, former Gatemaster of Jeweldance Keep. He is the one who has this day turned on his calling!" A stocky man of medium height, with short brown hair stood before Summersong. He held his head proudly high and bared his teeth defiantly but made no other move. The crowd roared with anger, how dare a Keeper turn against his brethren! It was unthinkable!

Summersong held his hands up for silence and waited for the crowd to quiet down. He turned once more to Argos and addressed him loudly, so that all might hear. "You have this day turned against your own kind and against the laws that we hold. Have you anything to say for yourself?" Argos sneered at Summersong and replied, "You don't know what you're going up against! You have no idea how close to death you all are! The laws of the Keepers hold no more power in this world and your days are numbered! Brimstone will prevail and all who have chosen to follow freely will survive the days to come. We will be awarded positions of power and glory; we will be feared and famed throughout the land as rightful rulers!"

Thunderstroke could take no more; she stepped forward and faced off with Argos, while Summersong held out a protective arm to keep her from getting too close. "How dare you abandon your dragons like that? How could you do such a thing? And then you come trying to steal our dragons?" Argos raised his eyebrows a little, "Oh-ho, aren't you a tough little thing! Only ten of our dragons agreed to accompany us to Brimstone, therefore we needed more. We did not abandon the other dragons though; we used their power to transport our Keep into Brimstone. They are dead, which serves them right for refusing to obey us! That is why we need your dragons – breeding takes too much time, especially with only one female dragon and nine males." Summersong held his hand up for silence before the crowd exploded; Argos didn't realize some of their dragons had escaped and he didn't want the man to know.

"Explain to me please exactly what you did?" he asked Argos sternly.

Argos obliged, obviously enjoying the spotlight despite his predicament. "Why, it is simple! We needed a home in Brimstone, and we liked our Keep enough to move it there. But to transport an entire cave system, well, that takes more power than we had. So, we simply barricaded the unwilling dragons into their stable, to harness their power. For you know that the Keeps are located directly above the stables. Once that was done, we simply drew on the power of the dragons, using some special crystals provided by our new Master, and drained the life force out of our dragons, thus propelling our Keep into Brimstone. If I were you, I wouldn't try to transport to Jeweldance; it is no longer there!" He grinned maliciously at Summersong.

The crowd was silent, stunned, unable to fathom how an entire Keep full of people could willingly kill their dragons in such a cold and heartless manner. Thunderstroke looked back at Silverwing in the crowd, raising a questioning eyebrow at him; she realized that Argos didn't know most of the Jeweldance dragons had escaped. Silver shook his head slightly, signaling her to keep silence. Summersong spoke again, "You have shown terrible judgment, Argos. You have not only turned against your brethren and the world of Arkady you were sworn to protect, but you have turned against your dragons, willingly trying to kill them to further your own ends for power and control. Duty and service are more important to the Keepers than power or fame. You and your people have long strayed from the true path we hold to, I wish we had acted sooner. This day you have forfeited your life, and we will put an end to the others as well before more damage can be done."

Argos kicked out swiftly at one of the Keepers holding him, and making him falter just enough to loosen his grip. That was all the desperate man needed and he wrenched his weight against the other guard, throwing him bodily into the first who was still unsteady on his feet. Summersong flashed his sword out, but Argos was just as fast, grabbing the sword off one of the guards and swinging wildly at Summersong, then leaping back and transporting away in a blue glow, laughing hysterically. "No!" Summersong shouted, and then spun quickly to the crowd "Everyone, from now on no dragon is to be left unattended at any time! We will have to sleep in our stables for the time being. Steele! How soon until that rift is mended? We will all come and lend a hand this day, for haste is needed!"

Chapter 26 – Talking With Dragons

Steele ran a fine-bladed knife along the edge of the last pillar, sending off a fierce shower of blue sparks as the final seal was completed. He looked up at the tall row of pillars now surrounding the old stable cave of Jeweldance and watched as arcs of magical blue electricity snapped between the pillars in a fine meshing net and reached up into the sky to seal off the area where Jeweldance Keep had once been, invisible to the naked eye, but still there. Steele watched the net until the arcing blue magic faded and disappeared, still there, but invisible; now all that could be seen were the four, enormous pillars and the jungle stretching away in every direction. He turned at last to the waiting people and dragons behind him and said, "That should do it, everyone! It is finished at last! We should have no more breakthroughs from Brimstone, and we can all return to sleeping in our beds once more."

Gatemaster Moonshadow smiled and replied, "Good work Steele! You said this same technique has been applied to all the Dragon Gate pillars as well?" Steele nodded, "Yes, we should have ended the threat of invasion through those routes as well, and we are now working on the new guardian pillars. I used some of the crystals we recovered from this last batch of Brimstone folk to make the seals stronger, powdering the crystal and mixing it with our diamonds. The crystals contain a magic that proves to be useful on many fronts, not the least being that it should repel any future attempts by Brimstone as it turns their magic back against them. Furthermore, my men and I will install a set of guardian pillars around each Keep as we did here at Jeweldance to prevent future attack along those fronts to stables and to Keeps. We will need at least a week to complete that work, but once it is done we can all breathe a little easier. Now, you should be able to concentrate on getting that seed planted."

Silverwing turned to the crowd of Keepers and their dragons and said, "We've had a hard couple of days, let's take this evening to relax at our homes and tomorrow we will meet once more in the Gathering glade to finalize our plans. I know we are all tired after what has happened, so if Steele has bought us some breathing space, we should take advantage of it to recoup before heading into the next phase because it will only become more difficult from this point on."

Later that evening after dinner, everyone sat around in the common area of Kingscannon Keep, sprawled comfortably in various chairs and Summersong asked Thunderstroke "So how did you know the dragons were in trouble when we were in the meeting room at Grimhold last week? It's been such a hectic few days helping Steele with those pillars that I forgot to ask you, but I thought you'd taken ill for a short bit. What happened?" "Oh yes, tell us!" said several voices as the men chimed in, leaning forward in their chairs, and waiting to hear the story. Thunderstroke looked up at the cave ceiling as she searched for words. "I – I'm not really certain how," she began, "but what I do know is that there was a voice in my head suddenly crying 'Help me!' and as I was wondering who's voice it was, suddenly it was joined by dozens and then hundreds more all crying for help. I just knew somehow that it was our dragons! Then as the realization came, pictures formed in my head, and I could see those evil men from Brimstone with their whips at all the different stables."

The men glanced around at each other, confused. Finally, Baldy spoke up, "Is that possible? Do dragons have voices and human speech?" Sundowner said tentatively, "They do understand human talk perfectly, and they can communicate with chirps and barks and such to those who understand their speech." Sapphire spoke up, "They cannot talk like humans, or they'd use words instead of dragon-sounds, wouldn't they? Is Thunder psychic?" Thunderstroke said, "No I'm not! I know it was the dragons, and what's more, I heard all of them talking to me in the cave after the fight. That's why I knew they were scared and that's how I knew their powers were gone, they told me in my head!" Then Summersong stood up and said, "Wait here, all of you. I'm going to find someone that knows more about this, I'll be right back." He took his sword out and transported.

He returned within five minutes, having with him both Harold the Tender of Beasts from Arkady and Lady Songbird "Birdie" of Jumpriver Keep. "Both of these folk understand dragon talk the same as Thunderstroke," Summersong announced, "so, perhaps with their help we can get to the bottom of this." Just then, Gatemaster Firestorm transported in, "Don't leave me behind now! I'd like to watch my Lady work!" He twitched his neat mustache rapidly, making Thunderstroke giggle. There was general laughter about the room and Lady Songbird kissed Firestorm. "So, Thunder, tell these three what you told us and then perhaps we can figure this out." Lady Thunderstroke obliged, telling Harold, Firestorm and Birdie just what had occurred when she heard the voices of the dragons.

The men of Kingscannon were silent while they watched the three visitors take it in, thinking. Lady Songbird spoke up tentatively, "I have always wished that I could get Firestorm to understand the dragons. Perhaps this is the way? Can they speak to any Keeper or just to those of us who understand dragon speech? I didn't hear anything at the time you did, and I was in the meeting room with you." She said, turning to Thunder. Harold cut in swiftly saying, "The best way to solve this is to go to the stables and enlist the dragons' cooperation. I for my part do not doubt this has happened. As you all know, the owls and foxes are always willing messengers for me and my kind, but did you know it is because we can all hear their voices in our heads and also communicate telepathically with them in that manner?" A babble of excited voices broke out as everyone started talking at once. "Thunder, Harold, Birdie," said Summersong, "will you three guide the rest of us in hearing the dragons, and talking to them in this manner?" The three nodded eagerly and with an expectant hush everyone transported out to the stables.

Chapter 27 – The Great Pairing

The scene the following afternoon at the Gathering glade was one of excitement and festivity. Dragons were all brought along, not just the ones belonging to Keepers but even those that had not yet been paired. There was a total of forty-three unpaired and untested young dragons all hopping with excitement off to one side. A smaller group of the twenty-eight dragons remaining from Jeweldance was also in attendance. Thunderstroke had talked to the abandoned dragons the previous night using the new telepathic method of communication, and the dragons of Kingscannon Keep had lent their voices to the conversation as well. The twenty-eight had agreed to come to the Glade, although there was some doubt that they would pair again, since it had never been attempted before.

The amethyst dragon stayed near the Jeweldance group, just to be safe. News had gone out the night before among all the Keeps that the dragons could communicate with their Keepers telepathically, even with those humans who couldn't understand dragon speech. This morning all had gathered extra early and there was a feel of electricity in the air from the excitement of the crowd of humans and dragons. Little sleep had been gained the previous night as all Keepers and dragons experimented with their new method of communication and enjoyed long conversations with each other.

The Keepers had sent their Messengers out across Arkady early that morning to find people willing to join the Keepers' world, and there were several hundred people in attendance in addition to the Keepers, mostly Tenders of Beasts from the world of Arkady, but also others who had shown special preference for dealing with animals, or those who had a special knack for metal-working, crystal-working and stone-working, tasks which Keepers excelled in due to their work with the Gates and with weapons; it was hoped this day among all that the Keepers ranks would be increased and all unpaired dragons would find their chosen Rider. The new Keepers would then join Farhaven Keep to increase their presence in the southern jungles, the most-exposed flank in the Keeper's world.

"Summer, you told me that the Arkady folk will give up their names entirely, or combine them with their dragon names, once they have paired with a dragon." Summersong looked down at Lady Thunderstroke who was watching the pairing procedure with a critical eye, "Yes, all Keepers share their name with their dragon, it's tradition. What of it, does it still confuse you?" he asked her. She shook her head and turned briefly to look at him before putting her attention back on the spectacle in the field, "No, but I was just wondering about the dragons that were paired with Jeweldance Keepers, what will happen with them? Do they keep their old names? Would we then have Keepers with names the same as the Keepers of Jeweldance? That might be confusing for anyone who knew the Jeweldance Keepers."

Summersong sighed heavily and shook his head, "I do not know how it will work because nobody has attempted to do this before. We are uncertain whether the dragons can even let go of the bonds with their previous Riders to allow a second

pairing once they have lost their first Keeper, or if
they will rebel and go wild. I am not sure how they
will feel about their names. We do not know. I was
amazed last night when you said you wanted those
dragons to come also. Firestorm and I were
uncertain, but we decided that it would not hurt so
long as the dragons themselves were willing to try.
That they are here is proof enough that they're
willing. But what will happen when the pairing
moment comes is something that none of us now
know. We are in new territory this day."

They both returned their full attention once more
to the scene before them. The field was filled with
dragons, but it was unlike the usual pairing of a
Keeper's Ride, as Thunderstroke had experienced.
Dragons had one and all decided that talk was
more important to them than anything else and
each of them desperately wanted a Keeper that
could hear their voice. Instead of stomping and
roaring, or pushing the potential Riders around to
test for courage, they sat quietly in a long line
opposite the audience of humans, trying to

communicate with the people as the humans walked around before the dragons.

Thunderstroke kept her eyes on Harold, certain that he would be the first to choose a dragon since he could talk to all of them easily and hear their voices. She was curious to see which he would choose to pair with. She was also pleased to know the tall, blue-eyed Tender of Beasts from Arkady would be joining the Keepers; she had a soft place in her heart for this man who had helped her through Arkady in those first awkward days. She knew now that it was through Harold's efforts that she had been reunited with Summersong after what felt an eternity, even though it had been only two days. She shuddered as she remembered the "old goat" Silenus, and then sighed heavily, leaning against Summersong as he wrapped his arms around her. "Heaven," she breathed softly, smiling to herself happily.

A few of the Arkadians had already retreated to the edge of the field, frightened by the size of the great beasts, yet still wanting to be part of the Keeper's world. Silverwing was going around to those people now and talking quietly to them, encouraging, and reassuring them. One of them took courage and went back out on to the field to try her hand once more. She was smaller in stature like Thunderstroke, a quiet girl with a pale complexion and long, curly blonde hair, barely into adulthood. She walked tentatively up to one of the Jeweldance dragons that was sitting quietly at the edge of the activity and reached out to touch the soft pink fur, then stopped as the dragon turned a wary eye towards the young woman. Amethyst Thunderstroke sent a warning message to the pink dragon "Do not fear! She is too small to hurt you. Listen to her thoughts first and see how frightened she is, then perhaps she will hear you in return."

The dragon glanced over at the amethyst dragon without moving her head and then shifted her eyes back down to the diminutive human girl still frozen in place next to her. The pink dragon edged her face a little closer to the girl and closed her eyes, concentrating. Suddenly the pink dragon snapped her eyes open and began to purr and shuffle her paws. The woman smiled and reached up to bury her hands in the feathery mane of the dragon. "We have our first pairing this day!" Shouted Firestorm, who was in the field officiating over the activities. The crowd quieted and all the other dragons and people on the field stopped and looked over to watch. Firestorm walked over to the new pair and said, "Now you must ride your dragon and then," he hesitated, suddenly realizing that this dragon had a previous name, "Then we will see." He finished lamely, rubbing a hand over his buzzcut in uncertainty. He motioned her up and the dragon crouched down for her to mount.

The woman clambered unsteadily on to the pink dragon's back and grasped tight handfuls of fur in her fists, then looked up uncertainly. Firestorm backed up and motioned the dragon into flight. The dragon walked forward and spread her wings, lifting gently off the ground, and whirling gracefully up into the air as the girl hung on. The crowd cheered as they watched the girl loosen her grip and catch the motion of her flight; the dragon was talking her through. "That is a much tamer ride than my first ride!" Thunderstroke said in hushed tones to Summersong. He smiled and glanced down, answering her, "Not all dragons are as feisty as Thunderstroke, and her temperament matches yours, my lady!" She giggled.

Finally, Ride and Rider landed gently back down, and the girl jumped off as the dragon sat down and shoved her head forward for pets. Firestorm approached once more and watched the pair. They watched Firestorm in return. Finally, he spoke, "We are unsure this day how to go about this, you see the dragon you have paired with once belonged to another and she has a name already." The pink dragon lifted her head and shook her mane fiercely, and all the Keepers heard the pink dragon's voice "I have new life now; give me a new name!" Firestorm smiled and said to the young woman, "You have heard her as have we all. This time I speak the words of tradition. It is time for you to name your dragon here in front of us so that all may witness."

The young woman looked up into her dragon's eyes and then turned back to Firestorm, saying, "I shall name her Velvet Rose because she is as soft as velvet and as beautiful as a rose." Firestorm looked to the dragon and said, "Do you accept this name, dragon?" The dragon pranced in place, crooning happily, and arching her neck, mane fluffed out to full. "Then let it be so!" said the Gatemaster, turning to the audience, "This day the Ride has found a Rider and the pink dragon shall be known as Velvet Rose!" He turned towards the new Keeper again, "Lady, when this day's ceremonies are complete, you will take your ride back to Farhaven Keep, where she shall make her new home along with you – who shall now be known as Keeper Velvet Rose of Farhaven Keep." The audience erupted into cheers and shouts of joy as the first pairing was made, then all went silent with anticipation as the remaining dragons and people squared off on the field once more. "Alright!" Gatemaster Blackwing said in a delighted whisper as he watched from the audience. Summersong, sitting nearby, said quietly to him, "Do you like her, Blackie? Are we looking at the new Lady of Farhaven?" Blackwing grinned back at Summer and said, "I hope so! That will depend on whether she likes me that much, but I'm gonna try!" Lady Thunderstroke leaned over Summersong and said conspiratorially, "With your quirky charm, how could any woman not like you?" The three of them laughed and turned their attention back to the field.

Eight more pairings were made in quick order after the first one, dragons and people having lost some of their shyness and warmed towards each other. Surprisingly, of the nine pairings so far made, seven were of the older dragons from Jeweldance. The Keepers were one and all pleased to see that dragons could and did form new bonds at need. Lady Thunderstroke watched eagerly as Harold still walked among all the dragons back and forth, as if he weren't in the least concerned about choosing one; he had yet to make a motion toward any dragon. She was confused by Harold's actions and said so to Summersong at last.

Summersong hugged her close and leaned down to whisper in her ear, "Does it surprise you that he would wait? You know he will pair because it has already been decided that he must, and he is aware of that. But Harold seems particularly good at working with people as well as beasts, and I believe that he is waiting so that he can lend encouragement to the others who are not as sure of themselves as he is. He is known to all the other beast handlers and most of the Arkadians as one who can talk to all beasts, if he had been first to choose, then the others would perhaps falter, but because he has waited while allowing others to choose, it gives them hope that they can indeed do this thing. Do not fear, he will choose one yet, there are still plenty of dragons to go around."

Twelve more pairings were made quietly and without fuss, and three pairings with a small show of dragon antics, bucking and aerial tricks from pure joy. Many of the Keepers in the audience were now sitting on the ground to watch the proceedings, relaxed, and enjoying the day. Laughter and quiet talk had become general throughout the audience as people discussed the new pairs and marveled at the Jeweldance dragons' resilience shown this day. "Summer," Lady Thunderstroke said as they watched the proceedings, "why is Firestorm calling all of the women who pair today 'Keeper' instead of 'Lady', like he called me when I paired? Shouldn't they all be called ladies?" Summersong looked down at her as she sat next to him, and asked a return question, "Lady is a title, I thought you knew that?" She nodded, answering, "Yes, but they're ladies too, only he's calling them Keepers."

They both looked up as a loud dragon snort echoed, and watched a dark green dragon take flight, then Summer looked down at her again. "Lady is the title we use to refer to the Gatemasters' mates. The other women of the Keep are ladies, yes, but their official title is Keeper. You are a Keeper, but your title is Lady, I am also a Keeper, but my title is Gatemaster. The leaders of each Keep are known officially as Gatemaster and Lady. Does that clear things up?" She nodded thoughtfully, "Yes," she said after a moment's thought, looking out at the field to watch the dark green dragon and its Rider land, "I guess it does. I just thought you folks were all being polite to use the term. I mean, that first night in Kingscannon with the meeting, you called me, Caroline, and Daisy Mae by lady, so I assumed it applied to all." Summer laughed lightly and said, "Well, sometimes we do use the term in politeness, which is what I did that night. With you, however, I also used it because you didn't have a name and I didn't want to say, 'hey you!' and besides, I already knew that you would accept me as your mate, which meant that you would be carrying the title of Lady very shortly." They both laughed and turned their attention back to the field.

Two of the Jeweldance dragons had shown reluctance to be placed in Farhaven, so close to their old home and the memories associated with it, so it was decided that those previously paired dragons uncomfortable with the proximity to their old home would be placed in other Keeps. Thus, Meadowbrook and Greyweather Keeps both benefited from the addition of a new pair that day and other Keeps looked forward to also adding to their ranks. The new pairs of Keepers and dragons were all sitting quietly along one edge, happily getting to know each other more fully as the remaining dragons and people continued searching for each other.

Suddenly a young dragon, dark violet in color, broke from the ranks of untested dragons and went galloping up and down the field, knocking people over and charging right into the middle of a starting pair, sending both dragon and man falling backward to the ground. The heavily built man was up quickly to his feet, running toward the black-furred dragon he had been talking with, his white ponytail flying behind him; already protective before the full pairing had been completed. The black dragon roared angrily as he jumped to his feet and beat his wings, taking off into the air to chase down the young upstart. The man jumped swiftly and grabbed hold of the black dragon's foreleg just as it left the ground, then swung himself up onto the dragon's back with lightning precision and the polished moves of a rodeo cowboy. He leaned in on the dragon's neck and desperately tried to soothe the angry beast as it roared after the violet dragon, which had now turned and started squealing with fright.

Firestorm shouted out above the din, "Oh, blast! That's the third time that young dragon has interrupted the proceedings! Somebody do something!" Harold stood in the middle of the field admiring the older man's moves; he was one of the Tenders of Beasts that Harold himself had taught. Harold threw his arm out and pointed towards the young purple dragon, saying sternly to him, "You go apologize right now!" The purple dragon hung his head until his sweeping, spiral horns almost scraped the ground in front of him and belly-crawled over to the black dragon hovering a few feet above the ground. The black dragon was still extremely angry but had been brought in check by the man on his back and held his position, snorting furiously at the young dragon. The crowd was silent and still, watching the drama unfolding before them as the young violet dragon finally reached the larger black one and collapsed on the ground, crying piteously for forgiveness.

"There now," said the man on the black dragon's back, "I've never seen a sorrier dragon in my life. It's your move, will you forgive?" The black dragon snorted again, sides still heaving with anger and fur spiked, claws still splayed out for a strike. "You must admit, he didn't mess up our pairing now, did he? In fact, we came together quicker with his help." The black dragon paused and rolled his head back on his long neck to look upside down at the man on his back. He snarled at the man, baring all his teeth, and the man reached out and playfully ruffled the dragon's furry, bearded chin, "You don't scare me one bit!" he said, leaning his face in towards the large maw, "Now what are you going to do about it?" The dragon gave a sharp ruff of annoyance and then flipped his head back around to view the young purple dragon still groveling beneath him. He snorted a final time and then tilted his wings and flew up into the air, circling twice around the field before alighting in his former place. The man jumped off and walked to the dragon's head, then both turned and waited for Firestorm to make the pairing official.

Firestorm approached the pair and stopped a few feet in front of them, saying to the man "It is time for you to name your dragon here in front of us so that all may witness." The man answered immediately "I shall call him Night Shadow." Firestorm looked to the dragon and said, "Do you accept this name, dragon?" The dragon reared up on his hind legs, roaring with all his might and then came back down, arching his neck, mane fluffed out to its fullest. "Then let it be so!" said the Gatemaster, turning to the audience, "This day the Ride has found a Rider and the black dragon shall be known as Night Shadow!" He turned towards the new Keeper again, "Sir, when this day's ceremonies are complete, you will take your ride back to Farhaven Keep, where he shall make his new home along with you – who shall now be known as Keeper Night Shadow of Farhaven Keep."

The audience roared their approval, applauding loudly to welcome the new pair. Night Shadow and his new rider moved off to take a place alongside the other new pairs at the edge of the field. Summersong nudged Thunderstroke and said to her, "Watch! Harold is going to take that purple dragon!" She turned her attention from the new pair and watched intently as Harold approached the still slumped and groveling violet dragon on the ground in the center of the field. Firestorm was also watching from where he stood, waiting as if he knew the two would pair off.

Harold walked up to the young dragon and gave him a friendly shove in the shoulder with his boot, "Get up! It is time you were paired off; you have caused enough trouble this day, you wild and crazy thing!" The purple dragon looked over to Harold and moaned pitifully, squirming around until he was belly-up on the field. "You're shamming and I know it." Harold said to him. Thunderstroke giggled quietly as the young dragon began to cry, howling and turning his face away from Harold. "What are you laughing for, Thunder?"

Summersong asked her curiously, "Listen to Harold's voice," she answered him; "he is trying not to laugh! The dragon really is shamming, to see what he can get away with!" Harold looked up across the dragon at Firestorm, who had begun to walk over, and rolled his eyes before turning once more to the young dragon. "That's enough, goofball! Stop playing around and get off your back! I know you're fooling around because you're just like me and you're too happy with life to be upset for long!" The dragon quieted suddenly, and then turned to look at Harold, trying its best to look affronted and indignant. "No, that doesn't work with me." Harold answered him. The dragon pushed his bearded chin out in a good imitation of a pout. "No, sorry, that doesn't work either." Harold answered again.

By this point most of the Keepers in the crowd were trying not to laugh at the play being enacted before them. The dragon stuck his tongue out at Harold and the man laughed saying, "Oh, let's see how you like a tummy-rub!" He reached forward and rubbed his hands along the furry purple belly

345

as the dragon rumbled approval and chuckled, squirming around on the ground. "Okay, that's enough games! Get up this time and let's go so we can get this day done and over! There are a lot of pairs yet to be made!" The purple dragon rolled over and bounced to his feet, shaking the dust and grass out of his fur and then turned to Harold and licked him from top to bottom with a large, sloppy tongue. Firestorm chuckled as he waited nearby to make the pair official, and the purple dragon promptly turned around and licked Firestorm, leaving him soaking wet. The crowd did laugh that time, and two men out in the field joined in.

Firestorm said to Harold "I do not doubt that you can ride him, therefore it is time for you to name your dragon here in front of us so that all may witness." Harold looked over at the purple dragon and ruffled his mane, saying, "I shall call him Happy Harry because he's just like me." Firestorm looked to the dragon and said, "Do you accept this name, dragon?" The dragon thumped his tail like a large puppy and stuck his tongue out and crossed his eyes, arching his neck, mane fluffed out to its fullest. "Then let it be so!" said the Gatemaster, turning to the audience, "This day the Ride has found a Rider and the violet dragon shall be known as Happy Harry!" He turned towards the Harold again, "Sir, when this day's ceremonies are complete, you will take your ride back to Meadowbrook Keep, where he shall make his new home along with you – who shall now be known as Keeper Happy Harry of Meadowbrook Keep."

The audience roared their approval, applauding loudly to welcome the new pair as they moved off to take a place alongside the other new pairs at the edge of the field. The audience relaxed once more after the tension and comedy of the last two pairings and watched eagerly as the activity on the field resumed between the remaining people and dragons.

Chapter 28 – Lady Thunderstroke's Bad Day

Two weeks after the Great Pairing, as the Keepers now called that day, Lady Thunderstroke stood in the middle of the Kingscannon Keep common room. She stood with hands on hips, looking around in exasperation at the men sprawled out in various chairs sound asleep. It was early evening but even the few new women that had been added to their Keep were similarly dozing off. She had questions that she wanted answers to, she wanted to talk, but most of all she wanted Summersong's arms around her. He had gone off angrily to Grimhold Keep and the others had fallen asleep one by one, uninterested in conversation. She shook her head and transported out.

A few minutes later she was walking along the edge of the lake that Summersong had first brought her to that morning she learned to transport. She looked out at the setting sun barely visible above the horizon and sighed. She had fought with him this day and he had been angry with her, as had all the Keep leaders. She hadn't tried to fight, but only wanted an answer to a question, and when no one answered her the first time, she asked a second time. She did get a response then, but they had responded with angry words rather than answers. Summersong had ordered her to her home Keep in no uncertain terms; her face was hot with embarrassment as she had transported out, to be sent away like that as if she were a small child sent to her room for naughtiness. When he had come home, he hadn't been any calmer, berating her for "going against the judgment of the Historians," but she hadn't gone against any judgments, she simply didn't understand. She shook her head to shake the memory of this past day away from her mind; she truly didn't care to remember it. She sighed again and sat down on the bench, tried to think everything through, there was so much that had happened in the past two weeks.

The Keeps were now stronger than ever, seventy-three new Keepers and dragons had been added to the Keeps, most to Farhaven who needed them so desperately, but every other Keep also benefited that day. The Gates were fully operational once more, with the new Keepers being trained at their work. In addition to the new Keepers added, the remaining Arkadians who had come to try out but hadn't paired off still wanted to remain in the Keeper's world. It was decided that they would remain and that any other folk from Arkady would also be welcome. Thus, the Keeper's world now sported dozens of new leather workers, metal smiths and stone masons alongside many other occupations that had not been seen before in this world and the little groups of workshops and houses that had first been built when the Arkadians were saved out of Arkady were now grown to villages. It had become a self-sustaining world without the need to draw on resources from Arkady. Thunderstroke liked the changes and thought the world felt more home-like and less wild than it had been.

Moonshadow and his Smiths had finished installing the new protective pillars around each of the Keeps, making them invisible to anyone standing outside the four pillars, and were now busy installing single guardian pillars in each of the little villages that had sprung up, to protect those not living in Keeps. The world was secure and safer than it had been. Thunderstroke sighed again as she reached that part of her thought where the trouble had started for her this day. The scouts that had been sent to the living world the day after the Great Pairing to find the planting area had returned, and a meeting had been held of all Keep leaders this day, along with the cartographers to best ascertain their next move. The report which the scouts had brought back had not been good at all: the living world was at war between several major countries as well as many minor ones. The planting area was smack in the middle of the worst war zone and no seed planted there could survive for long. The scouts reported hundreds of Nevilem from Brimstone all around the living world, fueling the war, although the living had no idea of the invisible host around them.

The Keepers then changed their plans once more and started talking how best to defeat the evil presence in the living world so that peace would return, and the seed could be planted. Thunder had spoken up saying she didn't think that was the best way to go about it, to have a ghost war happening alongside the living war, and wouldn't the seed stop the evil? She had been told curtly to hold silence. As the talk progressed, she asked what would happen if the seed were planted in the Keeper's world, or even in Brimstone. No one had mentioned that before. That was when her trouble started, with the leaders all turning on her and Summer sending her home to be out of the way. She shook her head angrily, realizing she was starting to remember the same embarrassing thing over again. She wanted to think of answers, not remember bad memories.

Suddenly a telltale blue glow filled the air, and she waited nervously to see who was coming in. She studied the electrical blue color a moment, realizing that there were none of the new sparkles associated with the reworked weapons, and then sprang away from the bench to a more open area, drawing her sword and one of her little throwing daggers as she moved and crouching low in preparation for a fight. The glowing stopped and before her stood Argos. "How did you get here?" she demanded of him angrily, wondering why Steele's guardian pillars hadn't prevented this. She sent out an immediate, silent plea for her dragon to come and bring help, opening her mind as fully as she dared and hoping Argos wouldn't know what she was doing.

Argos laughed at her, sheathing his sword, and then standing calmly before her several feet away, keeping his arms out from his sides and away from his weapon belt. "Do not fear, I am not here to kill this time, or to kidnap dragons. I have been sent to talk to you." Argos had a raspy voice, yet he was not speaking unkindly, and there was a certain charm about the man. She stood up from her crouching position but still held tightly to her sword, keeping it out in front of her while holding the small dagger in her other hand, hidden by her side. She repeated her question, "How did you get here?" He grinned, answering, "Well, well, to think Steele forgot the ordinary; yes, I know there are magical glyphs in this world to seal it, I can feel them. But I didn't try to break in at all. I simply transported. Any former Keeper may do that without hindrance." He stood quietly, letting her take in the significance of his words. Of the fifty-two original Keepers from Jeweldance, seven had been killed that day of the kidnap attempt. That left forty-five former Keepers now working for Brimstone who could transport into the Keeper's world at will. This was indeed a serious oversight.

She looked at Argos, "What is it you want to talk about? Why come here to this out of the way part of our world?" He smiled a deceptively charming smile at her and said politely, "Why, because you are here of course, and it is you I wish to speak to, Lady." He waited, knowing her next question and smiling as she asked it, "How did you know I was here?" She was getting curious, that was good, and he could throw her off her guard that way. He answered "Because of course the power of the seed calls. It sends out magical emanations that can be felt to those trained to detect them. I am not one, but my Master can feel and see the seed wherever it travels. He gave me the coordinates and I transported. Now, shall we talk?" Thunderstroke was tense, worried, he was a smaller man than Summersong, but still larger and stronger than herself, and she was alone.

She sent another silent plea to her dragon and then questioned Argos again, "What do you want to talk about?" Argos smiled, "That is better! I want you to plant that seed for us, of course. It will benefit everyone once that task is done. I fail to understand why the Keepers have held you back from planting it for so long. We will give you safe passage to the planting glade in Snowmelt Wood if you go." She looked at him curiously for a few moments, and then asked, "You will of course want me to plant this seed in Snowmelt Wood and not in the living world?" He shook his head in surprise, "Of course not! You may choose. We will allow you to plant the seed in the world of your choosing and give you safe passage to that world's planting glade – we ask only that you plant it so that we can all move on from here and get back to normal. We do not wish to be spending our time in war any more than you Keepers."

She looked at him curiously, thinking, and then asked the question that had so angered the other leaders earlier this day, "If the seed is planted in Arkady it tends to evil, if it is planted in the living world, it tends to good, but what if it is planted in either Brimstone or the Keeper's world? What will happen?" He nodded his head and answered calmly, "Ah, so you have been trying to decide where it is best to plant? I will tell you the answer you seek, since your information is a bit incorrect. The seed planted in Brimstone will tend to evil, planted in Arkady will tend to good, and planted in the living world or the Keepers world will tend to both good and evil together. Snowmelt is the best place for it, if you wish only for good to come of the planting."

He waited, sensing her indecision, and wondering if she might be swayed already. She looked up at him again, "And you will let me plant this seed anywhere, even if I want to plant it in Snowmelt where it tends to good? Doesn't that hurt Brimstone's purpose?" He smiled that charming smile again, "You may plant it in any of the worlds you wish, and we will give you safe passage. We ask only that you plant it quickly." Thunderstroke dipped her sword down to rest its point on the ground as she thought. She remembered Harold's words about Silenus long ago: "Do not trust Silenus, he will tell you some truth, but only that truth which he thinks will gain him your cooperation" Now, as she looked up at Argos' sparkling brown eyes and saw his quirky, yet charming smile, she wondered how much truth this man was giving her. His reply truly did not answer her question – and yet perhaps it did. If they were so willing to allow her to plant the seed anywhere, then perhaps the seed should not be planted after all.

Argos stood quietly and let her think things through, knowing that he was close to a victory. He didn't know what had happened to her this day, but he sensed that she was open to suggestions, and it made his job easier. She asked curiously, "This may not have anything to do with things, but I'm curious why you aren't angry at me for asking these questions. At the meeting today everyone was upset with me and accused me of causing trouble. Why are you being so helpful to me when you're on the side of evil and I on the side of good?" He smiled again as he realized he was indeed winning her over, "I have no reason to withhold the answers you seek, since your cooperation will benefit us all, in all worlds good or evil."

She looked intently at him, stalling for time yet anxious to know more, "Who is your master? Is he the man that killed me in the first place? The one they call a Daimon?" He smiled widely, relaxing further, and thinking she was falling nicely into his hands, "The man who killed you is the Master's General, not the Master himself. The General is over all of us, and the Master is over him. We do not name the Master – it is forbidden. Indeed, I do not even know if the Master has a name, since I am still new to Brimstone." She fired another question his way, "What happened to Silenus?" She was trying to stall until help arrived, but she truly was curious. Argos shook his head in some confusion, "I do not know this name, who is Silenus?" She told him that he was the steward of Greenfield town.

"Oh, that Silenus! I did not know that was the name he went by in Arkady!" She cocked her head curiously, waiting for Argos to continue. "Didn't you know? Didn't you feel something when you confronted him upon arrival? He is known in Brimstone as The Silencer. I should have known he would take a false name in Arkady. He is the General's right-hand man, of course. It is he who has turned the town into the newest center of evil and he still makes his home there, only he has kept himself hidden from view since you went missing, because he fears the Keepers are hunting him. He is responsible for notifying the Master of interesting new arrivals to Arkady – arrivals that might benefit Brimstone. He has many men at his disposal in each town and city to inspect new arrivals and there are men who watch the Keepers as they bring arrivals to the towns, searching for good candidates for Brimstone."

She frowned, not liking this latest answer, but then seemed to come to a decision and looked up, replacing her sword in its sheath to throw him off guard. "If I choose to plant this seed in Arkady, you will allow me to go there without interfering? And if I go to Snowmelt Wood, you will allow me passage? I do know that there are hundreds of evil soldiers in those woods." He nodded and said, "Yes, we will. If you choose to plant in Snowmelt Wood, we will either allow you passage or leave the area entirely and watch from a distance if you so desire. But the seed must be planted soon. If you have not heard, I will tell you, the living world is in serious war at this moment, and it cannot continue much further. The seed must be planted soon to stop that war!" She sighed heavily, wondering why help had not arrived yet, and then looked up as the field behind Argos began to fill with multicolored sparkles. Argos spun around and took his sword out of his belt, transporting away in a blue glow as he called to her, "I will await your decision!"

Summersong and his dragon were there, along with Thunderstroke's amethyst dragon and the other leaders with their dragons. They were too late to capture Argos; his transport finished as they arrived. Summersong ran over to her and immediately started yelling at her once again, "How could you put your sword away and leave yourself defenseless like that? How could you? You should know better!" She turned her face from him to hide the tears brimming in her eyes and walked away, the dagger in her left hand now visible to him as it shimmered and transported her away in a cascade of falling purple sparkles. Summersong hung his head in shame, disgusted at himself for not trusting her. He turned and looked at the amethyst dragon saying quietly to her, "Thunder, find her. Let Summer know where and we will follow."

He ran back over toward the others and jumped on his golden dragon as amethyst Thunderstroke disappeared, and then turned to the other leaders still astride their dragons, "I have made more mistakes this day than I care to count and treated my mate very badly." He said in a defeated voice. Silverwing gave a half-hearted smile and said, "We are all guilty this day of the same. She has proven to be the clearest thinking of us all ever since she arrived. Now we have had it proven beyond doubt. That was an interesting scene played out for us this evening." Lady Songbird spoke up then saying, "I remember she said something about seeing scenes from the stables in her head when the dragons first spoke to her, that day of the attempted kidnapping, but never did I imagine what that must have been like. Now we have seen and heard this day just what transpired between Argos and Thunder, we will be more careful in future." Suddenly Summersong's tawny golden dragon gave a sharp bark and tossed his head up, horns glowing brightly. The other dragons followed suit, taking their cue from him.

Thunderstroke didn't realize at first where she was, she had transported with only one thought in her mind, to go away. Without any location in her mind, she had ended up in the only place she could: the empty remains of Jeweldance Keep. It was dark, too dark to see anything, and bitterly cold. She began shivering immediately and wrapped her arms around her body for warmth, still holding the dagger. She thought of transporting back out, but then decided that it was better to die – to die forever – than to continue any further. Even when she had first arrived in Arkady, trying to remember her name, and her past life and felt that nagging, continual sense of urgency and fear, she didn't feel this terrible. Now, she felt nothing but hopeless despair and fell at last to her knees, teeth chattering and body shaking violently with the cold. The dagger clanged to the stone as her numb fingers lost their grip and she tumbled sideways, unable to keep herself upright any longer. As she lay upon the cold stone, she had a sudden idea, an understanding about the locket, but it was too late. She could no longer control her hands or feel them. She couldn't reach the dagger lying so close beside her in the dark; she closed her eyes and waited for death, listening to the moaning howl of wind. It should be over soon. Suddenly warmth enveloped her, and bright purple light glowed softly around her. She opened her eyes and found herself on the earthen floor of the Kingscannon Keep stable with her dragon's paws on either side of her and the great bearded chin hovering protectively over her as her dragon watched the other dragons transporting in. She didn't want to face the others, she couldn't. She closed her eyes again and lapsed into unconsciousness.

"Come on, Thunder, please?" Summersong was standing before the purple dragon, trying to reach his mate, but Thunderstroke was fiercely protective of her Rider, growling steadily in her throat and showing her large fangs to the man standing before her; the great, curving claws were exposed and dug deeply into the earthen floor. Summersong turned at last to his dragon and said "Summer, do something?" The large golden dragon walked over and stretched out alongside the amethyst dragon, reaching one paw around her back, and holding his face close to hers, joining the snarl. "What!" Summersong burst out in amazement, "Guys! She's cold! I can feel the cold coming off of her from here! We need to get her warm or she'll die; body heat alone is not going to do it."

Firestorm's red dragon came forward then, nudging Gatemaster Summersong away from the two dragons and lowering his snout close. "Careful, Firey!" Firestorm said to his dragon, dropping off the dragon's back to walk over and join Stormchaser, whose red dragon had followed Firestorm. The red dragons Firestorm and Stormchaser breathed gently out from their nostrils, warming the entire stables. The amethyst dragon Thunderstroke shifted a little to allow the warmer air to circulate around her rider. The red dragons breathed out repeatedly until the stables had warmed up to an almost intolerable heat. Riders began sweating, taking layers of clothing off as they stood around and fanned themselves. "That's enough there, Firey!" Firestorm said at last, wiping sweat from his brow with his shirt.

Stormchaser said, "That should be plenty warm, Stormy!" As he too, wiped the sweat from his forehead.

Lady Thunderstroke stirred and opened her eyes, feeling warmth in her limbs. The amethyst dragon nuzzled her and purred as she woke more fully. "Thunder!" Summersong exclaimed, kneeling, and trying to peer under the bearded amethyst chin, "Come here, Lady, let me hold you. I'm so sorry!" Lady Thunderstroke turned her head and looked out from under the fringe of purple fur and feathers surrounding her; she could just barely make out Summer's kneeling form. She sighed softly, she didn't want to talk anymore, didn't want to do anything, she felt strangely drained of all energy and ambition. Finally, she shifted and scooted forward until she was out from under Thunderstroke's bearded chin, and then sat exhausted from the effort and unable to do more. Summersong reached out and picked her up in his arms, holding her close and saying over and over to her "I'm so sorry! I'm so sorry!" She fell asleep once more, unable to retain consciousness any longer.

Later that night she woke, feeling warm and secure. She opened her eyes as wakefulness returned to her and looked straight into his dark brown eyes as he held her in his lap and gazed down upon her, still sheltering her tightly in his arms and holding her to his chest. She was too comfortable to speak, too relieved to have him close to struggle against the tight hug of his arms. She knew time was running short and that they had to move fast, yet she knew only at this moment that she wanted to be close to him, to be held by him. Nothing else mattered to her then. She wanted to feel his love all around her as she felt it then, wanted to be closer to him than she had ever been. "Then you shall be." His voice echoed in her head, startling her into wide-eyed alertness. She had spoken no words; neither had he, yet he had heard her thoughts and responded in kind. He smiled at her and rose, carrying her over to the bed and placing her gently upon it. He turned down the oil lamp in their private chambers and then joined her.

She reached around him with her arms, and he pulled her into a close embrace, kissing her softly before gently pulling her shirt off.

Chapter 29 – A Way In

It was late morning before they arose and discovered the Keep empty of all save the two of them as they left their private chamber the following morning. The others had arisen and breakfasted, then taken their leave for the day, reporting for various duties about the Keeper's world and Arkady. Raindance had left a note on the kitchen counter for Summersong to let him know where the company had been assigned for the day.

They moved quietly about the kitchen, preparing a small breakfast for two. No words passed between them and yet they spoke volumes to each other, exploring this new facet of telepathic communication. Later that day they would report to Grimhold Keep for a meeting of all Keep leaders so that they could discuss the information Thunderstroke had gained from Argos, but for the time being, they were both satisfied to take things slow, reveling in their new closeness, both in communication and love, and wanting nothing more than to remain alone for a short while longer. They sat down and enjoyed a leisurely late breakfast before their day began.

Later that same day the group of Gatemasters and Ladies, along with Weaponsmith Steele, once more assembled in Grimhold Keep. After filling Steele in on yesterday's event with Argos, everyone sat silently, not entirely sure where to begin. Steele started the conversation going at last with a question to Lady Thunderstroke, "How did you manage to get into Jeweldance Keep? The magic I wove around it to seal it off from breakthroughs also should prevent any deliberate transport into the Keep by anyone. I removed the Keep name with the magic glyphs so that it simply doesn't exist anymore and someone thinking of that Keep cannot reach it. How did you get in there?"

She shrugged and shook her head; she didn't know the answer. Firestorm stood up and said, "Let me try going there now and perhaps we'll discover a break in your net, Steele." He took a small knife out of his pocket, and it glowed brightly red, but the glow didn't spread from the knife to engulf him as it should have, and he remained standing where he was. "Oh, I say, that didn't work at all, did it?" he said with some surprise, returning the knife to his belt. Several more then stood to try and transport but all failed. Steele turned to Thunderstroke once more and said, "How did you do that? I can understand your dragon getting there because she can follow your mind, but how did you get there in the first place?"

Summersong stirred and spoke then, "Would it be the locket she carries? Can that be how she got in?" Steele shook his head, "No, that locket is a simple locket carrying a seed for planting and," he broke off, eyes wide, and turned to face her suddenly. "Have you ever looked inside that locket to see what the seed is like?" A hush fell over the room as she pulled it out from under her shirt and held it out, saying "No, I can't get it open, it's sealed tightly." Steele reached forward to examine the locket, turning it over at the end of its long chain as it hung around her neck and trying to pry it open with his fingernails. He tapped it suddenly and then held it quickly to his ear, "Hmmm, this thing is not what we originally thought. It is humming." He let the locket drop and then said, "Transport to the old Jeweldance Keep and come immediately back, do not stay. I simply want to see if this locket does indeed allow you entry. That will answer some questions for us."

She stood and took a dagger out of her belt, and everyone held their breath as it glowed purple, but she did not go anywhere. At last, she gave up and replaced the weapon in her belt, shrugging, "Does this really matter, Steele?" she asked as she sat down again. "Yes," he replied, "if I can understand how you got into an area that should be protected from transport, then I can better build our defenses against transport to outsiders. It disturbs me that Argos and his people can enter so easily to our world, and I must find a way to prevent future incursions."

Lady Rose turned to Thunder then and commented, "I'm surprised you'd choose to go to Jeweldance at all! So many places to choose from and you chose to go there!" Thunder looked at her quickly and said, "But I didn't think of Jeweldance! I didn't think of anything. My mind was blank except for the thought to leave." There was a sharp intake of breath all around the circle at this and Steele stood up, holding his knife out and saying, "Wait here; that is the answer." He disappeared in a sparkle of falling silver before anyone had time to respond and was back a few heartbeats later, shivering and stamping his feet to warm up. "That's it!" he said to the waiting group, "That is how she arrived there – she thought of nothing! The place doesn't exist anymore, it is nothing."

Everyone looked around at everyone else, taking in this strange information. "There is something else though, something strange there," Steele continued, "it is no longer black there; it is filled with purple mist, and there is no longer a wind like Raindance reported encountering." He looked at

Thunderstroke curiously, hoping she might have an answer. She shifted uncomfortably in her seat and said at last, "I was holding one of my throwing daggers in my hand when I transported in. My fingers became too cold to feel anything, and I dropped it there. But there was a wind while I was there, and it was dark." She looked up to Steele to see if that answered his question.

Steele nodded slowly, mumbling to himself but not answering. At last, Thunderstroke stood up and everyone watched her, waiting. "Yesterday," she began hesitantly, "I had an idea about this locket, and Steele confirmed it just now when he examined it. There is no seed inside, at least not in the way we have all thought; I think the locket itself is the seed. I felt the idea more than thought it. This might sound stupid, but I could feel the locket suddenly come alive in that place, almost as if it were a breathing, living thing. This is not the seed that ancient lore has spoken of. This is another seed, but no less important. It does indeed need to be planted, only not in the planting glades of any world. It needs to be planted where no one can get to it. We need to plant it within that empty Keep. I am as certain of this as I can be." Everyone stared at her in disbelief and Blackwing spoke out saying "But how will it grow in a cold and dark place?" She shook her head, answering them all, "This is not that kind of seed. It is something else. I don't know exactly what, but it is something else."

Steele was staring intently at her, his dark eyes boring into her. She looked over to him, but he made no sign, simply waited for her to continue. "Listen to me," she said, "the enemy is seeking this thing because they think it is the Seed of Growth that the legends speak about. That is a seed which will grow and expand any power which plants it. They don't care where I plant the thing because they have already imbued all the planting glades in every world with magical seals which the seed will pick up and grow through, and that seed will tend to evil and grow the powers of evil no matter which glade it is planted in, no matter who's hand plants it. But this is not that seed. This is something else." She looked over then to the small group of Loremasters who had been sitting quietly in a corner of the room and said to them, "There is another seed, am I right?"

The small group fell in upon themselves, talking quietly and nodding their heads gravely. Finally, one of them stood up and addressed the gathering "Lady Thunderstroke is correct. Our ancient legend speaks of three major seeds. One is the Seed of Growth, which we originally thought this to be. The second is the Seed of Understanding. The third is the Seed of Power. The three seeds are equally important, and all have been lost for many, many generations. Each needs to be planted to come to fruition and do the work it was designed to do, but each must be planted differently.

The seed of Growth must be planted in the Planting Glade of Snowmelt Wood in Arkady. The Seed of Power must be planted where no power can reach it – thus we believe now that Lady Thunderstroke is correct, and this is the Seed of Power." He sat quietly down, and the gathering waited hushed for a moment before Silverwing finally asked the question that was on everyone's minds, "What of the Seed of Understanding? Where must it be planted?" The Loremaster stood once more and said with a quiet smile, "I do not mean to leave your question unanswered, but we simply do not understand the Seed of Understanding! There are not many words written about that one in our scrolls. Doubtless if it is ever found, more will be made clear to us at that time!" The assembly laughed as the Loremaster returned to his seat.

Summersong stood up and addressed the assembled gathering, "So it is decided. This day my Lady will plant the Seed of Power in the empty place. But she must not go alone. I would ask that the leaders of each Keep accompany her to witness this event along with the Loremasters and Historians to witness and record the event in the scrolls and Steele to oversee the venture in case some sort of Smith protection is needed for it. Also, I ask for some help from the dragons. I do not know which dragons should come, but I suggest at least one or two red dragons, since they have the powers of both fire and heat and can warm the place enough for us to work in; and a white dragon to light the place so we can see what we are doing." Everyone agreed with this and Gatemasters Firestorm and Stormchaser immediately offered their red dragons for the task while Lady Evenflower, Lady Starmist, Lady Shimmerwing, and Gatemaster Jasmine offered their white dragons.

Steele spoke next, saying, "I will add to Summer's suggestion on the dragons and say that the silver dragons should also accompany this group, since they have the power of invisibility and once this seed is planted and we are ready to transport out, they can impart a degree of security to this seed so that it can grow in peace, by masking it from detection. That may be all the protection it needs." Everyone agreed once more and this time Gatemaster Zephyr of Plainsrunner and Gatemaster Silverwing of Grimhold volunteered their dragons. "Steele," Summer said, "You have a silver dragon also, bring him along when we go."

Once more agreement was reached, and everyone turned to look at Summer for further instructions. "Do we go now?" Lady Songbird asked, "Or is there something else we wait on?"

Summer turned at last to the Loremasters and asked, "Are there any preparations we must make in planting this Seed, or are we ready?" The Loremasters huddled once more as everyone waited, and finally one stood and spoke, "We do not have a full understanding of any of the Seeds of legend, but of this one I will say the seed might require some help to grow. We suggest you add one dragon from each of the other colors, since we do not know which ability may be of help until we arrive there. Is there room in the Keep for this to be done?" Summersong nodded, answering, "Yes indeed, Jeweldance was the largest Keep of all, and it is larger inside than many of the stables, especially now that there are no walls within but only empty space!"

He turned to the entire group once more, "Let us all bring our dragons, so that the dragons may also witness for each Keep this day. We will thus have all the color abilities covered in this manner. We will meet in the stables of Grimhold in one hour; dress warmly, for even with the red dragons heating the place, I do not doubt that it will still be very cold. In the meantime, I ask each of you to inform your Keepers of this day's coming planting so that they can lock down all Gates in case there is a breakthrough attempt when the planting occurs. Also, it would be wise to bring every resident of the villages in this world to the Gathering glade where the Keepers can protect them, since I believe that if the enemy's strikes fall, they will fall within our world to try and stop us." The meeting broke up.

Chapter 30 – A Seed Is Planted

One hour later the leaders of each Keep, along with Steele and the Loremasters sat upon their dragons, which were grouped in a circle inside Grimhold Keep stables preparing for transport. The small group of five Loremasters had been separately placed with the Gatemasters since they had no dragons of their own. Summersong turned to address the two red dragons, "Firestorm, Stormchaser, prepare to heat the area once we have transported, and come in from opposite sides to cover as much area as possible; it is very cold there."

The two red dragons fluffed their manes out in confirmation and moved further apart from each other as Summersong spoke once more to the entire gathering of both people and dragons, "Remember all to think of nothing when you transport. That is how we will arrive there. When we leave, we will report to the Gathering glade where all will be awaiting us to hear of the deed.

Let us go." The group disappeared from the stable in a multicolored shimmer of falling sparkles.

The entire group arrived in the empty remains of Jeweldance Keep and looked curiously around at the changes. The red dragons were already hard at work heating the place and though they did not dispel the entire chill of the place, it was warm enough for people and dragons to work in. The white dragons had added a small globe of white light which surrounded the gathering and left all outside of the globe in darkness too deep to penetrate with the eye. Everyone sat silent upon their dragons, looking towards the center of their circle at the strange sight. The floor of the empty space held the imprint of a small dagger in the exact center, but no dagger remained.

Jagged cracks in the floor spread out in all directions from the dagger, filled with a strange purple light, almost a liquid yet not so. The purple light pulsed softly, and a faint hum could be heard throughout the great empty cavern. There were several minutes of silence as everyone took in the sight and wondered at it before Lady Thunderstroke finally dismounted and walked over to the dagger indentation in the floor. She took the locket off and held it up, turning around the circle so that all might see it one last time, then stooping down, she placed it carefully into the dagger indentation and backed up a few steps. Nothing happened.

She went forward again and tried to remove the locket to look at it, but it had become firmly embedded within the stone. She looked around at the others, unsure what to do, and then she caught sight of Gatemaster Sharptooth's and Lady Sundancer's orange dragons. The dragons were fluffing their manes out and swishing their tails in agitation, so she motioned the two dragons forward. The dragons approached and Sharptooth reached out a single claw, carefully touching the metal locket as it lay within the stone indentation. The locket responded immediately to that touch, full of the power to bend and shape metals, and the edges of the locket peeled back as if the petals on a flower had opened. Everyone leaned forward to get a closer look at the metal thing and then Sundancer breathed out over the locket, causing it to hum loudly. The dragons both retreated quickly to their places in the circle once more and Thunderstroke, sensing something was about to happen, retreated likewise and scrambled atop her purple dragon to watch. The purple liquid light in the floor cracks began to pulse softly as the locket gradually melted out and filled the dagger indentation completely with a molten gold. The hum increased until the entire cavern was filled with the sound as the molten metal expanded impossibly outward to fill all the cracks in the floor with its golden hue.

The floor was vibrating steadily underneath of them as the pulsing light slowly subsided and the metal hardened. Everyone breathed in hushed tones as they waited for more, but it was soon evident that the metal had no more to do. Finally, Lady Thunderstroke dropped from her dragon once more and went forward to look at the center. She bent over the dagger indentation and studied the molten gold filling it, then straightened and motioned Lady Rose's dragon forward, "Come! It is your turn now; there is a crystal inside." She backed up to allow the pink dragon Rose to come forward. The dragon studied the crystal for a long moment before finally placing a paw on either side of the indentation and tilting her head back to sing a strange, crooning dragon song over the crystal lying within. A sound like that of shattering glass could be heard suddenly throughout the cavern and the pink dragon leapt back quickly to her place in the watching circle as her Rider held on tightly. Thunderstroke retreated once more to her dragon and stood next to her.

A moment later she scrambled hastily to the side of her dragon and up as the crystal exploded in sudden growth, filling the spacious cavern impossibly fast upward and out. The cavern floor shook and crumbled as the crystal tree expanded and grew, filling the cavern swiftly with a purple crystal form, its crystal roots tracing a jagged pattern along the cracks in the floor, crumbling the stone underneath as they ate into it and grew downward. "Everyone get out now!" shouted

Summersong. Steele bellowed over Summer's voice as the Rides and Riders one by one began to transport away "Silver dragons, power on the way out!" Silverwing, Zephyr and Steele and their Riders left the area last as the crystal tree continued to expand. There was a brief, momentary glimpse in their minds of a huge crystal tree, its trunk and roots reached down into Arkady and the Keeper's world and up through the sky, impossibly high and out of sight, branches splayed out over the worlds with shimmering amethyst leaves, then it was gone as the invisibility spell of the silver dragons hid the tree, protecting it.

Moments later they transported into the Gathering glade where the entire population of the Keeper's world awaited them. There was stunned silence throughout the large audience: the image of the tree had been seen by all that day. A soft tinkling sound of glass could be heard as if in the far distance and then it too faded away and was gone, leaving the world as it had been before the planting, yet all knew with certainty that a special power had filled their world and that of Arkady this day and overcome the evil forces of Brimstone – for a time. A power they had yet to explore.

EPILOGUE

Thus ends the story of Snowmelt Wood, but it is not the final story of the Keepers of Arkady.

Ahead remains the story of the finding of the remaining Seeds of Legend, and the adventures they faced along the way.

CAST OF CHARACTERS

Ajax "Jax" – A man of medium height with long, straight brown hair kept pulled back in a ponytail. He has a ready smile and friendly demeanor. He is the head Crystal Smith of Stonyvale Keep and has a red dragon.

Argos – A stocky man of medium height with a large nose, short brown hair and brown eyes and pale skin. He was the Gatemaster of Jeweldance Keep, who defected to Brimstone, taking his entire Keep and company with him. He has a black dragon.

Balderdash "Baldy" – A younger man with a mop of tousled blonde hair and a ruddy complexion. He has a cheerful, playful countenance. He is the Messenger of Kingscannon Keep. He has a bright green dragon.

Bert – An older, slightly heavyset man of medium height. He has grey hair and blue eyes set in a pink, cleanshaven face. He used to work as a sentry for the town of Greenfield in Arkady. He joins the Keeper's world to help them against Brimstone.

Blackwing "Blackie" – A tall man with a ruddy complexion, green eyes and long, straight, sandy brown hair which he allows to fall freely down his back. He can't remember where he's originally from. He is the Gatemaster of Farhaven Keep. He has a black dragon.

Bluebell – Keeper of Grimhold Keep. He has a blue dragon.

Caroline – A short and somewhat plump older woman of Polynesian descent with short, curly brown hair. Caroline comes from Arkady to join Windspeak Keep as a Healer.

Daisy Mae – A young woman from Arkady with long, curly, dark brown hair. She joins Grimhold Keep as a Cartographer. She was trained under Greenfield's chief Cartographer, Maximillian, and she was Thunderstroke's first friend in Arkady.

Evenflower "Eva" – A tall, slender woman with twinkling green eyes set in a tanned face. Her long white hair is usually kept in a braid down her back. She originally hails from Australia. She is the Lady of Grimhold Keep, and the mate of Silverwing. She has a white dragon.

Firestorm – A tall, sturdy man with piercing blue eyes set in a deeply tanned face. He keeps his red hair in a short buzzcut and sports a neatly trimmed red mustache under his long nose. He has a habit of twitching his mustache when amused. Firestorm originally hails from Glasgow, Scotland. Firestorm and Silverwing knew each other in the living world. He is the Gatemaster of Jumpriver Keep, and the mate of Songbird. He has a red dragon.

Harold /Happy Harry – A tall, muscled man with blue eyes, tanned skin, and short brown hair. He's a friendly man with an almost continual smile on his face. He is a "people person" and gets along readily with everyone he meets, and he has a deep love for all animals. He begins as a Tender of Beasts from Arkady, and later becomes Keeper Happy Harry for Meadowbrook Keep. He has a violet dragon.

Jasmine "Jazz" – A tall, long-legged man with short, feathered blonde hair, smiling blue eyes and a ready smile. He's a good storyteller with a teasing manner and is always ready for a laugh. He no longer remembers what country he originally came from, but he has a distinctly Scandinavian appearance. He is the Gatemaster of Meadowbrook Keep, and the mate of Sundancer. He has a white dragon.

Jubilee – A woman of average height and sturdy build, with dark brown hair falling in ringlets around her face and shoulders, and hazel eyes. She originally hails from ancient Athens, Greece. She is the Lady of Greyweather Keep, and the mate of Talon. She has a green dragon.

Maximillian – An older man with white hair and beard and a slightly stooped appearance. He has trained many students in the art of map making in his day. He is the chief Cartographer from Arkadian town of Greenfield who joins Grimhold Keep to continue his work there alongside his favorite student, Daisy Mae.

Moonshadow – A tall, dark-skinned man with wavy, shoulder-length white hair and a deep, rich voice. His smiling brown eyes are set in a cleanshaven, square-jawed face. He originally hails from California. He is the Gatemaster of Stonyvale Keep, and the mate of Shimmerwing. He has a light blue dragon.

Nightfall – Keeper of Grimhold Keep. He has a black dragon.

Night Shadow –A tall, heavily built man with craggy features, long white hair kept in a ponytail, and a cheerful demeanor. He is a Keeper of Farhaven Keep and has a black dragon.

Raindance "Rainy" – A tall, muscled but slender older man with blue eyes and s smiling, cleanshaven face. His short white hair contains a hint of strawberry blonde. He originally hails from Sweden. He has a friendly demeanor and deep knowledge of the Keeper's world. He is a Keeper of Kingscannon Keep and has a chocolate brown dragon.

Rainsong – A tall woman with dark brown skin, a ready smile and laughing eyes. She keeps her thick, curly black hair pulled back from her face. She originally hails from the island archipelago of Vanuatu. She has a love of people and cares deeply for the sick and injured who come to the infirmary almost as much as the Healers. She is the Lady of Windspeak Keep, and the mate of Stormchaser. She has a golden yellow dragon.

Rose – A tall woman with pale skin and high cheekbones, wavy strawberry blonde hair, freckles, and green eyes. She originally hails from Kilkenny, Ireland. She is the Lady of Redrock Keep, and the mate of Sharptooth. She has a pink dragon.

Rudy – Keeper of Grimhold Keep. He has a red dragon.

Ruffian "Ruff" – A large, burly man with a ruddy complexion and large nose. He sports a thick brown beard and shaggy, shoulder-length brown hair. He is the Armory Keeper and a member of Jumpriver Keep. He has a black dragon.

Sandstorm "Sandy" – Keeper of Farhaven Keep. He has a light brown dragon.

Sharptooth – A tall, athletic man with broad shoulders, a sandy complexion, dark eyes, and a ready smile. He keeps his wavy black hair short and sports a neatly trimmed goatee. He doesn't remember where he's from. He is the Gatemaster of Redrock Keep, and the mate of Rose. He has an orange dragon.

Shimmerwing – A younger woman of medium height and white skin who wears her reddish-brown hair pulled back in a ponytail. She has blue eyes and a ready smile. She can't remember where she's originally from. She is the Lady of Stonyvale Keep, and the mate of Moonshadow. She has a white dragon.

Silenus – A short man with short white hair and beard and a pompous manner. He is the leader of Greenfield Town in Arkady; he works under the General for Brimstone and is known there as The Silencer.

Silverwing "Silver" – A tall, muscular man with shoulder-length wavy brown hair and blue eyes. He originally hails from Glasgow, Scotland. Silver and Firestorm knew each other in the living world. He is the Gatemaster of Grimhold Keep, and the mate of Evenflower. He has a silver dragon.

Songbird "Birdie" - A slim woman of medium height, with long brown hair and green eyes. She originally hails from Portofino, Italy. She is the Lady of Jumpriver Keep, and the mate of Firestorm. She has a bright blue dragon.

Starmist – A tall woman with shoulder-length wavy blonde hair, blue eyes, and a snub nose. She originally hails from Kyiv, Ukraine. She is Lady of Plainsrunner Keep, and the mate of Zephyr. She has a white dragon.

Steele – An extremely tall and heavily muscled man of Spanish appearance, with dark eyes, short, curly black hair, and a long curly black beard. He is the head Weaponsmith of Stonyvale Keep. He has a slatey-blue silver dragon.

Stormchaser "Stormy" – A tall, muscular man with crinkly blue eyes and a ready smile. He keeps his black hair styled in a mullet. He originally hails from Santiago, Chile. An affectionate man, he is concerned for the welfare of the people and dragons brought to his Healers for care, and very protective of them. He is the Gatemaster of Windspeak Keep as well as a Healer, and the mate of Rainsong. He has a red dragon.

Summersong "Summer" – A tall, broad-shouldered man with high cheekbones and a cleanshaven face with dark brown eyes, and long, silky black hair which he sometimes pulls back in a ponytail. He originally hails from a territory near the North Saskatchewan River in southern Alberta, Canada and was a member of the Siksika Nation (Blackfoot). He is the Gatemaster of Kingscannon Keep and the mate of Thunderstroke. He has a tawny golden dragon.

Sundancer "Sunny" – A taller woman of medium build who keeps her long, silky black hair pulled back in a braid. She originally hails from Lima, Peru. She is the Lady of Meadowbrook Keep, and the mate of Jasmine. She has an orange dragon.

Sundowner – Keeper of Kingscannon Keep. He has an orange dragon.

Tabitha – A caustic yet caring older woman who is very possessive of her patients. She keeps her long, silvery grey hair pulled back in a bun on her neck. The short and stout woman is Head Healer for Windspeak Keep and is usually attired in a gold and white Healers outfit of lightweight linen. She doesn't have a dragon but can understand and speak to all dragons telepathically.

Talon – A slender, willowy man slightly taller than average height with an angular face and short, straight black hair. He originally hails from Kyoto, Japan. He is the Gatemaster of Greyweather Keep, and the mate of Jubilee. He has a brown dragon.

The General – A tall, muscled, and foreboding man who is more comfortable with a sneer than a smile. This Daimon is the Brimstone Master's right-hand man.

The Master —He is the leader and creator of the evil world of Brimstone.

Thunderstroke "Thunder" – A short, and slender woman with a round face and long, dark brown hair and eyes. Extremely friendly, yet stubbornly courageous, Thunderstroke originally hails from the countryside of Nepal but was living in Kingston, Canada at the time she enters Arkady. She is the Lady of Kingscannon Keep and the mate of Summersong. She has an amethyst/purple dragon.

Velvet Rose "Rosie" – A young woman of smaller stature much like Lady Thunderstroke. She has a pale complexion, long, curly blonde hair and blue eyes. She originally hails from Kentucky in the United States. She was brought from Arkady for the Great Pairing and paired with a pink dragon.

Zephyr – A tall and muscled man with dark brown skin tone, twinkling eyes set in a bearded face. His shoulder-length, curly black hair is sometimes pulled back in a ponytail at the base of his neck. He originally hails from Dodoma, Tanzania. He is the Gatemaster of Plainsrunner Keep, and the mate of Starmist. He has a silver dragon.

ABOUT THE AUTHOR
Jo Erickson

Raised in the Northwoods of Wisconsin, Jo grew up with long days spent exploring woods and field on foot or horseback in search of adventures. She spent her evenings drawing and writing about mythical and magical animals imagined and places discovered during each day's exploration. Reaching adulthood, she promptly filed away and forgot about the adventures and writings as the day-to-day realities and responsibilities of life took over. Now, half a lifetime later, Jo has rediscovered the joy of writing and started to adventure again, this time seriously. (Serious fun, that is!)

Made in the USA
Monee, IL
25 February 2024

53423694R00221